2/15/23

Brian

I hope you ~

Best,

TJbz

All That She Brings

By Toby Brookes

ISBN: 978-0-57838-618-8

Table of Contents

Part I Hartford...1

Chapter 1......................... 3   Chapter 8......................... 61

Chapter 2......................... 6   Chapter 9......................... 66

Chapter 3........................ 15   Chapter 10....................... 73

Chapter 4........................ 18   Chapter 11....................... 84

Chapter 5........................ 28   Chapter 12 93

Chapter 6........................ 38   Chapter 13 106

Chapter 7........................ 51   Chapter 14...................... 114

Part II Pasadena...131

Chapter 15 132   Chapter 27 222

Chapter 16...................... 141   Chapter 28 226

Chapter 17...................... 151   Chapter 29 232

Chapter 18...................... 157   Chapter 30 247

Chapter 19 162   Chapter 31...................... 263

Chapter 20 177   Chapter 32 272

Chapter 21...................... 185   Chapter 33 274

Chapter 22 190   Chapter 34 279

Chapter 23 194   Chapter 35 295

Chapter 24 205   Epilogue........................ 300

Chapter 25 210   About the author 305

Chapter 26 217   Acknowledgments............. 306

This book is dedicated to the memory of
Constance Lamb Brookes

1924-2018

Come down off your throne
And leave your body alone
Somebody must change
You are the reason
I've been waiting here so long
Somebody holds the key

And I'm near the end
And I just ain't got the time
And I'm wasted and
I can't find my way home

—*Steve Winwood*
"Can't Find My Way Home"

PART I

Hartford

Chapter 1

September 1999

"Tell me you love me," the woman said.

"I love you," her husband echoed.

"Say it like you really mean it."

"I did."

On the morning after their third anniversary, the young lovers, Julia and Matthew Banks sat up against their headboard, bare bodies glistening in the brightness of the early sun. A damp lock of Julia's hair hung in her eye. Matthew reached over and brushed it aside. They were looking at themselves in the mirror hanging above the dresser opposite their bed. The chime of crickets sounded outside their screened windows. It was an unseasonably hot September weekend in Hartford, Connecticut.

"What made you say that?" Matthew asked.

She thought about the question for a few seconds.

"I like to hear it once in a while," Julia said.

"But I just said it when we were making love."

"That doesn't really count."

She continued to stare into the mirror, her eyes shifting the tiny amount required to study him, and then turning back to herself and the reflected image of them both. His cheeks were rosy; she looked pale, tired.

Matthew rose from the bed and went into the bathroom where he turned on the shower. Julia remained covered up with the top sheet to her waist, gazing out the window overlooking the tiny front yard. From the bedside table, she pulled out a cigarette and lit it, expertly blowing a plume of smoke to the window where it was immediately sucked outside. She'd promised to quit, but there were times when the urge was over-whelming. She smoked and thought about the day ahead, what needed to be done before she left.

Now Matthew was washing his body, and then rinsing his hair, evident by the sound of shampoo splattering on the tile. Seconds later he turned off the water. A pleasant quietness invaded the bedroom. Julia stubbed out her cigarette in a dish on the table, a scalloped saucer he once made for her, normally used to hold her earrings.

"I hate it when you smoke in our bedroom," Matthew yelled from the sink. "You know that."

There was a time the faint, musky scent of their lovemaking was a kind of feral pleasure. Today, she was anxious to wash herself. Their lovemaking had felt hurried, perfunctory. As much as he had enjoyed himself, shouting at climax, she had moved quietly through their eight-minute session. It had been months since they last had thrilling sex, and she conceded that notion was now a distant memory.

"Did you leave me any hot water?" she said.

"No, it's ice cold. Of course, I did, silly."

Matthew came back into the bedroom and put on a pair of shorts and a T-shirt while Julia watched from the bed. Outside, their peculiar one-armed neighbor had started his lawnmower and was cutting the

4

grass in his front yard, pushing the machine back and forth as best he could, the drone of the two-cycle engine ringing off the plaster walls.

"You know," Matthew said as he sat on the bed to put on a pair of socks, "saying 'I love you' always counts."

Julia stared blankly out the window.

"*You know*," she said mimicking him, "saying 'I love you' when you have an orgasm is for a man nothing more than a primal reflex. All guys do that."

Pushing aside the sheet, she climbed off the bed and stood over the table to remove her earrings, which she had forgotten to take out after their date the night before. She placed the studs beside the cigarette ashes then walked into the bathroom and turned the shower back on.

'*All guys?*' he thought as he stepped into a pair of moccasins.

The shower door clunked shut and Julia talked over the hissing water.

"You know I leave for Atlanta on Monday."

"You're gone till Thursday."

"You and Bella will be alright alone, while mommy is away?"

Chapter 2

Julia hadn't picked Atlanta as the rendezvous destination. She would have preferred somewhere more exotic to meet her secret lover, like Marblehead, or south to the Cape. Bryan Kane was a boat builder from Maine, and their affair had been going on for exactly three months. Atlanta happened to be the city where the national pharmaceutical association was holding its biennial convention and her company, a leader in chemotherapy, was sending her and two other scientists as representatives. The convention was being hosted at the Peachtree Plaza, where a special room rate was available. Because she wished to inject more excitement into their two days together and also needed to avoid her two colleagues, Julia had found a boutique hotel tucked away on Magnolia Street half a mile away.

"Can I offer you a refreshment?" the owner asked as Julia sat in the lounge the afternoon she arrived.

"I may have a glass of wine," Julia said, turning her engagement ring upside down.

"Will your husband be joining you?"

Julia was startled by the apparent success of her lie.

"He's on his way. Traffic, you know," Julia said.

"It's abysmal," the woman said. Her voice carried a southern weariness.

Neither woman made a move to the Honor Bar where several inexpensive varietals were lined on the table, so Julia stayed on the couch, staring out the front window in search of Kane's taxi. It was a suffocatingly hot early autumn afternoon in Georgia, and the heat was visible as a shimmer rising off the paved sidewalk. The only unfortunate souls out of doors now were laborers and domestics, people with no choice. The forecast called for hotter temperatures tomorrow.

Julia was almost giddy as she sat there with the excitement of her covert adventure and the lusty thrill of meeting up again with this man Kane. Just months ago they were complete strangers to each other. It began at a gathering in Boston. Julia was up from Hartford without Matthew, visiting a college friend. Bryan was there sourcing wood for his racing sloops. They spoke very little that evening but he got her contact details and called her at work a few weeks later. He was very forward. "I like the cut of your jib," he'd told her. Not sure exactly what that meant, she was uncomfortable and avoided him for weeks. But he persisted, mixing his Yankee humility with an irresistibly cute style of flirting. She eventually agreed to see him when he called one day. He was in town on a business trip and was in a bar near where she worked. Two glasses of wine was all it took to agree to meet again, and they would plan their first romantic liaison. "There she is," the deep voice growled from behind her. "My girl."

She turned and saw the big man, suitcase in hand, standing at the opposite entrance to the room. He filled the doorway.

"I asked the driver to drop me off in the back. Wasn't that the right thing?" he asked.

Julia, smiling broadly, shook her head no.

She rose to embrace him. "They're all at the other hotel, silly."

Kane put down the suitcase and she disappeared into his massive clutch as he lifted her off her feet and swung their joined bodies back and forth. In his brief show of masculine desire, she abandoned any feeling of guilt or hesitation and was reminded of what was lacking at home.

"Let me show you our room," she said. "It's so cute."

The owner had disappeared into the kitchen. Outside, another couple was coming up the steps with their luggage. Julia wanted to avoid them. It was a small, intimate setting after all. She hurriedly led Kane up the wooden stairway.

He closed the door behind them and looked at his younger lover, now stretched out on the small double bed. Julia seemed sexier every time they met up. She wore a light cotton dress that reached halfway up her lean thighs. She had let her hair grow over the summer, and long, streaked, blonde was now reaching down to her modest breasts. The lasting richness of a deep summer tan was still evident on her angular face. He stood and stared, basking in his good fortune.

"Come here, you big lug," Julia said, patting the covers of the bed.

Kane hung his sport coat on the bedpost.

"What a trip," he said, kicking off his shoes. "The drive to Portland took longer than the flight. Foliage people have taken over the freaking state." He sat on the bed beside her.

"I've been one of those foliage people," Julia said as she pulled him down to her. She put her open mouth on his as their heads dropped to the pillows, and the kiss grew more intense until he sat up and took off his shirt. She buried her face in his chest as he lay back and unbuckled his pants. Outside their window in an alley, a delivery truck beeped obnoxiously as it backed up. They made love quietly between the thin walls and dozed before going out for an early dinner, returning to the hotel for an 11 p.m. bedtime.

Julia awoke the next morning exhausted. Through the night, Kane had more than proved his manhood, which she initially considered the most exciting change. She may have gotten two hours of uninterrupted sleep, and now she turned off the alarm and walked slowly to the shower, feeling disoriented and slightly beat up. Kane remained in bed snoring while she dried her hair, put on some lipstick, and got dressed, and it wasn't until she turned the doorknob that he stirred and lifted his head from the pillow.

"Sorry, Jules. I should have gotten you coffee." She hadn't heard the nickname before.

"Go back to sleep, you sex maniac," she said.

"Is that all you love me for?" He asked.

Julia sat through the morning conference–a droll discussion on patent protection– dreamily replaying the various permutations of the prior evening's carnal extravaganza. At twenty-eight, sex was still somewhat of a novel pleasure, an endeavor in which she was still discovering how to get what she wanted, having only enough lovers so far to count on one hand. It was her third time with Kane, and the two previous meetups, while exciting, were more a process of familiarization. But last night the man was unbound, ravenous, and she wondered if this was intended as a show or simply standard procedure. His reckless sex, at first eye-opening, hardly seemed sustainable.

At lunch at the Westin, a buffet of cold cuts and seafood salads served in the Grand Atrium, she sat with a co-worker, a brilliant, taciturn middle-aged woman from the lab named Carey.

"Get in a run this morning?" Carey asked, noting the high color in Julia's cheeks.

"No, it's the heat," Julia said. "I could never live here."

"It's just so *lazy*," Carey said. "People move like sloths."

After lunch, Julia endured three more hours of dry scientific presentations and skipped the cocktail reception, also held in the atrium, and hurried back to the hotel. Kane was waiting for her at the Honor Bar, a glass of wine in one hand.

"You're late for the party," he said with a sardonic smile. "I started without you."

"Did you open that?" she said, looking at the nearly empty bottle.

He gave her a cunning smile.

"Make sure you fill out the chit," Julia said. "What time is our reservation?"

He emptied the bottle into his glass and rose from the couch. She could see him list slightly, straighten, and walk carefully toward her. His eyes weren't synchronized. She realized he was drunk.

"Shit, I forgot," he said with an exaggerated frown. Julia had left him with the name of a restaurant she picked out.

"How could you forget? The city is teeming with executives demanding the best places to eat. We'll be lucky to get a table at IHOP."

She had the sinking feeling they were on the verge of their first fight. They only had one more night together.

"Leave it with me," Kane said as they walked from the lounge.

Upstairs he began to undress, suggesting she do the same. But Julia was overheated, sticky after the walk from the Westin. She took a cooling shower while he was on the phone in search of a reservation. When she came out of the bathroom he was shirtless and opening another bottle of wine he had brought from the Honor Bar.

"Why don't we wait till later with the wine?"

"No time like now!" he said, pulling the cork with a pop. "By the way, you were right. I struck out with the reservations. We can still go to the place you wanted. I'll man-talk my way in."

He poured two glasses.

"Man talk?" she said.

"Yeah, I'll be the pissed-off guy from out of town saying they must have lost the reservation. Works every time."

Two hours later they were sitting at the bar of the restaurant, waiting for a table that never came. The place was as reviewed – romantic, small, some kind of fusion cuisine, drinks she'd never heard of. And it was wildly popular, at least tonight. Kane was less surly after some pot stickers but his mood was growing steadily darker and Julia now had the unsettling feeling she was with a different man. When he ordered his third Kamikaze she leaned onto the bar, putting herself squarely between him and the bartender.

"He will not be having any more, thank you," she said to the man holding the lime juice.

"*Bullshit!*" Kane shouted. There was a lull in the buzz at the bar and people were looking over toward them. Julia glared at him and he passed it off with a chuckle and turned back to the bar. She got the check and paid and told Kane she was going back to the room.

"I thought we'd have an after-dinner drink," he said as she rose to leave.

She stood from the bar. "I have a breakfast meeting."

In the room, Julia found a note slipped under the door with a bill for two bottles of Rosé: *Next time please remember our honor code.*

She got ready for bed and thought of calling Bryan to tell him the key was at the desk but changed her mind. Setting her travel alarm for six o'clock, she turned out the light and instantly fell asleep.

She was dreaming of drowning and jerked awake. Kane was on top of her, his six-foot-four frame smothering her entire length, stinking of vodka and cigarettes. He was reaching down between them and she felt her panties torn aside and then his hardness driving into her.

"*Bryan!*"

11

She was unable to budge him. He put his hand over her mouth.

"Don't," he whispered coolly.

She squirmed and he clutched her neck and squeezed, crimping her windpipe. She moved just enough to put some space between them and pulled her knee violently up into his groin. He gasped and drew his legs up and she leapt from the bed to a corner by the closet and crouched, ready to fight.

"I'll scream," she said across the room, catching her breath, her eyes wide. "Everyone in this whole fucking place will hear me."

Kane sat up against the headboard and said nothing. She began jamming things into her suitcase, keeping an eye on him while the bag filled. Clothes worn earlier in the day were hung on the bathroom door and she hurriedly slipped them on, grabbed a handful of toiletries, and was gone.

* * *

The next morning, Julia sat on the edge of Carey's bed at the Peachtree Westin.

"Do you want to talk?" Carey asked. She had met Julia in the lobby just after midnight and led her to her room on the 12th floor. Now Julia was silently sitting on the opposite side of the queen-sized bed, staring into a corner.

"Were you raped?" Carey said.

She hadn't slept. After getting into bed, she stayed awake listening to her workmate's gentle breathing, unable to stop trembling, her throat aching, and she tried to come to terms with the terrifying sense of powerlessness she felt in the face of violent sexual intent. It only made matters worse that she had in some manner set herself up for it. How does a woman get that far with someone only to find she has been so thoroughly duped? He was not only a mean drunk but a misogynist, a rapist. She felt broken in so many ways: Humiliated, embarrassed, but most of all violated. Now she had to go meet her boss for breakfast.

Carey said, "I understand your reluctance to talk about it, but you need to talk to *someone*. Consider filing a police report." She was standing beside Julia, her arms crossed. "And I have a scarf you can wear."

Julia looked up at her, puzzled. Carey gestured to her neck. Julia got up and looked in the mirror and saw the bruise.

"*Shit*," was all she said.

Julia's flight out of Atlanta was delayed on Thursday afternoon by a fast-moving cold front headed north. The storm had lightning and gusts up to forty mph and as she sat in Hartsfield-Jackson Terminal 4, she wondered about getting a room. But her need to leave town exceeded the fear of facing Matthew.

There had been no word from Kane since she fled their room Tuesday night. Julia spent a second night with Carey after calling the hotel and authorizing the charges, which included another bottle of wine. Kane had paid for nothing. Before they went to bed the second night, she haltingly told Carey what happened, opening up out of a desperate need to tell someone, a need that transcended her shame. Carey was too politic to comment on infidelity but didn't hold back in voicing her alarm. She told Julia it angered her, the thought Kane would walk free, and insisted she report him, even threatening to go to the police herself. The tone of their conversation softened when Julia began crying, repeating Matthew's name, saying her husband wasn't the perfect mate but was honest and sincere, and without an ounce of violent behavior. This tryst with Kane, she admitted, was one colossal, stupid mistake, and she finally broke into long, exhaustive sobs. Carey, knowing more now about her coworker than she ever wished, could only offer a shoulder to cry on.

The androgynous voice blaring out of the overhead speakers in the waiting area announced the unexpected weather window that would allow Julia's Hartford bound flight to take off in ten minutes. She put away a notebook of contacts and information on competitive drugs and entered the line to board. In three hours she would be home. Matthew would be waiting with the bottle of champagne he'd promised and her favorite dinner. It was a devastating reminder of the man's unwavering sweetness.

Chapter 3

Rain pelted the clapboard siding of the old frame house on the edge of Hartford, driven by a hard southeast wind. The curtains were blowing into the rooms like spinnakers as Matthew Banks scurried about, closing windows and turning on lights, his 12-year-old yellow Lab, Bella, following close behind. He had been in the middle of preparing dinner for his wife's homecoming when the storm hit and was taken by surprise. In the kitchen before him on a cutting board lay a pile of sharply green basil, a chunk of pecorino cheese, an extra bulb of garlic the color of bleached bones, and a half-liter bottle of extra virgin olive oil. Everything was artfully aligned in the order of processing, and when combined, these ingredients would become a simple yet tangy pesto sauce; what he considered the perfect complement to a bowl of steaming linguini. He filled the mortar and began pulverizing the basil leaves. Bella, sensing he'd be in one place a while, lay curled at his feet.

Thoughts turned to the evening ahead. The minute Julia walked through the door he would lift her off the floor and cover her face with kisses. Next would come the bubbly; their reunion tonight called for a celebration worthy of newlyweds, which technically they were not, but he was determined to keep the embers burning. Candles on the tiny kitchen table would barely light the room, toasts would be exchanged, and following the meal, they would linger only long enough to finish their wine before retiring to bed.

Since leaving his busted childhood home in California eight years ago, the gains in Matthew's emotional equilibrium had been steady and sure. Never a pious person, he was convinced this was heaven sent. Twenty-nine years old on the eve of the new millennium, Matthew Blevins Banks was safely ensconced in a life poised for liftoff, the realization of whatever he and his aspiring wife might envision. Both were gainfully employed, she as a biochemist, he in the banal but well-paying insurance racquet. It wasn't his first choice as a profession, but still, he was able to cautiously claim his life was firing on all cylinders. (Even if what he achieved came faster and with less handwringing than ever imagined.) A half dozen years with the lovely Julia was surely the main contributing factor. She'd lifted him to an entirely new level of confidence, with loads of intelligent advice, a veritable prescription on how to pursue life, coming from someone who grew up in a relatively normal, loving family. All of this and more was wrapped in the prettiest of packages.

He'd graduated near the top of his class at a "potted ivy" school in New Hampshire, been aggressively recruited by a historic New England insurance company, and found a partner he was certain – as certain as any man could be – was the right and final one. They married at the edge of a golf course, on a country club by the sea, and now he had a mortgage on a 150-year-old home on a tree-lined street at the edge of Hartford. There were funds in multiple accounts and talk of children and most nights, with a faint smile on his face, Matthew Banks drifted off wanting for nothing.

Dinner's ingredients were now chopped, grated, and diced. The little frame house shook as he stirred the bright green pesto. Bella rose and dragged her body to the bed in the kitchen corner on stiff legs, where she performed her ritualistic circular turning before settling back down. The clatter of rain hitting the house was so loud Matthew thought perhaps it had turned to hail, and now he worried about Julia on the freeway, heading home from the airport. He pictured her compact sedan hydroplaning over the wet highway, wipers flapping furiously.

He sat with a glass of wine and checked the weather on the small kitchen TV hanging beneath the cupboard. The meteorologist was pointing to a map splashed with color depicting the autumn storm. Forty-mile-per-hour gusts were now blasting some areas, felling trees, and backing up sewer drains. The coverage cut to a live feed from a helicopter sky cam zooming in on a crash scene. A tanker truck had slid off the highway into a passenger car on the main artery, pinning it against a temporary cement barrier. Police cruisers and two boxy EMT vehicles were nosed into the wreckage at random angles. Blue and red light pulsed into the watery night. The only evidence of the crushed car was a tire jutting from the truck's undercarriage. A tow truck had connected a winch and was pulling the massive tanker off the car. Traffic was backed up for miles in both directions. Matthew turned off the TV and listened to the wind and rain beat against the windows. Moments later his phone rang.

"Hello? It's Sargent Mathers of the Connecticut Highway Patrol. May I speak to a relative of Julia Banks?"

Chapter 4

December 1999

"Just behave yourself, Banks. That's all we're asking."

It was the day before the company holiday party, and Lawrence Holmes, Director of Human Resources, stood behind his desk addressing his young protégé. Given the young man's recent lapses in judgment, Matthew Banks' good behavior was far from a sure thing.

"And remember, people will be watching," Holmes added.

Lawrence Holmes called everyone at the company by their last name, including women, and Matthew ignored both the insinuation and the blunt tone of his request. The larger concern was that a tally was being kept, a record of his behavior, sitting on a hard drive somewhere in Human Resources. Since the death of his wife in the grisly crash earlier that autumn, Matthew's attendance followed no predictable routine; he often showed up at the office late, disheveled, looking as though he'd gone with little or no sleep. Projects he once commanded with authority and verve were gradually being pulled from his portfolio and given to other managers. At a monthly Directors' meeting, Holmes had agreed to take the young executive under his wing, even at the stern warning of his peers. He argued the boy deserved a chance to recover from his nightmarish loss, find his footing, even though the company party was like a Siren song tempting him to rocky shores. Everyone knew a significant *faux pas* could spell the end of his brief career at *Connecticut Life and Casualty*.

"I'll stick with the punch," Matthew assured him that afternoon. The truth was Matthew had decided to skip the holiday party altogether, but now felt obligated. He acknowledged the opportunity to prove his self-control and would seize on it. Plus, the prospect of Christmas and New Year's had put him in a terrifying place of dread and uncertainty. It would be his first holiday alone, in the house in Hartford he and Julia painstakingly renovated. Here he had no family, few friends he wanted to see, and just his dog Bella to spend it with. The stretch between Christmas and New Year's, when his employer closed the office's doors, loomed before him like a prison sentence.

Connecticut Life and Casualty's annual holiday party always fell on the last workday leading up to Christmas. Janitors cleared the cafeteria and erected a make-shift bar by covering the steam tables with plywood, allowing plenty of floor space for the 225 employees to order their drinks and dance. They would show up in their holiday outfits, not as flagrant for the men as the women, who often pushed the limit on the company dress code and wore revealing, even sexy attire. The gathering had not only grown in size, but as the company expanded through various acquisitions and its culture diversified, it had become a raucous, booze-fueled free-for-all. It was Lawrence Holmes' charge to tame it down. This year, the party would begin at 4:00 pm sharp, an hour earlier than previous years, to get everyone home by dinner time.

"My treat, Matthew!"

Sarah Finnegan from Underwriting held a glass of champagne up to her co-worker. Her eyes were dancing, and she was dressed in a tiny cocktail dress deeply cut, showing at least half of her buxomness.

Matthew had arrived later than planned, having just finished signing year-end expense reports, and he groped for the best way to get out of it. The party was in full swing, the decibel level of the crowd's excitement as it rang off the glazed ceramic brick of the cafeteria walls nearing a jet at take-off. A towering blue spruce adorned with kitschy ornaments rose from the center of the cavernous room while generic holiday music droned overhead.

"I can't, but thanks anyway," Matthew said sheepishly. "I've got people watching me."

Sarah frowned and took a long sip from her glass.

"One won't hurt you. Come on. I'll cover," she said, stepping closer. "And by the way, who cares if anyone's watching?"

Matthew looked around and saw no one of importance and emptied the glass with practiced ease. The effervescence made his eyes water and he quickly handed the glass back.

"Mum's the word," he said.

From behind Sarah, three junior managers stepped into their space. Brad Simms, from Risk Assessment, was the first to address Matthew.

"*Goddammit* Matt! How are you holding up?" He was always loud and curiously serious, and tonight his face was lacquered with sweat. At least his was an oblique reference to Matthew's tragedy, but still, Matthew was reminded why he didn't want to be there.

"I'm okay Simms."

"Hey," he said abruptly, "there's a more fun party in the mailroom if you want to ditch this scene." He gestured to the back of the cafeteria and turned to lead them out. Matthew held back.

"Come on, you stick in the mud," Sarah said, tugging at his coat sleeve.

The four made their way through the crowd and exited the cafeteria toward the back of the building. The mailroom was located next to a loading dock. Simms knocked on the closed door.

"It's me," he said.

The door opened slowly and a middle-aged man who ran the mail looked through the crack and let them in.

"Lock it," Chad Knowles said from across the room. The young manager in charge of marketing stood over a sorting table with a rolled-up bill in his hand. He assessed the group and then bent over a line of cocaine and snorted it up. In the corner, a small bar was set up with several bottles opened.

"Banks, get over here," Knowles said.

Matthew looked at Sarah. She nudged him forward and the next thing he knew Chad was handing him the makeshift straw.

"I can't," Matthew said. "Really – I have to leave."

Sarah came to him with a glass of tequila.

"*Matthew,*" she said, drawing out his name. "This is good for you."

Matthew looked at Chad, and then back to Sarah.

"Maybe just one."

He threw back the powerful liquor and his throat caught fire. Now Chad was holding a mirror to his face with the bill in his hand and Matthew, as if this were a chaser, made the white crystals, in the shape and size of a caterpillar, disappear into his nose.

He stepped away from the group and observed the gathering: six people in their thirties, white, with various management roles, all apparently willing to risk their careers on this back-room delinquency. They liked and respected Matthew but were at a loss as to how they might help.

21

The junior managers, or *fine young cannibals* as Holmes once labeled them, had developed an esprit de corps other departments envied. They collaborated effortlessly, competed just enough to avoid rancor, and often gathered outside the office for happy hours and barbeques. Matthew and Julia had joined the cohort just months before she died, and the group's support for him now manifested only in their sense of obligation to provide whatever it took to get him through the night.

Now his upper palate was numb as a stone, and his heart hammering. Fortified with a sense of uber control and all-knowing wisdom, he had the confidence of a Russian tsar. How could one more shot of tequila hurt? Chad stepped up and was peppering him with insurance-type questions about Julia's accident: Was there legal liability on behalf of the trucking company; did he identify her body; was there any pending settlement. Having ingested enough cocaine to make this a one-way conversation, his inquiries were so rapid-fire Matthew was thankfully spared having to respond. The net effect of this was the dire need for reinforcements, and he indicated to Sarah what he needed in a series of *Charade* like gestures. In minutes she was making her way over with the mirror and a shot. It wasn't until the fourth tequila that voices and events in his immediate sphere separated from space and time, and some kind of avatar of Matthew Banks hovered just above the fracas.

They had a disco ball going in the cafeteria. Sarah was escorting him across the dance floor, the two of them dodging in and out of shimmying dancers, all moving in sync to electronic sounds of the 1970s. Shards of light ricocheted off the steam tables, creating a strobe that obscured the horizon. Matthew had asked her to take him out by way of the rear parking lot, but the back entrance was locked. He swayed amidst the queasiness of the combined intoxicants and was forced to lean into Sarah's exaggerated bosom as they approached the main entrance. Standing in the light of the dimmed sconces twenty yards away was Lawrence Holmes. Beside him stood the company psychiatrist, the highly regarded Dr. Madeleine Batiste. They both clutched drinks but still looked more like sock hop chaperones. Matthew tugged Sarah's arm in the opposite direction and as they turned his name was called out.

"Banks!" Holmes yelled.

Sarah halted and held fast to Matthew's elbow.

"Come say hello!" Holmes was waving.

There was a brief tug of war and Sarah prevailed when he realized there was no escaping. She led Matthew toward the couple. Holmes greeted Sarah with a corporate hug.

"I'm Sarah," she said, turning to Dr. Batiste, extending her hand. "We worked on project Jetstream together." Sarah was remarkably clear-eyed and upright.

"Yes, hello Sarah," Dr. Batiste said. She was known for her aloofness and intellect, and tonight she appeared entirely in character.

Sarah said, "And of course, you both know Matthew Banks."

Holmes stepped around and leaned into Matthew's face.

"Someone spiked the holiday punch!" he said with blistering sarcasm.

Sarah seamlessly looped her arm inside Holmes' and pulled him toward the center of the floor, immediately launching into an improvised version of the Hustle. All by himself, listing beside Dr. Batiste, Matthew moved to the wall.

"You're in Data Analytics, isn't that right?" Dr. Batiste asked, with the same measured smile. Matthew blinked hard to sharpen her features. He said yes, that was correct.

"I've seen your file," she added. "We're lucky to have you."

Matthew began scouring the crowd for Sarah, praying for her to rescue him the second the song was over. From the corner of his hazy vision, he could make out Dr. Batiste studying him with an odd intensity. Had he spilled food on his lapel, or worse, could there be cocaine on his nose?

"Dance?" she asked.

Matthew leaned harder into the wall. Not waiting for an answer, Dr. Batiste pulled him onto the thumping floor and began moving freely to the music. Now he could tell she was at a party. Her attire was tasteful but not particularly seasonal, a fitted burgundy gown with a high neck. Her curves were well defined and Matthew couldn't take his eyes off her mid-section as her hips swayed with flowing synchronicity, mystifyingly, a cobra under the spell of a snake charmer. Matthew stood several yards away, shuffling his feet in no organized pattern, his heart still sprinting, feeling whirley and on the verge of a cerebral hemorrhage. But Dr. Batiste maintained her cool smile and seemed to be enjoying herself and when the music shifted to a livelier classic tune, she adjusted elegantly and with seamless precision. It took every bit of his youth and fear for Matthew to remain upright. They made it through the song and as the DJ started to cut in a Marvin Gaye classic Matthew gestured to the sidelines. Sarah and Holmes had returned and as they approached, Matthew shot Sarah a look of horror. Small talk lasted only minutes, generated mostly by Sarah, bless her heart. She and Holmes talked about industry trends while Matthew and Dr. Batiste talked about something else, the precise nature of which would be lost to the night. In the days to come, to his great distress, all that remained of that final interaction was the fear he'd uttered to her something inappropriate, possibly vulgar, words he would probably take back given the chance.

* * *

The next morning, the start of Matthew's Christmas break, he awoke nauseous and dry-mouthed. He vaguely remembered saying goodnight to Sarah. She had driven him home and invited herself in, but he declined. He'd gone directly to bed, apparently, for he was still wearing his shirt and pants. The coolness between his legs and a faint acrid scent could only mean one thing. He threw back the covers and sat up, eyeing the wet spot spread evenly beneath him. He immediately stripped off his clothes and climbed into a hot shower, letting the water beat on his neck and shoulders for ten minutes.

Downstairs, Bella had left evidence of her own loss of control. Two piles sat reeking in the living room and a puddle spread across the kitchen linoleum floor. He cleaned her messes, went back upstairs to wash his sheets, and sat on his bare bed waiting for his head to stop pounding. Outside his bedroom window, a cornflower blue sky offered a cruel suggestion of hope and possibility.

He spent the rest of the day padding around the little frame house waiting for the unrelenting grip of his hangover to ease. A jumbo bottle of Coca-Cola couldn't quell his thirst. He tried to rest quietly in his favorite chair, a Swedish black leather recliner someone suggested he acquire in the aftermath of losing Julia. They promised it would become a comfortable place of solace, and sure enough, it was his go-to spot where he'd lately been making his way through *Anna Karenina*. Now he merely sat in full recline, legs slung over the ottoman, gazing through his front window at the goings-on of his quiet neighborhood.

He had slipped into a light doze when the phone rang mid-afternoon. As had become his custom, he let it go to voicemail. His machine allowed him to hear messages as they were recorded and he sat back as his mother's shrill voice came through the speaker.

"It's me, Mattie. Would you please call back? The holidays are hard for us all. Love you."

It was her favorite time to call, just when he would be returning from work, which was after her lunch and before five o'clock, her etched in stone cocktail hour. Her calls were more frequent these days, since Julia's death, and his track record for picking them up was roughly one in ten. Dorothy Banks, who also lived alone, had a way of infusing guilt, however subtle and undeserved, into every message she left. *The holidays are hard for us all?* She lived alone in a big home in Pasadena, left by her parents. It was a grand Spanish-style affair designed for a large family, and Matthew often pictured her rambling around the enormous hacienda, talking to the portraits hanging in the downstairs great room; it was no wonder she drank so much. If she called in the evening, he automatically ignored her, for her condition deteriorated as the day progressed. He had not seen her since Julia's funeral when she came for three days and lapsed in and out of coherence while numbing herself with vodka and valium. To say their relationship was on shaky ground would be optimistic. Even so, he briefly considered calling her back on this dreary afternoon, if only to break up the suffocating ennui that had settled in.

His hangover began to lift as dusk seeped into the living room. He could sense the outside temperature dropping and got up from his chair to build a fire in the living room hearth. He used a combination of oak and birch, the latter igniting quickly and providing a soothing *crack*, the oak burning more slowly and heating the room with its dense, glowing embers. (He was never sure if the fire truly added warmth or sucked the home's heat up the chimney, as his know-it-all neighbor Hughes once insisted.)

The house was drafty as a strainer, built in 1879, and the furnace dated back to the mid-20th century. It was a beastly boiler that consumed nearly half the space in the basement, and it heated and sent the water toward the iron radiators strategically placed in each room. In the winter, they hissed and creaked as the pressurized steam coursed through the system, and the dry heat caused the air to be desert-like, turning skin to parchment. All this mattered less because the windows no longer fit properly in their frames, allowing cold air to seep in so freely that in a high wind the metal blinds rattled. The windows were the last planned renovation Matthew and Julia had budgeted for; a project quickly dropped upon her death.

He heated some canned soup and finished the day reading by the fire, its embers dusted with ash as the warmth dissipated. He let Bella out the back door to do her business, which she completed in record time, and the two climbed the stairs as the hallway clock struck nine, an early end to another empty, lonely day.

Chapter 5

"Tis the season!"

The greeting cut through the darkness as Matthew climbed from his car, the unmistakable patrician voice of his one-armed next-door neighbor, Hughes Billingslea III. Matthew reached into the backseat of his old Volvo station wagon for a bag of groceries and looked up after shutting the door to see him standing on his front porch, cocktail in his one working hand.

"Not tonight, Hughes," he shouted back. "I'll take a rain check."

"Come on, Matthew, don't be a bore! It's nearly Christmas for God's sake!"

Matthew stood by his car and stalled for an excuse. The sky was spitting rain, a northeasterly gale blowing it sideways, hitting his face like pins. His Christmas party hangover had taken two days to run its course and he still shuddered at the thought of alcohol.

"Just one?" Hughes said.

Hughes lived alone in the big Victorian house on the north side of Matthew's lot, the original homestead built on what once was a sprawling dairy farm. He had owned it for over ten years, restoring it to its former glory with detailed artisan trim, a new Mansard roof, and decorative period colors. A covered porch wrapped around the front of the house, and a brick walk ran to the street.

It was an unspoken mystery, what exactly happened to Hughes' left arm. All that remained was a stub, sticking out from his shoulder like a chicken wing, enough there for an artificial limb to be affixed. He usually wore the prosthesis beneath the sleeve of a sweater or coat, but on hot summer days he could be seen *sans* the piece, the stump wagging pointlessly as he worked in his garden. Unless he hugged you, when the stiff plastic was apt to dig into you rudely, the artificial arm was quite convincing. A neighbor once told Julia it had been severed when he was at Princeton, in an accident on the train tracks, but this had never been verified. In the wintertime, he curiously wore two gloves.

What everyone did know was that he owned a valuable and extensive art collection, a small portion of which hung on the walls of his home. In the early days of their friendship with Hughes, when Matthew was away on business and Julia visited him for a glass of wine and hors d'oeuvres, he had explained to her that his father was a collector, a serious one. The man had brought countless paintings over from Europe, mostly Impressionist works out of France and Italy, several by known artists and even a few masters. The senior Hughes had operated a quiet business in Boston, on Beacon Hill, with global distribution. He left it all to his son after dying under mysterious circumstances, on a buying trip to Romania. There were rumors the paintings were of questionable provenance, possibly stolen by Nazis during World War II. Investigations were rumored, but as the years passed nothing came of it, and Hughes continued to proudly display many of the most valuable works in his house. He sold several a year, a source of income, and apparently somewhere off-site was a warehouse containing dozens more. Above his hearth hung a large, vibrant Matisse, which he claimed was his favorite, and valuable originals were thoughtfully placed throughout the rest of the big Victorian structure. An imported alarm system guarded the collection, and every so often Matthew could hear the beeps shrieking next door as Hughes performed operational checks.

Matthew was too tired to argue and said he'd be back after putting away the groceries and taking Bella for a quick walk.

"I'll get a fire going!" Hughes yelled through the opened door. "It's not fit out here for man nor beast!"

By the time Matthew and Bella returned Hughes was standing beside the roaring hearth in his velvet smoking jacket, martini glass held at his midsection, as though posing for a society magazine.

"There's more in the pitcher," Hughes said, mechanically gesturing toward the bar with his prothesis. Matthew hung up his coat and suddenly the idea of a little holiday cheer sounded more appealing. He poured himself a smaller version and joined his neighbor by the fire.

"Glad you came around to your senses," Hughes said.

"I was thinking of a Coke, but what the hell," Matthew said.

"To the holidays, my boy!" Hughes said, raising his glass. "It's good to get you over. It can be deathly quiet in this house, as I suppose it is next door."

Matthew took a coward's sip to ease into it and stared into the fire.

"You're better at this than I," Matthew said. "Sometimes I feel I'm going looney over there. But I guess I can always count on you for a drink, Hughes, and some sarcastic commentary."

It was true. Regardless of the time of day, Hughes could be expected to proffer a drink and lively conversation, typically as the two of them crossed paths in their normal comings and goings. Since Julia's death, which hit Hughes especially hard, his invitations had been more frequent. Matthew accepted he was nothing more than a stand-in for his departed wife, with whom Hughes had established a more intimate relationship during their two-year acquaintance. Their friendship revolved around a shared love of gardening, fine art, and white Burgundy. He enticed her to visit with expensive wine, and he was a creative chef, convincing her to stay for impromptu dishes of pasta Carbonara or some dish he would throw together with leftovers. Their many evenings spent on his artistically flowered back patio or in the elegant parlor were filled with enchanting conversations focused on Hughes' deep knowledge of fine art. Each painting seemed to have a fascinating back story. Matthew soon realized, after her death, he and Hughes would need to find something else to talk about.

"So really Matthew, how do you plan to keep busy, with all this time on your hands? Do you have a hobby?"

Matthew looked to the ceiling. It was a topic he'd rather avoid.

"No hobbies, to speak of."

"If I remember, Julia said you met in a pottery class."

"That's right. She was pretty good, better than me."

"She told me you were the better one. Why not take it back up? Keep your hands busy, tap into your creative reservoir, keep yourself out of trouble."

"Let me get through the holidays."

Matthew began to perspire and retreated from the hearth, moving to one of the wingback chairs. The martini tasted like insect repellant, and he set down the glass.

"What are your plans for the holidays? Hughes said. "I assume a man of your organizational skills is entirely prepared."

"I'm trying to forget about it," he said. "It'll be just another day, as far as I'm concerned."

Hughes scowled.

"Don't be a nincompoop. You will at least have dinner with me. I'm roasting a goose."

Matthew shook his head. "I'm really not feeling too sociable these days, Hughes. I'm sorry."

"I've invited no one else! I can't possibly eat the whole thing myself," Hughes said.

"Can I bother you for that Coke?" Matthew said, changing the subject.

"You look a bit green around the gills," Hughes said.

"I'm still recovering from the party at work."

Hughes instead poured a glass of water at the bar and handed it to his guest.

"Must have been some party. Drink this. It's better for you. So, any hanky-panky with the pretty lady in accounting, or some such thing?"

"No hanky-panky. Just way too much to drink. I think I made a fool of myself."

"Such a tender boy, still wet behind the ears. I had you all wrong."

Matthew, suddenly wishing to change his perspective, emptied the martini glass and stood from the chair. He was feeling suddenly queasy, anxious, not sure whether it was the juniper berry or Hughes' sudden intimacy.

"I need to feed Bella," he said.

"Was it something I said?" Hughes said.

"Of course not."

"Then I'll see you Sunday night?"

Matthew considered the invitation for a moment and changed his mind.

"Can I bring anything?"

"Just your usual charm," Hughes said.

* * *

During the eight years he'd lived in the Northeast, Matthew learned New England winters are something to endure, like a case of hives. A five-month stretch of monochromatic environs under thick grey skies matched precisely the ashes that mounted up in his fireplace, and with every passing week, the desperation grew.

His first winter as a freshman in college in New Hampshire had come as a total shock. Growing up in the dry warmth of southern California, he'd never experienced this kind of environmental abuse, a cold that seeped through any number of layers and settled into your bones for months at a time. He nearly went home halfway through his second semester, when a freak snowfall closed the campus for a day in April. But his roommate from Vermont insisted it 'had to snow once on the daffodils' and spring was around the corner. Matthew remained, mostly due to the alternate dread of living at home with his tortured mother. But another less obvious reason for sticking around was a woman named Julia Bancroft, who he'd met in the early weeks of the second semester. It was a casual coming together, by way of a ceramics class, a course he had signed up for as a break from the banal business classes his mother had insisted on. He'd loved working with clay as a child in his father's studio and had shown great dexterity and imagination. So it was more than just a passing interest when he signed up for the course. But it soon became interesting in a different, more exciting way. Most days he was working side by side that spring with his pretty classmate, together shaping clay in new and innovative ways. A slight competition arose between them, each pushing the other to extend their skill by taking risks, creating wild shapes, and he noted right away she was less inhibited and seemed to draw from a cool confidence and unfettered creativity. Hers was an energy he found so refreshing to be around. Inspirational, hopeful, unencumbered. For the first time in his life he imagined what it would be like to spend the rest of his days with one such woman. Several platonic dates followed, and a budding romance was in its early stages.

By the end of the semester, they each had several respectable pieces to show for their final grade –finished pieces each had labored over– and each received the highest grade possible. The teacher featured both their works in a department exhibit, and they gushed in their shared success. The connection they'd formed was compelling enough to bring him back for his sophomore year, capped off by that kiss she gave him the last day that hit him like a lightning bolt, a charge that would reverberate the entire summer.

* * *

Christmas day was spent on the black leather recliner with his Russian novel. A light snow fell intermittently, and the temperature had dropped into the low teens. The only sign of Christmas at the Banks house was a red ribbon looped around Bella's neck. Matthew had intended to put up a tree but the spirit never materialized. He couldn't bear digging out the lights and ornaments and trinkets from the basement, where he'd stored many of Julia's belongings. A single Christmas card, from his mother, sat unopened on the bookcase in his living room. He knew from every previous Christmas here it contained a check for $100.

In the early afternoon, still in his pajamas, the phone rang. He knew it was his mother, but he picked it right up anyway.

"Merry Christmas mother," he said.

There was a pause as he heard her take a sip of something and then she said, in a grave tone, "Are you alright?"

"I'm fine, mother. How about you?"

"I didn't hear from you and I got worried. I'm getting through the day. You know what it's like now. Holidays are the worst. At least you have your dog. What's her name again?"

"How's the weather in Pasadena?" He always asked this, despite the inanity of the question. The weather there rarely changed.

"Perfect, of course. Do you have snow?"

"Yes, we're having a white Christmas."

"Well, stay off the streets. I don't want you in a snowbank, freezing to death."

She spoke for some minutes about trivial things and he listened as she continued on and sipped her drink and at one point light a cigarette. Usually, toward the end of a call, she would bring up his father, who had left years ago to pursue a dream of becoming a painter in France. From there it was all doom and gloom, and she became boringly morose and then angry, letting loose a jeremiad of complaints and condemnations at a fever pitch. It was all so predictable.

"Do you have anything for dinner?" she said.

"Have you ever had goose?" Matthew asked. "I'm going next door."

"No. It's popular in England. It sounds dreadful. But you should expand your palette, whenever you get the chance."

He could always count on her for one of these random motherly axioms, which when induced by alcohol bordered on non-sequiturs, and he passed this one-off and wished her a merry Christmas. After hanging up, he was surprised by her relative normalcy. She was tipsy, but the usual vitriol hadn't entered their conversation. She didn't once bring up Mr. X, as she called him. And she showed less exaggerated concern for Matthew's emotional state, which in the past had forced him to lie.

He went upstairs and got dressed, putting on his flannel-lined chinos and a thick turtleneck sweater, a pair of wool athletic socks and his Bean hunting boots. Downstairs, he called out to Bella and together they stepped outside into the near darkness as the fine, delicate snowfall continued to flutter down. At the end of his driveway, it clung to his mailbox like white moss.

Inside Hughes' living room, a bluish smoke had gathered at the ceiling. Matthew called to him from the door.

"Everything alright in there?"

"It the damn goose!" Hughes yelled from the kitchen. It was a thick, gamey smell, one you might find in the air of every Yorkshire village on Christmas night, Matthew thought to himself. Hughes was at the sink in full chef's regalia, with a tall white hat and an apron that reached below his knees. Parsnips and brussels sprouts were rinsing in the sink and a pot full of Yukon potatoes boiled on the stove. Matthew had brought a bottle of wine he'd been saving, a coveted Bordeaux, and asked Hughes if he'd like it opened.

"I prefer Pinot Noir with the fowl," Hughes said with his back turned, "Not to appear ungrateful. I've opened a bottle to breathe. In the meantime, do help yourself to a martini. I'm tired of drinking alone." His words were syrupy and stuck together, evidence he'd been at it for a while.

"I prefer a single malt, not to appear ungrateful," Matthew said from the bar in the living room.

Hughes came out grumbling, reached to an overhead cupboard, and pulled down a cut-glass decanter.

"It's the best in the house," he said. "Mind you, I don't offer this to anyone."

Dinner was a mixed affair. The savory roasted seasonal vegetables were perfectly cooked with a hint of chicory but the goose tasted like sweat socks. Hughes repeatedly apologized and Matthew did his best to appear gracious but found himself downing the Pinot like water, backed by the peaty malt Scotch. After a dessert of pecan pie with a brandy glaze, they retired beside the hearth, where Hughes piled on more logs and then poured them each a glass of vintage Port. The two sat watching the fire for some time, lulled by the food and drink, and finally, Hughes snapped to attention.

"Perhaps I'll try ham at Easter," Hughes said.

"That was my first goose," Matthew said.

"I'd venture a guess it will be your last," Hughes said. "You sent most of it back to the kitchen."

Matthew sipped his Port.

"I'll fill in with this," Matthew said, nodding to a plate of bleu cheese, grapes, and salted crackers on the coffee table.

Hughes offered another glass and Matthew said 'no, thank you,' and rose to get his coat. Surprisingly, Hughes didn't protest and walked him to the entrance, opening the door.

"Thank you for coming tonight. In all frankness, you don't bring as much to the party as the lovely Julia," Hughes said drunkenly, "but you're a perfectly respectable dinner partner."

Matthew let the comment go, responding with a fabricated smile. Hughes plopped his prosthetic hand onto Matthew's forearm, its sharp edge digging through his coat sleeve.

"Someday, she'll be a distant memory, my boy. Part of a life you left behind, not the bright new one before you," he said.

Chapter 6

The span of days between Christmas and New Year's passed at a punishingly slow pace. Matthew was floundering all by himself. Christmas and New Year's, in their major holiday status, by themselves presented a depressing challenge. Combined and drawn over a ten-day stretch, it was like crawling across a desert, unlike any kind of loneliness he'd ever imagined. He might as well have been in the middle of the Sahara, for all anyone knew. And with January upon him, the slowest month of the year, he realized he'd need to get creative to find ways to fill the hours. Of course, there were always menial chores, reading, or cooking, long walks with Bella. But he knew, no matter what, doing things alone was often the equivalent of doing nothing at all. He thought back to Hughes' suggesting he return to pottery, and this was tempting. But it was repressed by a combination of visceral memories, good and bad.

When Matthew was just five years old, Albert Banks had assembled a small studio in their basement in Pasadena. A lawyer by day, the senior Banks was a weekend ceramicist and painter of landscapes not without talent. He'd sold paintings through law school to help fund his tuition and had a small following of wealthy benefactors who continued to encourage him. It turned out his passion for art would far exceed that which he felt toward his family, and he walked out the front door unannounced one Saturday afternoon while Matthew was eating grilled cheese sandwiches with two pals in his kitchen. His brief note said he was headed for France, to pursue his dream. Matthew's mother tried to hide the ugly reality, saying he'd been called from town on emergency business, but in time the truth would be revealed: he was not coming back. Matthew's world was turned upside down. Everything he had been taught while at his father's side, throwing pots and shaping small figurines, along with the nurturing father-son rapport developed during the hours together, would be negated, buried beneath a heap of bitterness that eventually became abject hatred for the man.

The second reason was less complicated but equally deep -seated: Having met Julia amidst the romance of art, the sensuousness of caressing soft clay, the mutual indulgence of their creative instincts, was forever burned into his memory. The remembrance of those potent early days would be more than he could bear.

This feeling mysteriously disappeared when he found himself crawling the walls, in the days between Christmas and New Year's. The all-consuming post-Christmas ennui, as he sat in his drafty house, bored with his novel, jittery from espressos, anxiety-ridden by his life *writ large*, would all contribute to a readiness to pursue a lost craft. By New Year's Eve, after scouring the want ads for used equipment, he'd found most of what he needed to construct a rudimentary pottery studio.

The first accessory was an Austrian kiln made in the '50s that he'd seen pictured in manuals, owned by a retired artist in Philadelphia. He was also selling a foot-powered wheel that was exactly like the one his father had. Matthew paid the extra shipping charges through eBay and his new used equipment was soon on its way. Hand tools were easy to find locally and by the last day of December, the last day of the century, he had picked up or ordered all the equipment he needed. By the time it was assembled, his basement, half-filled with the old furnace and water heating system, would be cleared, making way for a studio he could call his own, a place he could retreat to, create, hold at bay the frightening specter of insanity.

But first, at the invitation of Sarah Finnegan, he would attempt to celebrate New Year's Eve. It found him on his usual stool in the jam-packed neighborhood bar called Rico's. He arrived early to take advantage of free champagne and Alec, the owner, was handing them across the bar to any and all takers.

"Fancy meeting you here," a woman's voice said from behind. Matthew turned to see Sarah up against him with a girlfriend jammed in on either side.

"I think you owe me one," she said, nodding to the champagne. She was dressed fancy for the evening's festivities, with a mini black dress and sparkles in her eyeliner. "Glad to see you've recovered," she said.

"No thanks to you," he said. "You dragged me into it."

"What a party! So much for the two-drink chit program! That Holmes is such an idiot. But I thought you and Dr. Batiste made a stunning couple on the dance floor, by the way," she said.

"Oh God," Matthew said.

"For a shrink, she had some moves," Sarah said.

"I haven't thanked you for the ride home," Matthew said.

"Yes, you did, at your house, don't you remember? In bed?" She said with raised eyebrows.

Matthew strained to recall. She could see the look of horror on his face.

"Just kidding!" she said, laughing uproariously.

Matthew yelled to Alec. "A round of bubbly for the ladies!"

Thus began the last New Year's Eve of the century. Matthew Banks, tragically single but surrounded by people who would remind him he wasn't all alone, helping him, for now, forget he was a widower. Allowing him to pretend Julia was simply not there, perhaps off on a business trip, and tonight he could relax in knowing he was safe and welcome in the bosom of his ebullient friends. The bar filled beyond capacity as midnight neared, the music got louder, and the champagne was spilling all over the bar and the holiday attire of its devotees.

"Are you still buying?" Sarah asked right at 12 a.m.

"Of course," Matthew said.

She looped the air with her finger and ordered the group another round. The ball dropped on the television and Times Square was a blizzard. Everyone around him was kissing and hooting and throwing back drinks. Sarah's two friends were jostling one another in an effort to get ahold of Matthew, one of, if not *the* best-looking single man at the bar, and Sarah intervened and grabbed him by his ears. She planted a long, slobbery kiss on his lips, leaning into him. He could feel the cushion of her breasts and closed his eyes and compared it to kissing Julia. She was gripping the back of his head and she wouldn't let go. Matthew gave in and began feeling unexpected stirrings of desire. This business with Sarah felt foreign, yet nonetheless exciting, and their teen-age display of affection would continue well into the first hours of the new millennium.

* * *

"Are you alright?" she had asked when they awoke in his bed New Year's morning.

He didn't answer, couldn't answer, and got up to take a shower.

Downstairs, dressed only in his bathrobe, he made her coffee, poured it in a paper cup, and showed her to the door.

"My car is two miles from here," she said.

"Oh yeah," Matthew said, remembering she'd insisted on driving his car home.

He went back upstairs and got dressed. In the car, she apologized.

"We had to do that," Sarah said.

"To celebrate the new millennium?" he said sheepishly.

"No. Because it was time you got laid."

He stared at the empty road ahead as they made their way across town. He was feeling guilty and confused.

"Was it any good?" he finally asked.

Sarah smiled. "It was fine," she said. "Everything works."

When they got to her car, she looked at him endearingly, as if he were her younger brother.

"I'm always around if you need to talk."

She kissed his cheek and climbed from the car.

New Year's Day warmed to just above freezing, and in the early afternoon a light sleet glazed the sidewalks. Matthew lit a fire and settled into the black recliner. He wasn't so hungover; it was more a listless, unsettled feeling, one he remembered from the day he lost his virginity as a teenager. Rather than triumphant, he was cowed, as though he'd done something wrong, crossed a threshold from which there was no turning back. Had he been unfaithful? Of course not. Julia was gone forever, and for the first time he was face to face with the fact he was no longer legally married, which meant technically he hadn't broken a single vow. But it was cool comfort. With recurring glimpses of Sarah's naked body, the flowery scent of her perfume that clung to him, he couldn't help but try to recall their sex, wondering if it was any good for her. Something told him the answer was probably no.

Downstairs, the basement studio was shaping up to provide just the escape he had in mind. He'd gathered all the necessary hand tools, and the wheel and kiln were in place, ready to assist in the creation of art. Twenty pounds of clay sat on the table wrapped in cellophane, and when he stepped downstairs that New Year's afternoon it was like walking into a dream sequence. He heard his father's voice speak to him encouragingly. Visions of creatively shaped pots and vases passed before him, and he could see himself bent over his wheel, his hands working the wet clay into a hundred different shapes. He put on an apron and plopped a square of clay onto the wheel, added water, and began his first project. It would be a modest bowl, perhaps for nuts, and he focused on a perfect edge and uniform body. As he neared completion, the piece suddenly went askew, listing to one side and collapsing; some areas were paper thin. He smashed it flat and started over and would repeat this routine for several hours until he created an acceptable bowl.

As daylight dissolved beyond the half windows above, he set the bowl in the kiln and began the firing process. He then washed his tools and went upstairs to read his book, feeling he'd had a successful maiden session in his studio, certain he'd be back in the days prior to returning to work. He already had an idea for his next piece. It wasn't until later that evening, lying in bed, when he realized Julia hadn't once come to mind.

There was a January White Sale going on, and in the paper's Home Section he found a new mattress at a store that delivered. He would rid himself of the old, soiled relic, the queen-sized mattress that came with the bed, which had come with the marriage. Although he had a certain sentimental attachment, it gave off a faint unpleasant odor he blamed on his accident the night of the Christmas party. The offer included free recycling.

On the day scheduled for its delivery, the Friday before the last weekend of the holiday break, Matthew asked Hughes to watch for the truck, as he needed to go into the office. He'd promised himself during his break, one of several New Year's resolutions, to recommit to his job, as much as he dreaded the day-to-day banality. He realized the value in regaining management's respect lost over the previous months. Whether he stayed with the company or not, an involuntary dismissal could be emotionally and financially devastating. His office was in a complete state of disarray and he wanted to start the new year fresh. Hughes offered to wait at his house and showed up with several art magazines to keep busy.

Matthew pulled into his driveway later that afternoon to see the new mattress, sealed in plastic, standing beside the front door. Inside he found Hughes asleep, magazines scattered about the floor.

"Hughes – what the hell?" He said, walking into the room.

Hughes shook himself awake.

"Oh dear."

"The mattress guys?" Matthew asked, annoyed. "They were supposed to take the old one?"

"Oh my," Hughes said, still half asleep.

Matthew shook his head and told him to get up and give him a hand with the new one.

"Sorry, old boy," was all Hughes said as they stepped outside.

Matthew sized up the mattress and then looked at Hughes, standing there still disoriented.

"I know what you're thinking," Hughes said. "My good arm is as strong as both of yours"

They wrestled the mattress onto the stairs, Matthew leading them and Hughes, his natural and manmade arms locked in below, nudging them upward. Reaching the top, they waddled down the hallway into the master bedroom and stood it against the wall. Matthew stripped the sheets and mattress pad off the old one, releasing a faintly foul odor, and Hughes took one look at the stains and raised his eyebrows.

"If only this mattress could talk."

Matthew ignored the glib comment and grabbed the opposite side and they pulled it off the box spring.

"Letters from an old flame?" Hughes asked.

Matthew looked down to the box spring and saw the smattering of flattened envelopes, all with the postmark "Camden, Me."

"No flame of mine," he said under his breath as he picked one up. He pulled the folded stationery from one envelope and scanned the top half. *My hot little sex kitten.* He picked out key phrases: *Aching for you. Must plan our next trip.* He opened another. He scanned the postmarks and learned the writer had been sending them for three months. He let the letters fall from his hand to the floor and stared out to the front yard, where a light snow had begun to fall.

"Matthew?" Hughes was standing at the foot of the bed.

He didn't answer, shifting his blank stare to the floor. He turned and left the room and went downstairs. There was the jingling of keys and Hughes heard the door shut. After scooping up the letters, Hughes sat on the shiny new mattress and read each one, page by painful page.

It wasn't a total surprise. Julia had hinted to Hughes about gaps in her marriage, in the bedroom and beyond. She had withheld any direct reference to this Bryan Kane, but Hughes had sensed the presence of another man. From the sound of it, this man's infatuation was reciprocated. According to the letters, they had met up at least twice and had spent a lot of time, judging by the anecdotes, in bed. Hughes gathered the letters together and considered taking them away to avoid further trauma, but quickly dropped the idea. Maybe it was best for Matthew to do as he had just done, study each handwritten letter for clues to the relationship, determine if it was merely a tryst or something more. He put the letters on the windowsill, a three-inch stack of paper documenting a marriage in a death spiral. He cleaned up the mattress wrappings, went downstairs, grabbed his magazines, and went home.

An hour later, frozen like a mannequin, Matthew was driving through the snow-covered streets of Hartford, both hands gripping the wheel like he was trying to wrench it free. He was oblivious to the worsening weather conditions. What began as a light dusting now looked more like a Nor'easter. His wipers wagged ineffectually, spreading the snow without clearing it. People were shoveling their driveways. One man was hunched over a drift resting, holding his shovel, his breath coming in great clouds, the back of his navy-colored overcoat blanketed in white. On the edge of town, Matthew got stuck behind a snowplow, spewing a wave of slush, pounding the hood of his car violently. The found letters kept appearing in front of him like they were projected onto the windshield. This Kane's handwriting looked like a kid's. His expressions were trite, callow, no doubt poorly schooled, with sentences like "*Your SO fine*". The image of an illiterate, Yankee boatman came to mind. Kane worked with his hands, not his brain. What kind of a match was that? Julia was a scientist. She had a postgraduate degree! Matthew wondered if the son of a bitch even knew she was dead.

As dusk approached the snow was coming down in billowing clouds, turning each streetlight into a small hazy sun. He pointed his car toward Rico's and by the time he pulled in the employee parking lot darkness had fallen. In the kitchen, he walked passed Alec the owner without saying hello. Alec followed him into the bar.

"Everything cool?" Alec said.

Matthew nodded and took his usual stool.

"Give me a double Jack Daniels."

Alec first gave his friend a quick assessment, and then poured a tumbler without measuring. Matthew emptied the glass, winced, and asked for another. When he finished the second, less desperately, Alec leaned into him from across the bar.

"What the fuck?"

Matthew, his face already blotchy, eyes watering, looked back at him and said nothing.

"Dude – talk to me," Alec said.

He came around the bar and sat beside Matthew.

"Slow down," he whispered. "It's bad for business when I have to pick my customers up off the floor."

He gave him a one-armed hug and returned to the other side of the bar where he drew a glass of water.

"Drink this," he said, sliding it across the mahogany slab.

Five minutes later, Matthew spoke.

"Another."

Alec came down to him from the other end.

"First tell me what's going on."

Matthew's reptilian eyes slid from the rows of bottles in front of the mirror over to Alec.

"Julia."

"What about her?"

Matthew lowered his chin to his chest and began silently weeping, his shoulders rising and falling. Alec came around again, this time grabbing his friend's arm.

"We're moving you," he said, pulling him from the stool to a quiet corner table where he deposited him in a chair. "Sit here. Don't talk to anyone."

"Drink?" Matthew said.

"In a minute."

Five minutes later, Alec returned with a double and another glass of water. Matthew had settled deeper in his chair.

"I'll check back in a few," Alec said. "Behave."

A gust of wind blew the door open. Outside, the snow came in shrouds, bluish in the neon streetlight. Cars sat parked along the curb, caked with snow like igloos. The door slammed itself shut. Matthew drank all the whiskey and remained slumped in his chair, trying to calculate the likelihood of making it to the door. He could sleep in his car. As he summoned the courage to try, Alec came to the table.

"I'm taking you home." Alec stood patiently while his friend attempted a response.

"Unless you can get someone to pick you up," he finally said.

Matthew sat up unevenly and drank from the glass of water. His eyes floated across the room. By now it was filled with Friday dinner patrons. He fumbled in his pocket and pulled out his phone.

"I'll find someone," he mumbled.

Sarah was at the wheel of her Jeep as she navigated the snowy streets back to Matthew's house.

"Your timing sucks," she told him.

"Sorry," Matthew whispered, leaning into the passenger's side door.

"You caught me on the way out to a date," she said.

"I didn't know you had a boyfriend."

"I don't. Her name is Abbey."

48

"Abbey? Really?"

"*Hellooooo Matthew.* Sorry to break it to you."

"What about the other night?"

"I make exceptions in special situations."

Matthew closed his eyes as they pulled up to his house and begged her to come it.

"I have another special situation," he said.

Inside, Sarah helped herself to a beer and handed Matthew aspirin and a glass of water. They sat on the couch while, amidst the sobs, he explained the letters. She listened closely. Bella whined to go out.

"Just let her out back," Matthew whispered before passing out.

He awoke fully dressed the next morning, Sarah beside him, also dressed, lightly snoring beneath the thick duvet. They were on the bare, white mattress, which was extra-firm and smelled of fresh foam. The storm had passed and the sky outside the window was once again magnificently, brutally blue. Against the wall across the room stood the old mattress, a queen-sized billboard of past emissions, intentional and otherwise.

"Next time, I'm putting you on the clock," Sarah said, suddenly awake. "At an hourly rate you can afford."

"I'll pay, even without sex," Matthew said. "Why did you stay?"

"You made me."

She went into the bathroom and closed the door. Above the hiss of her peeing, she asked if he was alright alone.

"I think so," Matthew said.

He heard the toilet flush and then her washing at the sink. She emerged with a fresh face and hair brushed.

"Burn the goddam letters," she said sternly as she pulled on a sweater. "Do not, under any circumstances, read them again." She bent down and pulled the duvet to his chin. "And if I were you, I'd find a good shrink."

Chapter 7

Relieved the holidays were behind him, Matthew tried to embrace a new willingness to engage, and this started with his return to the office. There, he'd jump into new projects and mix with his peers. He'd given himself a head start during the break, organizing stacks of data piled on his desk and shredding old paper files.

The first day back at the office, he received an internal message on his desktop computer that instantly put everything into perspective.

"Please schedule fifteen minutes with me when convenient. Doris will arrange."

It came from Dr. Madeleine Batiste. Doris was her Administrative Assistant, a serious, unattractive older woman who had been with the company forever. He read the message three times. It was freighted with implications, none of them good. His thoughts raced back to the holiday party, the look in Lawrence Holmes' eye when he saw Matthew dancing with Dr. Batiste. And the murky conversation he'd had with Dr. Batiste before everything went kerflooey.

He wasted no time calling Doris and scheduled the meeting for the following day at 9:00 a.m., allowing himself time to prepare, although he acknowledged there was little he could do in that regard. He asked if anyone else was attending. Doris said it was just the two of them.

Dr. Batiste had wandered in and out of his thoughts throughout the holiday break like a pleasant fantasy. For the most part, he recalled their meeting as a tantalizing encounter. It was not merely her physical attractiveness; the most poignant memory included the aura she carried, which seemed all the more extraordinary considering his sketchy cognition at the time. And the way she so cavalierly dragged him under the disco ball; how she had danced like no one was watching. She was tall and lithe, her movements so sensual, almost tribal, as though from some distant civilization. Where *was* she from? Her racial origin was obscure: she had a voice that carried a faint Caribbean lilt and delicate features, with a perfect small nose and hazel eyes that stood out against her light brown face, giving her a faintly predatory, feline look. Her curly hair was nearly black. It was rumored she was not to be trifled with; she had fierce boundaries.

But all this only piqued his curiosity, and one night before the end of the break he called Sarah, who had mentioned Dr. Batiste when they worked on a project together. It seemed she attracted a lot of attention; people were talking about her, she said. Many men lusted after her, and a few women. She'd heard Dr. Batiste was orphaned at twelve, in New Orleans, and raised in a convent. She went on to Princeton, and apparently lettered in track, nearly qualifying for the summer Olympics her senior year. And from there it was on to med school. She had countless options for a career, and it was the subject of debate among many at *Connecticut Life* just how she ever came to choose the pedestrian world of insurance.

As Matthew made his way up the stairwell (one of his New Year's resolutions was to get in shape) he was casual in assuming his behavior at the holiday party was the subject of the called meeting. *Connecticut*

Life and Casualty was a conservative New England institution. A 170-year-old underwriter, it was still housed in its original structure, a stand-alone, four-story stone edifice in central Hartford. Dr. Batiste, as a member of the Executive Committee, worked on the top floor. Her relatively small office was wedged between Lawrence Holmes, the Human Resources director, and the CEO. She was often called on to provide expert level counsel for medical parameters of certain high-risk policies. That she had once been a psychotherapist, with her own practice, added value to the team.

"Please," Dr. Batiste said from her upholstered chair, gesturing where he should sit. Matthew stepped into her office slightly winded and noticed the faint but unmistakable scent of patchouli. A tiny stick of incense smoldered in the dark corner. The room was softly lit on this overcast January day, and a string of Christmas lights blinked around the perimeter of her wooden desk. She rose and extended her hand.

"Happy new millennium," she said.

She was taller than he remembered, wearing horn-rimmed glasses and a black turtleneck sweater, a cross between a university professor and an executive apparel model. Everything – from her cashmere top to her skirt to her jewelry, appeared perfectly curated. She came from around her desk and closed the door, silencing the chatter and commotion of the administrative pool just beyond. Matthew waited for her to start but found the quiet unnerving.

"Do you observe Christmas?" he blurted out, immediately embarrassed by such a stupid question.

Dr. Batiste looked startled by the question.

"I'm Catholic," she said without any expression.

Matthew shifted in his chair. "Sorry. I didn't mean to get too personal."

"My son and I went skiing in Vermont. It was magical. And you? What were you up to?"

He noticed a framed photo on the credenza of a smiling boy with a mouthful of braces wearing a Red Sox cap.

"I was here. The whole time."

"I understand you live alone now," Dr. Batiste said.

"I have a dog. Her name is Bella."

Her expression softened.

"I'm sorry for your loss."

The clock on the wall behind him ticked away, like an observer keeping time. The colored lights blinked ridiculously.

"So," she said, "we're meeting to talk about that loss. And any other issues you'd care to bring up."

Matthew had his elbows on the arms of the chair and steepled his fingers beneath his chin. He was trying to make out the brand of her stylish glasses, Italian, he guessed.

"Like the party?" he said, acting on his earlier decision to be preemptive.

"More than that," she said.

"What, then?" Matthew girded for the worst.

"Your work performance. Your emotional well-being, your future. There's a lot to unpack."

Unpack? Matthew looked over her shoulder and through the clear glass panes of the window. It had begun snowing. Large, cotton-ball-sized flakes were dropping slowly straight down in the rare vacuum of a windless day.

"I'm making some changes," Matthew volunteered. "I want to stay here." Now he was lying, for he assumed the worst.

"Then you mustn't lose control. And you might want to be more discreet about your interoffice relationships."

He wondered how she knew about Sarah.

Dr. Batiste leaned back in her chair and considered him.

"Where do you see yourself in five years, at Connecticut Life?" she asked.

"I don't know," Matthew said. "No clue."

"At least you're honest."

"I have no reason not to be."

She tightened her gaze, zeroing in on his eyes.

"How are you sleeping?"

Matthew wondered if this was a trick question.

"Like the dead."

Dr. Batiste paused, perhaps to determine if this was inappropriate, dark sarcasm.

"Well, that's good. You need your rest."

She stood abruptly and put out her hand.

"I hope this is a better year for you, Matthew," she said. "I hope it's a better millennium!"

He was shocked by the abrupt conclusion and tentatively rose from his chair and returned her firm grip.

"That's it?" he said.

"I mostly wanted to meet you, eye to eye, in the clear light of day. It's important, before getting our sessions started. Personnel files, and dancing to Marvin Gaye, can only give us so much."

Oh God, he thought. The party.

"What do you mean by sessions?" he said.

"Our regular consultations. Lawrence and I decided this is called for." And then, "He thinks quite highly of you, you know."

Matthew didn't respond as he turned away.

"Oh, and Matthew," she said as he reached the door, "How long were you married?"

"Why?" he said curtly.

"I think it's relevant."

He gave her a look.

"It's not, actually."

On the elevator going down Matthew felt his private life had become public property, to be analyzed and deconstructed by people at the highest levels of his company. He had prepared himself for a hand slap, commensurate with his behavior at the party, but apparently this would go beyond that. These people were charting his career and he'd given them reason for doubt, questioning his stability, his place in the company story, all based on a few bad decisions. Although Dr. Batiste mentioned Holmes liked him, what was that worth? And this Dr. Batiste – what was her story? He'd seen a therapist once in college, during a time of existential confusion. It didn't go so well. Dr. Batiste reminded him of the textbook shrink, the all-knowing mien, the off-putting demeanor suggesting *I know things about you that you don't, and probably shouldn't.*

As the day wore on, he found himself replaying their brief meeting. It wasn't so much what she said as the way she said it, and how she looked at him. Dr. Batiste's attractiveness flowed from her core; she was terribly pretty, but in an unconventional way. It was her cool, measured manner that he found more than a little intimidating. Forget the Ivy League diplomas adorning her walls; this was a woman of substance, a woman beyond degrees. She belonged in magazines, the glamorous genius. Two words echoed in his head: *these sessions.*

"Stop by when you're finished," Hughes called to Matthew that evening from his front porch. Matthew was scraping the last of the snow from his driveway. The weather forecast called for a clear cold front through the next three days.

"Only if you have something to warm me up," Matthew said, catapulting a shovelful into a bank.

"Indeed I do. And something else I think you'll like," Hughes said.

Ten minutes later, Matthew was standing by a crackling fire with a glass of whiskey. Hughes was down in the basement rummaging for whatever he had for him.

He appeared minutes later holding a small painting the size of a cereal box and set it on the mantel, its image facing the wall.

"This requires a brief introduction," Hughes said.

Matthew raised his eyebrows.

"You know how your Julia enjoyed my art," Hughes said. "I don't know if you're aware how much I enjoyed sharing it with her. She was so taken by the special pieces. She had an eye, that girl. She became quite keen and well versed, especially in post-Impressionist works."

"Hughes, where are you going with this?" Matthew said, impatient.

"Some time ago, well before the crash, I had decided to give her this piece." He motioned to the mantel. "It was one she especially adored."

Matthew's expression darkened.

"You *do* like the Impressionists, don't you?" Hughes said.

"Of course."

Hughes turned the painting around. It was of a light green pond with purple and white lilies and watercress floating on a rippled surface. The brush strokes were distinctly mid-19th century European.

Hughes' face lit up as he studied it.

"Painted by the French artist Turiot in 1872, an understudy of Monet but never gained any commercial fame. His paintings lately have become quite sought after. It turns out Julia's taste was not only spot on, but it was also quite prescient."

Matthew wasn't sure what to say. He studied the painting, acknowledging its aesthetic pedigree, especially the brushwork, but the composition was not anything to get excited about, not even close to a Monet.

"Tell me again, exactly why you are giving this to me?" he asked.

Hughes frowned. "I don't have to explain how much Julia meant to me," he said. "And I don't want to get maudlin, but with all that we've just learned, I feel an obligation to prop up her honor."

Matthew's face flushed.

"And you think a painting by some unknown Frenchman will make what she did alright? Are you *serious*?"

"Oh dear," Hughes said. "I was afraid of this."

Matthew walked to the closet to get his coat.

"I can't accept it, Hughes."

"Oh come now, man," Hughes said. "You have to put the Kane business behind you. Get on with your life!"

"My idea of getting on with my life would be to drive to Maine and put a bullet in the fucker's head."

Hughes stared in disbelief.

"Matthew! Please, rid yourself of this anger. It is extremely corrosive. Over time you will suffer. Plus, I don't fancy visiting you in Danbury," he said, referring to the Federal Prison an hour drive south.

Matthew said, "Goddammit Hughes! I have to do something, at least get in his face, give him some trouble!"

Hughes was shaking his head.

When his voice stopped ringing off the walls Matthew paused.

"I guess you don't see it that way."

Hughes' face softened.

"I *can* see the value in that," he said. "A man's slighted ego must somehow be made whole again. But killing your nemesis is not a long-term strategy. You need to cool down. Revenge is a dish best served cold."

Matthew stared into the fire. "I'm not entirely serious," he said softly. "But I would like to shake him up. Put the fear of God in him. How far is Camden, anyway?"

"Maybe five hours, or a bit more. It's a lovely drive."

They finished their drinks and Hughes asked him to stay for dinner. Matthew declined, put on his overcoat, and headed to the door.

"Aren't you taking the painting?"

Hughes lifted the artwork off the mantel and brought it to the door.

"Think of this as a steppingstone on your path to recovery," he said. "I'm not entirely sure how it all adds up, but it feels right."

Matthew took the painting without comment and stepped into the frigid night air.

"You know," said Hughes as Matthew went down the steps, "I love Maine. It's an easy drive. I'm not recommending you go, but if you do, let me know. It might be a fun getaway."

Back home, Matthew sat in his leather Scandinavian recliner staring into the cold empty fireplace. The whiskey had him at a crossroads. He could have another, enhance the buzz, or cut his losses, heat a pot of soup and go to bed. But his mind went back to Hughes' living room. His attempt to balance the scales with the gift only brought Julia's betrayal back to the present. Why would he want to stare at that every day? Now, as it sat on his mantel, facing forward, it seemed to telegraph Julia's name. He turned it back to the wall.

He remained in the black leather chair for another hour, choosing neither whiskey nor sustenance as he plumbed the murky coordinates of this new life. Drifting off, he got up to take Bella for a brisk walk around the block. The cold air was sobering but on his return he remained drowsy. He shut off the lights and climbed the stairs to bed. In minutes he would validate his claim to Dr. Batiste. He'd sleep the sleep of the dead, if only for a few hours.

Chapter 8

Matthew called in sick the next morning. He'd awoken at three o'clock, only to spend the rest of the night twisting in the sheets like a fish caught in a net. It wasn't the painting, or Julia keeping him up. Why was he so preoccupied with Dr. Batiste? She had steadily migrated to the front of his consciousness, becoming the most exciting thing about his job, and therefore his present-day life. He realized he loved the attention she was giving him, the sense of community their meetings would bring. But the day-to-day work remained vapid, to the point of utter despair. In a perfect world, he'd leave this corporate life and do nothing but create art, exotic pots, and even ornamental knickknacks. For it was only at his mother's insistence he pursued a business degree, and while he exhibited a quick grasp of numbers, economic models, and pro forma tabulations, it all left him stone cold. He had tolerated the job at *Connecticut Life* only because it paid him well enough to keep the house after the loss of Julia's income.

He was drinking a cup of coffee in his partially assembled basement studio when his cell phone rang that afternoon. He could see it was his mother.

"Your secretary told me you were sick," she said.

"You're up early," Matthew said. It was 5:45 am in Pasadena.

"Are you? Sick?"

"Sort of," Matthew said, cupping the mug to heat his hands.

"I have a proposition," his mother said.

Matthew rolled his eyes.

"Move back to Pasadena," she said.

He could hear her take a drag on her cigarette. At least she wasn't drinking.

"Return to your roots," she continued. "You and I can make another stab at a mother son relationship. And when I croak, you can have this place. I'll even change my will."

If it had been later, in the early evening, Matthew would know she was drunk and pass it off. But her voice was clear, true, and she was communicating a positive vision of the future.

"Another stab?" he said.

"You know what I mean. Let's not get technical. I'm all alone in this huge place your grandfather built. I hate to tell you, it's spooky. Oh, and I'm going to try to get sober. I could use your support."

Matthew held the phone from his ear and stared at it as if she had climbed inside.

"At least come for a visit," she said. "See how it feels."

Matthew's toes were getting numb, standing on the dirt floor. His coffee was cold. He dumped it in the sink.

"Maybe," he said. "A break in January would be nice. When do you quit drinking?" he asked.

"Soon. It might be February."

"Cold turkey?"

"They'll give me something," she said. "I'll be in Betty Ford."

Matthew paused, imagining her writhing with delirium tremens.

"Do you want me there, for that?" he said.

"You can come when you want, but I'd rather you wait until I'm out."

In an uncharacteristic show of support, Matthew told her she was brave. He'd think about it, he said, and then hung up.

Upstairs he built a fire to thaw his feet. The cold front gripping New England had lowered the temperature outside to near zero. The birch logs caught instantly, shooting flames into the chimney. He picked up his Russian novel and read through the chapter where Vronsky learns Anna's pregnant, and then falls off his horse in a steeplechase race. *Serves the bastard right*, Matthew thought to himself.

Dorothy hadn't been entirely forthcoming with Matthew about her plans for rehabilitation. Her doctor had already reserved a bed at the clinic in West Los Angeles. She would enter in early February. It was a six-week program, and at the end, she had the option to move to a halfway house. They recommended this, as she would work in a shelter for the homeless where she could live and serve free food and see daily what could be in store for her if she failed to get sober. It was this phase that gave her the most pause, living with other addicts and alcoholics from all walks of life, most of them destitute, she assumed.

It was a Christmas card from Matthew's father that triggered Dorothy's last round of binge drinking. Nearly fifteen years since she'd heard from the man, and the card, with its wispy calligraphy, suddenly appeared in her mailbox. It was a shocking blow to an already wobbly state of mind. One day later, she was in the emergency room with alcohol poisoning. The attending physician, an active member of Alcoholics Anonymous, shared his story of hitting bottom, an opiate overdose which nearly killed him. He tenderly asked Dorothy if perhaps she was nearing hers.

The card from Albert Banks contained a full *mea culpa*. He'd gotten caught up in a mid-life crisis. He'd reached the end of being a lawyer, even if it was his own firm. His job in Pasadena was destroying him, and he made vague references to having been fired for some act of impropriety. His dream, he wrote, was to paint, real art, like the masters. He admitted his decision to leave one Saturday, while fourteen-year-old Matthew and his mother were making sandwiches for his friends, was the biggest mistake of his life. He was never able to muster the courage to return, and he was seeking her forgiveness. There was no indication he wanted to come back.

When he left, all those years ago, Dorothy was already relying on vodka to get through the day. Raising Matthew alone, through his hormone fueled post-adolescent years, almost guaranteed her habit would become a full-on addiction. By the time Matthew left home for college they were barely communicating. He'd been accepted at a good New England school and made the mistake of telling her he'd be pursuing an art degree. She angrily insisted she would only pay for a business degree, and that if he wanted to be an artist, he was on his own. To have another member of the family chase a silly dream and fail to face the realities of life was unthinkable. He agreed to major in accounting.

On the day she dropped him at Los Angeles International airport for his first semester, she wished him good luck and pulled away as he stood watching from the curb.

Ten years later, trying to prepare for her sobriety, Dorothy was still drinking throughout the day, but on more of a maintenance level. The morning she'd called Matthew to ask him to return, she'd had just one glass of vodka to steady her nerves. If she could get Matthew to agree to come out after Rehab, her appearance and state of mind should be much improved. She vowed to make a second call in a week's time, when she would give her doubting son the full story. Preparation for that call would likely require more than one shot of vodka.

Chapter 9

"Banks – see me ASAP, please."

Returning to work the next morning, an email from Lawrence Holmes appeared on Matthew's desktop just as he arrived in his office. He called up to Holmes' administrative assistant on the fourth floor and they fixed an immediate time to meet.

"So, you've met with Dr. Batiste," Holmes said thirty minutes later from behind his desk. A balding fifty-year-old ex-basketball player, Holmes always wore his sleeves rolled up, as if he were about to jump into a game of one-on-one.

Matthew nodded.

"And?"

"And what, sir?" Matthew said.

"You agree to a series of sessions with her."

"Series?"

"We don't want to put too fine a point on this, but Dr. Batiste is highly skilled. We are very fortunate to have her on staff. You should take advantage of this, pull yourself out of the hole you've found yourself in. One hour, once a week for a few months, will hopefully get you back on track."

"I didn't realize I was off track, Mr. Holmes," Matthew said.

Holmes was leaning back in his tilting chair, tapping a pen on his blotter. He began nodding as if he anticipated the comment.

"What would you say if I told you we have videotape from the night of the holiday party?"

Matthew sat up.

"We have closed-circuit surveillance of the entire premises," Holmes said. "Twenty-four seven."

"Really, that's not necessary," Matthew said, visualizing the camera mounted in the mailroom.

Holmes smiled coyly.

"Check with Madeleine's admin. I've told her to make you a priority. Are we in agreement here? You will start right away."

Matthew had forgotten her given name was Madeleine. It was so perfect for a woman of her stature, her elegance. Suddenly the idea of spending fifty-minutes a week with this exotic woman with the sexy name seemed like a lightning bolt of good fortune striking out of the blue.

* * *

"You've succumbed to the winter doldrums!" Hughes said, bounding into Matthew's living room.

He'd let himself in and was at the door stomping the snow from his boots. Matthew was asleep on the couch, a heavy Hudson Bay blanket spread over his entire length.

"Sorry to wake you," Hughes said.

"Saturday is nap day," Matthew said, his voice sleepy. A smoldering fire was nearly out in the hearth, its embers still emitting a hint of heat. "What's up?"

"I've been thinking," Hughes said in his typical serious tone. "The restoration of Matthew Banks' honor is something we should not take lightly."

"What do you mean, exactly?"

"Since the night I gave you the painting…" He glanced around the room, looking for it.

"I hung it upstairs," Matthew lied. It was actually stashed in a corner cupboard.

Hughes continued.

"Facing up to this philanderer Kane is something you owe yourself," he said, sitting in the chair, his coat still on. "And the universe! Your soul won't rest until you've at least attempted to even the score. Now hear me out. You can't kill the louse, but you can stand up to him. It wasn't too long ago when a man in your position would draw a pistol at dawn. All within the law!"

Matthew nodded in amusement.

"You have given this some thought."

"I have indeed. And my offer to go with you to Maine still stands. I'll even drive."

Matthew furrowed his eyebrows. "I detect something else going on here," he said.

A grin spread across Hughes' face.

"If you must know, Camden is where a former boyfriend of mine lives. I haven't seen him in years. It turns out he's single again."

Matthew sat up, the Russian novel tumbling to the floor. It would be the first time Hughes made any reference to his sexual preference.

"Well!" Matthew said, gasping for words. "Have you been in touch with this –"

"His name is Carver. Peter Carver. I'm surprised Julia never told you about him. She was quite aware."

Matthew was standing now, folding the blanket.

"So, this trip isn't only about the restoration of my honor."

"You'll love Peter," Hughes said, his eyes twinkling. "He's offered to roll out the red carpet."

"Wait – you've already set this up?"

"We'll leave at dawn on Saturday. We'll take the African Queen."

He was referring to his vintage Jaguar sedan, a long, slender four-door model, the *Vanden Plas*.

"Hold on," Matthew said. "I think we're getting ahead of ourselves."

"I'm not. But if you have any reservations, I can go alone."

Matthew draped the blanket over the back of the couch and picked the book off the floor. He sat back down and faced Hughes.

"Just let me get comfortable with this," he said.

"You mean with Peter and me?"

"No – please. I need to decide what I'll do when I get there, when I look Kane in the eye. For the record, I always assumed you were gay. Thank you for trusting me with it. Why do you think I never complained about all the time you and Julia spent drinking wine and gossiping like a couple of bored housewives?"

"We never gossiped."

"Right."

Matthew threw another log on the fire, sparks bursting upward.

"How's the weather look for this weekend?" he said.

"Possibility of snow," Hughes said. "But that will only add to the beauty of Maine. You'll see, it's right out of Currier and Ives."

He'd never seen Hughes so animated.

"Maybe you can help me with my script," Matthew said.

"Script?"

"What I'm going to say. To put him on his heels, before I clobber him."

"We'll have five hours in the car," Hughes said as he stood at the door. "A little unsolicited advice. I say you visit him at home, hit him where he lives, and then we'll go to Peter's and raise a glass to the restored honor of Matthew Banks! It's got all the makings of an epic weekend!"

* * *

"Is this time on Fridays good for you? I don't want any excuses."

Dr. Batiste sat behind her desk as Matthew settled in his chair, one of two facing her. It was 9:01 a.m. on the third Friday in January.

"Sure thing," Matthew said.

He was silently trembling now that he was in her presence. All week he'd been anticipating this, guessing the subject of their talk today. Holmes had made it sound like it might be full-blown psychoanalysis. She looked so relaxed in her long-sleeved, tight-fitting cashmere dress, a soft coffee with cream color that matched her skin perfectly.

"So, how shall we start?" She was gently biting on the tip of one of the temples of her glasses.

"You tell me, Doctor. I'm not the one who called the meeting."

He instantly regretted the smart aleck comment.

"I'd like to talk about Julia," she said.

Matthew stiffened.

"I'd rather not, just now."

"But her sudden death is clearly part of your – shall we say, deviation from normal behavior. Accidental death of a spouse is one of the most traumatic events a person can experience. You are living with PTSD. People often don't realize this. It might be helpful to come to grips with how your life has changed, what is missing now, and how you will integrate going forward." Dr. Batiste's head was tilted slightly in sympathy as she addressed the young widower across from her.

She'd lapsed into insurance-speak. *Accidental death. Integrate going forward.* It all sounded so corporate, straight out of the actuarial manuals. He paused before speaking.

"What's missing," he said," is my *whole life.* I've lost everything. Jesus, I even lost what I *thought* I had with her."

He was struggling to breathe in the warm room. Dr. Batiste had wasted no time ripping off the scab.

"You still have yourself," Dr. Batiste said with a sympathetic smile.

"For what that's worth."

They sat in the morning silence of her office. The clock was loud and impossible to ignore, as before. The Christmas lights were gone. Her son continued to beam his shiny smile from the photo behind her. They'd only been talking for ten minutes and he was drained.

"Tell me about your family," she said, changing her tone slightly. "Back in California, right?"

"You mean *out* in California. *Back* is only for the east. Think in historical terms." Now he felt like a smart ass, but it was good to lighten things up.

"Okay, *out* in California."

"There's not much to tell. I have a mother who is threatening to get sober. I'll believe it when I see it."

"Father? Siblings?"

Matthew explained the situation. His droll delivery sounded as if he was reading from a newspaper. Dr. Batiste remained expressionless but focused. When he stopped talking she jotted some notes and changed the subject again.

"Do you think you had a good marriage? Did you love one another?"

The question knocked the wind out of him. He felt his emotions take off beyond his grasp. His throat tightened and tears pooled in his eyes. Dr. Batiste slid a box of Kleenex to the edge of the desk. He pulled two tissues and covered his face as the tears came full force. He was ashamed; he couldn't remember the last time he cried. It was horribly embarrassing, and he was stunned at how quickly it came on. Dr. Batiste rose from behind her desk and came over to sit beside him. She put her hand on his shoulder as he sobbed, then removed it.

"I think we've covered enough today," she whispered. "When you're ready, feel free to go."

Matthew caught his breath and straightened, dabbing his eyes.

"I'm sorry," he said, looking out the window behind her desk.

"There is nothing to be sorry for," Dr. Batiste said. "These talks are meant to help us understand your pain better, and now I see it is still quite fresh. I don't want to turn away from hard truths, but also we must not move too fast. We'll take our time."

Matthew stood to leave.

"I don't have any secrets about my marriage, if that's what you're thinking," he said. "I didn't do anything wrong."

"It doesn't matter, materially, either way. It's more about reconciling your emotions," Dr. Batiste said.

His face was flushed and wincing, a lost, frightened little boy.

"Think about what you want to share with me in our next session," she said.

Chapter 10

The highway was deserted Saturday morning at 6:45. There was no sign of the approaching dawn; the sliver of a moon hung on the western horizon. Hughes was at the wheel of his sleek car while Matthew poured two cups of hot coffee from his Thermos, mindful not to spill on the tan calfskin leather seat. He had talked Hughes into allowing Bella to come. She was stretched out in the back seat on her favorite blanket.

"Capital idea, bringing the coffee," Hughes said, "Use the cup holder please." He was leaning at an angle into the green-lit dashboard, his right hand working a knob on the wheel, prosthetic arm hanging down against the driver's door.

"What did you call this car the other day?" Matthew said.

"The African Queen. Bogart's gunboat. Don't you remember? It's the longest Jaguar ever made, a limited edition."

Matthew had his seat all the way back and his legs stretched out straight, thinking he might nap. But Hughes' specialized driving technique with the one-handed attachments, plus a concern about residual blood alcohol from the night before, was making that difficult. He sipped his coffee and looked out into the darkness of a mid-winter New England morning.

"Let's get on with it," Hughes said. "What are you going to say?"

"I have a newspaper clipping of the accident," Matthew said, speaking into the window. "Beyond showing that, I don't know."

"Promise me you won't get physical," Hughes said.

"I'm not planning to. Of course, if he turns on me –"

"Do you want me along?"

"I don't know. Probably not."

Hughes held the wheel with his knee now while he reached beneath the seat and pulled out a miniature baseball bat, the kind they give away at major league games.

"I brought this in case," he said.

Matthew laughed.

"I can hide it in my coat!" Hughes said.

They made their way north of Boston. The rotary at Portsmouth was quiet. Hughes said he needed to stop and got off at the next exit. As the two walked inside the rest area Matthew had to chuckle: He, in a leather bomber jacket and boots, the tough guy look, and Hughes dressed in a brand-new full length down parka, a senior metrosexual, his fake arm rigid at his side and a pair of Ray-Ban sunglasses with yellow lenses perched on his prominent nose. A young couple inside, the only customers, stopped talking as they gave them the once over. Hughes ordered extra-large coffees, paid for them, and headed back to the car while Matthew waited.

North of Kittery, a fine, granulated snow began falling. It hit the windshield with soft *ffffttttsss*. The Venti coffee had Hughes jabbering.

"You don't like the painting I gave you, just say it." he said.

"It's fine, Hughes. But it's really Julia's. I haven't figured out how to think about it."

"Don't think too hard. Just enjoy it. That's all it's meant for, to transport you someplace else for a moment or two. I thought that might be useful for you."

"But the whole thing with her –" Matthew said, staring out the side window. "If it was Julia's favorite, that doesn't automatically make it mine too. Actually, it's the opposite. Maybe I should have brought it along to smash over Kane's head."

"Now now. If you don't want it, tell me. I'll take it back. No hard feelings."

There was a long awkward pause until Hughes broke the silence.

"Really now, what *are* you going to do when we get there?" he said.

"I'll know when I see him," was all Matthew said.

The snow was gathering on the highway as the Jaguar pawed its way north on the Maine Turnpike, its tires leaving darkened contrails in the dusting. Somewhere behind the haze, the sun was brightening a swath of sky to the east. The only sound in the car now were the wipers working intermittently, and Matthew nodded off. As they left the toll road, the sun was up but the sky had taken on the leaden color of a battleship.

They headed east on a two-lane highway heading toward the coast and Matthew woke up and for the first time took note of the beauty of Maine, its granite walls reaching up on either side of the road, topped with the deep green of pine. Someday, under different circumstances, he'd return for fun, who knows, maybe with a woman; certainly, someone prettier than Hughes.

As they neared their destination, his mind flooded with doubt, questions around his motive, whether this was merely a post-adolescent, testosterone-fueled reaction to a bully in the schoolyard. Hughes tuned the radio to a pop station and the mood in the car instantly lightened as Matthew sang along to a well-known tune.

Camden, known for its quaint beauty and its boats, is often called the schooner capital of the world. The small coastal town sprouts up on the edge of Penobscot Bay and, as they approached, they were greeted by the colonial style homes and the flat steel-grey of the water. A low hanging sky appeared heavy with snow. It was lunchtime, and the sidewalks were dotted with residents running Saturday chores, shoppers returning Christmas gifts. The 19th-century street lamps were draped with colored lights and oversized red bows, and an antique sleigh sat in the middle of the town square loaded with pretend gift boxes and candy cane wrapping.

Hughes was hungry and suggested stopping at the Camden Inn, a majestic Victorian structure just off the square, known for its clam chowder. Matthew wasn't the least bit hungry.

"I'll sit with you," he said as Hughes pulled into the parking lot. "I need a telephone book for the address." He'd burned the letters and envelopes, at Sarah's advice, and destroyed any record of where the man lived.

They walked Bella around the lot and entered the formal entrance, cutting across the lobby to the bar. They were the first patrons, sitting at the bar, and Hughes ordered a martini. Matthew asked for a Coke. The bartender, a wiry older man with a grey ponytail, spoke with a Maine accent as thick as a Scottish brogue.

"Is there a local phone book handy?" Matthew asked as they watched him shake the cocktail.

"*Ayuh*," the man said. He poured the chilled gin into a glass, precisely to the brim, and carefully slid it over to Hughes. He filled a glass with Coke and reached down below the bar, pulling out the phone book.

"Who you after?" he asked.

"Just a friend of a friend. Trying to get his address," Matthew said.

"I probably know 'em. What's the name?"

"Kane," Matthew said tentatively. "Bryan Kane."

"Oh, *shoo-wah*."

Matthew closed the phone book.

"He's our mayor," the bartender said. "Lives on Osprey Lane, few blocks south. Or else he might be at City Hall. Prob'ly home though, today." He jotted the street number on a napkin and slid it over to Matthew. "I didn't give you this," he said with a wink.

Being in the same zip code, breathing the same air as the man he recently fantasized murdering, had Matthew's stomach churning Now it was real, it was happening. Two men Julia last loved were about to collide. Hughes sat quietly beside him, staring into his martini, sipping purposefully, while Matthew fidgeted in his seat in the darkly paneled bar. Christmas carols were playing overhead. He began weighing how much shame could come from calling the whole thing off. *The man is the goddam mayor*, he thought to himself.

"You might consider one of these," Hughes said, gesturing to his martini.

"I'd kill him if I drank one of those," Matthew said.

"Oh, I'd forgotten. Gin makes you surly. How about an Old Fashioned?"

"So does bourbon."

They sat staring at the bar and the rows of bottles lined up against the broad mirror. A series of stenciled schooners spanned the backdrop, artfully crafted wooden hulls with sweeping sails, each ship's bow spraying water high above the roiling waves.

"I better do this before I change my mind," Matthew said, sliding off his stool.

"I was thinking of having another," Hughes said. "Can you wait, or would you rather go without me?"

"Stay here," Matthew said. "If I'm not back in a half-hour let Bella out of the car." He snatched up the napkin with the address and hurried from the bar.

Crossing the street in front of the Inn, he made his way through the neighborhood, guessing at his direction. The heavy skies cast the neighborhood in a dim but even light. It would be dark in less than an hour. Lights were already turning on inside the modest houses. He found the address, a Cape Cod with two cars parked in the driveway. His boots were soaked through and his feet ached from the cold. Sweat slicked his forehead. He reached into his back pocket to make sure the newspaper clipping was there and walked up the driveway. He could see people moving inside, behind a sheer white curtain. His heart was racing. At the door, he rang the bell, a faint, antiquated ding-dong. The lock turned and a man large enough to fill the frame stood clutching an infant.

"Yeah?" His voice was deep, a baritone to match his size.

Matthew took a step back. With the interior lights casting him in silhouette, he managed to look into the man's eyes.

"What do you want?" the man asked.

"You're Bryan Kane?"

"Who are *you*?" His face reddened. His fierce eyes were drilling into him. For a second, Matthew considered saying he had the wrong address. But instead, he pulled out the clipping and held it out, his hand shaking slightly, for the man to read.

"She's dead," Matthew said as the man squinted to read the headline. "You'll never fuck her again."

The man's eyes moved down to the photo of the mangled car and then back at Matthew. Before Matthew could say anything more, Kane turned, taking the baby inside, leaving the door open. He returned seconds later, pulling the door closed behind him, and stood with his hands clenched into fists.

Matthew cleared his throat.

"I'm her –"

In a blink everything went blank but for a yellow starburst erupting squarely between Matthew's eyes, and now he was falling back, down, down until his head hit the ground with a *thump*. The frozen snow on his neck brought him to, and he began to make out Kane leering over him, preparing to kick his face. Matthew rolled to miss the boot and instantly was on his feet like a cat, desperately trying to focus, crouched to face the monster, who was shifting his stance as he maneuvered for another punch. The door opened behind him.

"*Bryan!*"

The woman's high-pitched yell rang off the house across the street and Kane paused. Matthew turned around and ran as fast as he could in the snow, slipping and sliding across the yard. He reached the street and gained speed, houses passing in his peripheral vision, his eyes bleary with what he thought to be tears, his face stinging and head aching in the freezing air. All the way to the Inn he ran hard until he burst through the entrance door and stopped short, heaving, in the vacant lobby. The clerk behind the desk, a frail, white-haired woman, froze as she took in the startling image before her. Matthew wasn't aware of the blood. His face was slathered in red, as was the collar of his white shirt and the front of his jacket. The clerk shrieked and ran into the back office. In the corner of the lobby, Hughes appeared as an apparition at the doorway of the darkened bar.

"Oh no – oh heavens *no!*" he said, advancing into the lobby.

* * *

Dr. Peter Carver lived two miles up the shoreline from the center of Camden. He'd built a sprawling modern multi-level house that conformed to nothing in an area known for its quaint salt-box architecture. At thirty-five, he was young for a senior physician at Methodist Hospital, where he specialized in emergency medicine. He had recently broken up with a partner of ten years, another, older physician who moved to Boston General. In the dying light, Hughes was trying to read the addresses on the mailboxes, leaning into the windshield, as they drove slowly through a forest of perfect Christmas trees. Matthew held a bloodied towel with ice against the bridge of his nose. Bella sat at attention in the back, whining, seemingly aware of her master's pain.

"I think it stopped," Matthew said, his voice muffled behind the pack.

"I certainly didn't think we'd be needing Peter's skills today," Hughes said. "Good. There it is."

He turned the car into a recently plowed driveway. Toward the shoreline they could see the lights of Peter's house, blazing on several levels, ornate chandeliers sending beacons like miniature lighthouses through huge gaping windows. Hughes parked the African Queen beside a black Range Rover and climbed out, retrieving their overnight bags, while Matthew crawled from the passenger side and opened the door for Bella. The sound of ocean waves crashing on the rocks could be heard from just beyond the tree line.

"Hughes! You old queen!"

Matthew looked to the deck above and saw a strikingly handsome man not much older than himself. He had blond wavy hair, a sharp jawline, and looked terribly fit. He came galloping down the steps and embraced Hughes while Matthew stood holding the towel to his face, clutching his small bag in the other hand. Peter turned to Matthew.

"Welcome Matthew! Hughes tells me you ran into some trouble," he said. "Fresh off the front lines? Let's see what we have here." He pulled away the compress and wiped off the blood. Now he could see a nose that was clearly displaced, and a purpling eye.

"Oh Matthew," Hughes whispered as he stepped closer. "Maybe we should run you to the ER."

"Hughes, I *am* the ER," Peter said.

Matthew whispered that it wasn't that bad, that he was going to be fine with the ice. Peter went silent and pulled Hughes aside and whispered something in his ear.

Inside, the house looked like a feature story in *Architectural Digest*. The living space was on three levels, with a fireplace on each, with modern Danish furniture and lighting hanging deep from cathedral ceilings. Woolen rugs from far away countries covered the lightly stained pine floors. In the open kitchen, a bar was set up with champagne in a silver ice bowl with hors d'oeuvres laid out. Peter showed them to their rooms and Matthew said he needed to lie down for a while. Bella followed him obediently into the guestroom and Matthew closed the door.

On the couch in the living room, Peter and Hughes were getting caught up.

"You look fabulous," Hughes said. "You are wearing your success well."

"And you, ever-youthful, haven't changed a bit," Peter said, his face beaming. Hughes was nearly ten years his senior. They kissed and clinked champagne glasses.

"I've missed you. I'm sorry about Paul," Hughes said. "That was a wedding I was not looking forward to, I must say!" Hughes said. They both giggled nervously.

They drank more champagne while Peter showed Hughes around his grand house and as it neared dinner time they hadn't heard a sound from Matthew. Hughes knocked on his bedroom door.

"Can I get you more ice? Perhaps some champagne?"

Matthew opened the door a crack and squinted into the hallway light.

"Hughes, can we go home?"

"Tonight? Heaven's sakes no. Peter has a lovely dinner planned. Come, please join in the fun."

Matthew stepped into the light of the hallway. Hughes gasped.

"Oh my lord, your left eye is shut," he said, wincing. "And your nose..."

"Can we go, please?" Matthew said, his voice breaking.

Hughes suggested he take a hot shower and offered to get more compresses. He stepped next door to his room, got three aspirin from his toilet kit, and delivered everything with a tall glass of water.

"Take these. Join us when you're feeling up to it."

Matthew never left his room that night. When Hughes checked on him before dinner he failed to respond and Hughes decided to let the poor young man be. He had his loyal pooch for a companion, Hughes thought, and after a good night's sleep he'd come around. Hughes and Peter savored the lavish seafood dinner and stayed up late, listening to jazz records and drinking freely from Peter's plentiful bar.

When Matthew rose the next morning in the gloom of near-dawn, sore, hungry, and dehydrated, he stepped into a kitchen cluttered with empty bottles and dirty dishes. Hughes' prosthesis lay disconnected on the couch. He cracked the door of Hughes' room and saw his bed was still made.

When Hughes and Peter emerged from the bedroom near noon they found the house empty. There was no note, no evidence of Matthew and Bella ever being there. Hughes stepped out into the even light of mid-day and looked down to the driveway. The African Queen was gone. Fighting to remain calm, he apologized to Peter for his troubled neighbor's lack of manners. Peter passed it off with a flick of his hand.

"I can't blame the poor guy," Peter said. "He's been through the mill."

"But how am I to get home?" Hughes asked.

"Who said anything about going home?"

Chapter 11

Turning onto Elm Street at noon, Matthew was agonizing as he tried to come to terms with his rash decision. Clearly, stealing the African Queen was an inexcusable, impulsive thing to do. He should have stayed, if for no other reason than to thank Peter for his care and hospitality. He could have caught a bus home if Hughes wanted to stay. Now, Hughes' house was dark and empty. The throb in his head was only intensifying and he had a new sense of existential worthlessness: that of a man all at sea, piling up a heap of bad decisions.

He pulled the Jaguar up to Hughes' garage, pushed the remote door opener, and got no response; probably a dead battery, which was not like Hughes. He would leave the car outside in the driveway, for he had no house key. He locked it up and made his way next door to his house, Bella running before him. He turned to look at the sedan, ghosted beneath a layer of highway salt. It had the nefarious look of a getaway car. Surely the neighbors would be talking.

Feeling defeated and lost, he moped around the house for the next hour before turning up the heat and going upstairs, where he could inspect his wounds, shed his bloody clothes, and take a long hot shower. Bella jumped onto his bed, unusual for this time of day, and watched him intently. He winced at the mirror, getting his first good look at his battered face. There was a deep split on the bridge of his nose, where Kane's big fist had landed, and the area around his left eye was bruised a deep purple. The lid was half-closed. The cut on his nose probably needed stitches but by now it was scabbed over and the bleeding had completely stopped. He'd have to keep ice on it to minimize the swelling. The rest of it would heal in time.

The shower's hot water beating down on him was a balm, taking the edge off the worst of the pain, plus the tension that had begun building in the car yesterday. He stood under the showerhead for ten minutes until the water grew tepid, a signal the tank was running low. He toweled off, put on some comfortable clothes, and headed downstairs where his cell phone was ringing.

"Were you ever going to call?" It was Hughes.

"I'm sorry. Of course I was going to call."

"You could have reached me from the road. You're lucky I didn't call the Highway Patrol. Or the mayor."

"I needed to get home. I tried telling you."

"I've been worried the brute might show up here. Turns out he's a creep," Hughes said.

"What was your first clue?"

"Evidently, he's facing a recall. Domestic abuse. Peter knows all about it."

"And now they can add assaulting a stranger on his front steps," Matthew said.

"How's the face?"

"Let's just say I won't be going out in public for a few days. It looks like I went ten rounds with Mike Tyson."

"The referee would have called it before it got that bad," Hughes said. "But don't lose any sleep. I'm quite sure the women will still find you irresistible."

There was a long pause.

"I'm sorry I stole your car," Matthew said.

"So am I. But sometimes these things happen for a reason. I've been invited to stay here a while. Perhaps I should thank you."

"Hughes," Matthew said as he ran a finger over the scab on his nose, "that was really awful yesterday."

"Yes, but you stood up to the reprobate, and that's the important thing. You should be proud of yourself."

"I ran like a scaredy cat."

"But you showed up. Who was it that said ninety percent of life is showing up?"

"How will you get home?" Matthew said.

"Peter wants me as his guest for an opening he's sponsoring later this week. It's so lovely here. I'm going to stay."

"He seems like a nice man."

Hughes sighed. "You have no idea."

When they hung up Matthew felt slightly relieved, a weight had lifted, knowing Hughes wasn't sore. He made some coffee and eggs and his usual fire, packed a fresh towel with ice, and retired to his black recliner. After two pages of the Russian novel he was softly snoring through his damaged nose.

✶✶✶

"You might as well tell me. I'll find out eventually."

Dr. Batiste sat behind her desk in her Friday casual attire; a pair of jeans, and a thick Irish knit sweater. Matthew had hoped his face would have healed by now, but the bruise around his left eye was going to take a while. He had called in sick all week; today was his first day back.

"Is there a rule that I need to tell you everything? In therapy?"

"No, but I would hope you'd be comfortable opening up. That's the fastest route to healing. That looks really sore, by the way."

Matthew looked around the room while he considered his response. The picture of her son had been updated. He was at the top of a mountain, outfitted in ski gear, complete with oversized reflector goggles.

"Your son looks like a downhill racer."

"He's a quick learner. I let him ski the black diamonds alone."

"How old?"

"Eight, going on eighteen."

She had her back to him now, staring at the picture, her head tilted slightly, and then spun around to face him.

"I'd love to brag about my son but we're here to talk about *you*. Shall we start with what happened to your face?"

Matthew winced.

"It's a long story."

"We have plenty of time."

He would get to the injuries last, starting at the very beginning of his list of disasters: his marriage, from the sublime to the tragic to the pathetic, and then he went on and on about the love letters, which still made his blood boil, even quoting one particularly outrageous passage. He was nearly shouting when Dr. Batiste interrupted.

"So this man Kane," she said pausing to confirm his name, "you thought you'd get even?"

"Well, yeah," Matthew said without hesitating. "I couldn't let the schmuck get away with what he'd done, even with Julia gone."

Dr. Batiste made some notes.

"So that brings us to your black eye."

Matthew sank into his chair and studied the white salt rings around his shoes, the result of walking through the company parking lot without boots. Left untreated, it would rot the leather. He made a mental note to pick up some mink oil on the way home.

"It was a mistake, going to his house," he said.

Dr. Batiste was easy on him, asking not so much about the physical details of the confrontation as his underlying emotions. Matthew told her about Hughes' recognizing and supporting the need to regain his self-esteem, even the offering of his car, and the congenial and impressive friend with whom they stayed in Camden after the incident. Her reply was encouraging, suggesting that by accepting his neighbor's help, Matthew was acting less like a betrayed victim and more like a problem solver. But in the final analysis, she said, Hughes had been an enabler of his revenge, and of course, his actions were wrong, on several levels. They talked for some time about anger management and he admitted to feeling a deep underlying rage but felt it had diminished after the trip. She began to say that was enough for one session, but Matthew interrupted and asked to admit to one more detail, specifically how he fled like a sissy after the brute knocked him down. She looked at him compassionately, and there was a long pause. Then she assured him there was nothing to be ashamed of, that it sounded like a wise decision given the man's size and demeanor.

"I commend you for opening up," she said at the end of the session. "It couldn't have been easy to admit your vulnerabilities. I can see you have weighed this carefully, and maturely."

Matthew lowered his gaze to the floor. "I didn't want to lose it with you again."

Dr. Batiste rose from behind her desk and came to the door.

"Sometimes we need to lose it. Let it go. That first session was more important than you know. It was the first time you dropped your disguise and let your emotions flow. Today you spoke earnestly, and you were more trustful. I think we're ready to do some real work now."

* * *

In the weeks that followed, Matthew's life slowed to monotonous execution of routine tasks in the office and cohabitating with his loyal pet Bella, who only needed to be fed once a day and walked every morning and night. His face healed, with just the hint of a purple line showing at the bridge of his nose where the skin had been split open. At work, he felt comfortably rejoined with his cohort, a group of roughly twenty younger employees who made up the Analytical Oversight Team. Sarah Finnegan popped in and out every few days to check on his state of mind. She had become a sentimental yet blunt reminder of his status as a single, celibate widower. He nearly forgot about that one night with her, his only post-Julia carnal experience, and given her motivation was based on pity, he figured that probably didn't count. Plus, her preference for women didn't bode well for any future encounters.

Somehow, his relationship with Hughes had changed. His neighbor returned from Maine a full week after Matthew stole the African Queen. Peter's black Range Rover appeared one night in the driveway and was gone the next morning. The two had exchanged pleasantries one morning across driveways, but there was an unspoken desire to minimize the extraordinary twenty-four hours they spent together. The sharing of such personal events – his run-in with Kane, Hughes' rekindled love affair, the stealing of the car, had pushed their relationship to a more intimate place, one he wasn't entirely comfortable with. He felt their connection had deepened in ways well beyond anything Hughes ever had with Julia, and this was unexpected and strange.

* * *

The sessions with Dr. Batiste grew more curious with each visit. The tenor of her questions shifted as she delved into some of the more remote reaches of Matthew's psyche. She asked random things about his childhood, even more about the relationship he had with his mother. His answers were generally forthright and frank, but every so often she'd hit a nerve, a topic that made him twist in his chair, sometimes searching for the right answer but just as often clamming up.

"There is no right or wrong answer," she'd tell him, observing his distress. "Speak from your heart." For the most part, he did.

On the Friday of their fifth session, Matthew showed up late for the first time.

"Late night?" Dr. Batiste asked, for she knew Thursday nights were for many the start of the weekend.

"No, I overslept," Matthew said. And then, "I got a call from my mother in the middle of the night. She's taken a turn for the worse. She's going into rehab this weekend."

"That should come as a relief to you," she said.

"Yeah, but they'll have to drag her kicking and screaming. I should probably be there."

"Does she have anyone who can take her in?"

"There's a neighbor. But mother sounds bad, like worse than ever."

"Maybe you should go," Dr. Batiste said.

Matthew didn't answer. After a long pause, Dr. Batiste asked about his studio and what projects he had going on. His mood lightened as he described some small figurines he was working on. He'd progressed from pots and goblets, he explained excitedly, and was now starting on animals. One, in particular, an leopard, was especially challenging, as he was trying to make it look about to pounce.

"You never make these things easy for yourself," she said.

"That's not any fun," Matthew said.

Dr. Batiste tilted her head and smiled warmly.

"I admire your pluck, Matthew Banks," she said. "You have only begun to tap into your reserves of talent and ability. Do you know that?"

Matthew blushed. She'd never offered such personal feedback, and it was awkward, the way her comment strayed from a therapist's clinical analysis to the realm of the personal. He could feel perspiration gathering at the back of his neck and when he looked up to find their time had run out he was relieved. When he stood to leave, she rose too and came around the desk. He could see now she had dressed up today, unusual for a Friday, wearing a skirt well above her lovely knees, with black tights. Her heels made her as tall as he, and when she put out her hand, something she rarely did, the grip was firm, and she held his hand for what seemed a very long time. Matthew was taken by the palpable charge coursing between them, something electric and sensual generated by a simple handshake. He let go and walked out, momentarily stunned by this phantom energy, wondering if she too had felt anything similar.

Throughout the afternoon, a hint of her perfume clung to his hand, and he'd catch the distinct scent of whatever it was, maybe patchouli, whenever he touched his face, launching him into a dreamy playback of their meeting. That evening, as he prepared to leave his office, an email popped up on his screen:

I'm available this weekend if you need to talk. I can be reached at 959-626-0743.

-MHB

Chapter 12

"Mrs. Banks, you'll be coming with us now."

The white-jacketed orderly stood in the foyer of *Las Palmas* with the door open, silhouetted by the rising sun behind him. Two EMTs stood just outside beside a stretcher with straps hanging off its sides. Dorothy Banks, still dressed from the night before, was visibly shaking.

"Dorothy, it's time." Paulina, her longtime next-door neighbor, held her close with one arm around her waist. "We've talked about this. This is what you want."

The rude smell of alcohol and cigarettes so early in the morning filled the hallway. Dorothy, swaying slightly, looked to each person desperately. She began weeping, straining to suppress it until she held out her hands as though being cuffed and let out a long wail.

"Oh, oh God – *oh God!*"

The man in the white jacket took her arm and they began escorting her through the door. She refused the gurney. A white van, its blue bar of lights flashing silently on top, sat in the driveway.

As they approached the vehicle, Dorothy Banks stopped and turned to face the enormous home where she had lived during two very different periods of her life. The sun cast it in brilliant illumination, the red tile roof beaming, its white stucco walls glowing like a shrine. She waved goodbye, as though she'd never see her home again, and allowed them to seat her in the back. The man in the white jacket sat beside her as the two technicians climbed in front and the van drove away.

* * *

In January of 1947, Harry Blevins, not long from fighting in the Battle of the Bulge, took out a VA loan to buy a car dealership in the heart of Pasadena. Recently married, he and his wife Eleanor were expecting their first child. The car business was on fire and the young entrepreneur wanted to sell the best damn automobile made in America. He persuaded GM to give him a Cadillac franchise. There was plenty of government money all around. The business would grow beyond his wildest expectations, and in five years he had bought up or started three more dealerships. By 1951, he was the largest General Motors dealer in the Western United States.

His fortune grew steadily. He purchased a five-acre residential lot on the edge of Pasadena, a former pear tree grove that rose from Western Boulevard and had sweeping views of the San Gabriel Mountains. He worked with an award-winning architect known for Spanish colonial design and they built a 9500 sq. foot hacienda they named *Las Palmas*, for the towering palm trees that marked the perimeter. Harry Blevins' vision was to build a house large enough for a brood of children and pets, with plenty of room for visiting relatives and guests, a veranda in the back that could host weddings and large summer parties, with fountains and lavish perennial gardens and statuesque palm trees strategically placed along the perimeter of the property. It would become the most talked-about home in Pasadena.

Hopes of filling the house with children fell short. His faithful wife Eleanor would only produce two girls, Dorothy and Elizabeth, both precocious and competitive swimmers, and although most of the hacienda would go unused day to day, they filled it with family and friends at Christmas and the Fourth of July, and the family became known for their opulent dinner parties and their once-a-year pig roast.

Dorothy would leave first to attend the University of Southern California, just a short drive south, as would her younger sister two years later. They would board there, hoping to put some distance between them and their watchful, manipulative parents. In her senior year, Dorothy met a handsome law student named Albert Banks, who at first shunned the pretty, younger ingénue. But she would, over time, win his heart and in the process get pregnant. They married shortly after she graduated, and three months into her pregnancy, they began their family life just a few miles out of town in a small starter home. Dorothy Banks would eventually return to *Las Palmas*, but under vastly different circumstances.

In the intervening years, she became a housewife, as her hard-working husband grew his law practice, and she raised their only child in their modest yet comfortable home on the edge of Pasadena. Matthew, born six months after their wedding, idolized his father, shadowing him when he was home and insisting on learning at his side. When Matthew was just four years old, Albert built a studio in the basement where he would paint landscapes and patiently teach his son the basics of shaping clay. She didn't mind their intersecting hobbies as much as she envied the amount of time they spent alone together.

Over the ensuing years, her husband became increasingly distant while his relationship with his son still dominated the household. She watched the man she once worshiped grow more disaffected and unloving. Her means of escape was easy and accessible. The drinking grew more frequent and heavier over time, and in just a few years they were estranged from one another. She was subsumed by drink, he by his art and fawning son.

And suddenly, mysteriously, Albert Banks was gone. One Saturday afternoon, when Matthew was a Junior in high school, Albert left no explanation. More importantly, he had abandoned his family without any means of support. Her parents helped keep them afloat, but as soon as Dorothy sent Matthew off to college back east, she was forced to sell the house and move into *Las Palmas* with her aging, widowed mother. Harry had died of cancer two years earlier. Gramma Eleanor committed to saving Dorothy, after having written off her sister Betty due to her joining a religious cult. Eleanor would die of a stroke a month after Dorothy moved in.

So when Matthew came home for Christmas his freshman year, it was just the two of them rambling around the cavernous hacienda, stocked with expensive western antiques, scores of memories of family gatherings, and little else. They ate a few meals together and spoke only when necessary. Finding the scene there so lifeless and austere, and his mother besotted with vodka, Matthew managed only three trips home his entire four years in college. The last was with a new girlfriend named Julia. Now that Matthew's focus was turned fully on the woman he'd ultimately marry, his mother only slipped deeper into the oblivion of drunkenness.

＊ ＊ ＊

Matthew got the call about her seizures at one o'clock in the morning. He woke from a deep sleep and picked up just before it went to voicemail. Paulina was calling from the hospital, panicking. They had administered drugs but she was not responding, and the concern was that her convulsions would lead to cardiac arrest.

"You need to come, Matthew. Your mother might not be long for this world."

"I appreciate your concern," Matthew said. "I'm not sure how much good it would do. She probably wouldn't even recognize me."

Matthew hung up and tried to go back to sleep. He had no intention of heading west. If she were going to die in the next twenty-four hours, there was nothing he could do about it. If she got through the next several days, maybe he'd book a flight. But he'd be ignoring a persistent urge to remain in Hartford, mostly to see Dr. Batiste at their regular Friday session.

✳ ✳ ✳

He found himself longing to bump into Dr. Batiste in different locations at work. He'd spotted her in the cafeteria, and then one day at an all-hands corporate gathering. There were several casual face-to-face encounters, one day in the middle of a snow squall, standing in the employee parking lot as she was preparing to get into her Mercedes. She was wearing a black cashmere beanie that was rapidly turning white, her long eyelashes catching flakes as they flew onto her face. He let her go, after learning of her son's hockey game, and after closing her car door and waving goodbye he dropped all pretenses and admitted to himself never before had a woman so fully captured his attention.

"I'm finding all this pretty boring," Matthew said during a session on the first Friday of February. "Is it alright if we just talk?"

Dr. Batiste smiled placidly, holding his gaze.

"That's a good sign. But I need to make sure we haven't left anything behind. The most important thing is that we've touched on the true source of your anxiety, your irrational fears, and then found way to manage it."

He sat back in his chair, legs crossed, with a dreamy look on his face.

"Do I look anxious?"

"You have made significant progress." She was intent, studying her patient. "Now tell me, how is your mother doing?"

He explained Dorothy's difficult struggle through the initial stretch, and she'd made it through but was a long way from being stable. He mentioned the brief phone conversation that ended quickly when a nurse intervened. Dorothy had left her room and was talking on a neighbor's cell phone. Two egregious infractions.

"How did she sound?" Dr. Batiste said.

"Like most recently recovering alcoholics. Hanging on by her fingernails."

"Shouldn't you be there? I can arrange some personal time off, which would not count as vacation," she said.

Matthew studied the woman across the desk. Today she had her black hair pulled back hard in a ponytail and was wearing those tortoise shell glasses, which seemed to magnify her almond-shaped eyes. She had on a minimum of make-up, barely detectable, and a slightly tart perfume, maybe persimmon.

"Matthew?"

"Sorry," he said, sitting up in his chair. "My mind was somewhere else."

"I'm not sure you are giving this situation the attention it deserves," she said.

"Am I a bad son if I don't go?"

"Where was your mind, just then?" she said.

His eyes rolled up to the ceiling.

"You don't want to know."

Dr. Batiste shifted in her chair, crossing her long legs. She leveled her gaze at him.

"Perhaps I do."

Matthew sat perfectly still and returned her stare.

"I think I may be falling in love with you."

The words burst from his mouth like water from a busted dyke. It was the most outlandish, honest thing Matthew Banks had ever said. Dr. Batiste blinked severely, jutting her head back in surprise. She leaned over her desk and straightened a stack of papers. She squared her ink blotter and repositioned her desk phone. She looked at the clock. It was 9:55.

"It's time to end," she said.

"We have a few more minutes," Matthew said.

"I need to prepare for a board meeting," she said.

"I understand, Dr. Batiste."

He rose from his chair.

"Just one thing," she said as he moved toward the door.

Matthew stopped and turned to face her. She was blushing and appeared upset.

"Oh, never mind," she said, waving her hand to dismiss him.

∗ ∗ ∗

Dorothy Banks was moved at the end of her first week from intensive care to a semi-private suite at the rehab center. Her roommate was a spaced-out woman with blue hair, a former rock star of some renown, although Dorothy hadn't heard of her. She was in for methamphetamine addiction and she was missing several teeth.

Since the worst of Dorothy's withdrawal symptoms had subsided, she was able to attend group meetings with the other patients in her wing, about twenty in total, who were suffering from addictions to everything from heroin to glue. She was allowed one visitor a day, and so far, it had been Paulina from next door, who dutifully came with magazines and a self-help book titled *Alcoholism is for Life*.

"What do you hear from Matthew?" she asked during her first visit.

"Nothing."

"I'll call him again," Paulina said.

"Don't bother. He's busy at work. He tells me he hates his job but he's there all the time."

It was true, almost. Matthew was spending an inordinate amount of time in the office, but not much work was getting done. He had a project to attend to, building a model for climate change exposure, but found excuses throughout the day to wander to the cafeteria or the men's room or run up to HR to get onto the Executive floor. Wherever he went, he still secretly hoped to cross paths with Dr. Batiste, and it was obvious to him now he had developed a schoolboy crush that had completely taken over his thoughts, his entire consciousness. But he wasn't a boy, and this wasn't school. They were two grown adults, ranking employees of the same company. Yes, she was a few years older, and a senior executive. Moreover, she was ostensibly his therapist. But none of this could counter his infatuation; in fact, it seemed to make it more intense. He carried with him her personal phone number from the email she had once sent, so that he could, at a random moment and if he had the courage, call her for purely personal reasons. He'd thought of asking her for coffee, or maybe to a museum. There was a Picasso ceramics exhibit in Hartford he'd been meaning to take in, but maybe that was too aggressive. Short of that, if a full week were to go by without any contact, there was always the Friday morning meeting. It had become an appointment that took absolute precedence over all others. Dr. Batiste cancelled their next session.

"I have a conflict. I'll get back to you with alternate times," was all the email said.

He was disappointed but not surprised. The message came on Thursday before their Friday meeting, and he'd gotten a haircut and was planning on wearing a new suit. He cursed himself. This change of schedule had to be the result of his unfiltered admission of his feelings, the blatant showing of all his cards. What a stupid lapse of judgment! Of course, she had to cut things off! He'd suddenly found a worthy recipient of his latent desires and it came on so fast and hard he was powerless to conceal it. His eagerness must have been written all over his face. But what about her? Didn't she have needs too? Still in her 30s, wildly attractive, a razor-sharp mind. Jesus, her mind! He often played back their most memorable discussions, that came in such a wide variety of contexts. He'd try to figure out the origin of a probe like, *"Did you wish for a sister or brother?"* Or *"What are your feelings about homosexuality?"* Were her inquiries rooted in analytic protocol, or was she merely curious for her own sake? And how had she processed all this analysis? Was there any attraction, physical or emotional? Was he crazy to think this was possible?

✳ ✳ ✳

Hughes had come out of hibernation and asked him to dinner that Friday. It had been nearly six weeks since their trip to Camden, and Matthew wasn't exactly thrilled but felt obliged. They sat in Hughes' living room on a freezing February night, huddled by a crackling fire.

"How's Peter?" Matthew asked.

"Wonderful, as usual," he sighed with a flip of his hand. "I'm planning my next trip up."

"Are you two back together?"

"We were never really *together*. It was originally a relationship of convenience if you will." Hughes got up to mix more drinks. "You're familiar with the concept of friends with benefits. That was us before you and I went up there. Thanks to your leaving me behind without a car, we had the opportunity to grow quite close, far closer than before."

Matthew looked up and smiled half-heartedly.

"I'm glad something good came from it," he said. And then, "I could use a friend with benefits."

"Of course, you could! And I'm bloody glad to hear you say that!"

Matthew was of course thinking of Dr. Batiste. Was she a friend? What would it look like, the two of them in a personal relationship? More than one night in the past few weeks he woke up in a fit of arousal, dreaming of sharing his bed with her.

"There's someone I might be able to work into that category," Matthew said.

"Is she in town?" Hughes said.

"She's the company shrink."

Hughes looked horrified.

"Dear me. Dipping your pen in company ink is *never* a good idea, Matthew. And with a therapist no less!"

They sipped their martinis. Matthew felt the febrile effects of the gin coming on. He'd cut back on drinking lately and his resistance was low. The heat first went to his face and head, a hot syrupy feeling between his ears. Hughes appeared pale and quite collected, barely batting an eye as he finished his second. Matthew declined another, asking for some wine.

At dinner in the candle-lit dining room, Hughes served a thick piece of broiled haddock sauteed with capers that was perfectly paired with a white Puligny Montrachet. Matthew began talking about Kane, a topic Hughes hadn't mentioned in weeks.

"What does Peter know about him?" he asked.

"Apparently he's a wife beater. She hasn't pressed charges."

"He would have killed me if I hadn't gotten up," Matthew said.

"Let's be thankful he didn't chase you down."

"That's the fastest I've ever run in my life – in cowboy boots in the snow no less!"

It would be the first time they laughed in the aftermath this shared, sordid affair. Hughes topped off Matthew's wine while they lingered at the table. He spoke about the weather. Unseasonable cold and snow were forecasted. There were the usual neighborhood developments. Agnes Shaw, his next-door neighbor, was going in for surgery after Christmas after they found a mass in her pancreas. The Murphy's dog, Scout, had been hit by the garbage truck and they had to amputate its hind leg. Larry Smoltz had been transferred to Buffalo and their house was about to go on the market.

"You really don't know any of these people, do you?" Hughes said, noticing Matthew's detachment. "I suppose you find it all quite dull."

"I'm tired," Matthew said after a long pause. "And drunk. I think I'll say goodnight."

They had moved to the living room and he was sprawled on the couch. He didn't move, his body buried in the down pillows, showing no indication to get up.

"Sleep there if you like," Hughes said and then, remembering Bella, "Oh, the dog!"

There was a tentative hug at the door and Matthew walked slowly to his house. He let Bella out the back and sat at the kitchen table staring into the blackness beyond the window. It was 11:00. His thoughts were of Dr. Batiste. He wondered if she was still awake. He remembered her offer to take his call at home, not that he ever forgot it, and pulled her number from his wallet and dialed. It rang three times before a sleepy voice answered. Matthew froze and hung up. He had woken her. Now he was angry with himself. He let Bella back inside. His cell phone began buzzing on the kitchen table.

"Matthew?" She sounded annoyed.

"Yes," he said.

"Is everything alright?"

"Not exactly – but yeah, I'm fine Dr. Batiste. I just wanted to hear your voice."

"Have you been drinking?"

"Yeah."

"Are you home?"

"Yeah."

"Go to bed. If you need to talk I'm here tomorrow. Good night." She hung up.

Matthew's heart was beating inside his chest like the wings of a sparrow. *Do you need to talk*? Was that the same as wanting to talk?

In bed, he turned out the light thinking he could make something up, a reason he needed to talk.

✶ ✶ ✶

Her name was Perseid, and the story she gave at the rehab center was that she fell to earth out of a meteor shower. Friends called her Percy. She'd just changed her hair from blue to platinum and was leaning out the window smoking a cigarette when her roommate Dorothy Banks returned after a one-on-one with a therapist.

"Do any good?" Percy asked, sucking on a cigarette.

"I'm a drunk," Dorothy said. "How much good can they do?"

They'd become closer because of their common disease, living the addict's code. They had a million axioms. "One day at a time." "Lies get you drunk." "If I could drink like normal people, I'd drink like that all the time." "One is too many, a bottle isn't enough." Their means of escape may have differed, but the psychopathology of their behavior was similar. Now they smoked cigarettes, multiple packs a day, one last addiction they could get away with. The No Smoking policy at the rehab center was a joke. Most patients shut themselves in their private bathrooms with the fan on high. That these two were in a first-floor suite was a minor perk. Their window opened.

"I heard you talking to someone. Was it your son?" Percy said.

"He finally called. I've been here for two weeks. Some son."

"Is he coming?"

"He's too busy at work."

"I'm sorry, darlin'," Percy said.

Chapter 13

It came to him that Friday night after hanging up with Dr. Batiste. Deep in inebriated slumber, Matthew's subconscious conjured up a scheme that could justify seeing her. In a dream, his father called him from France on a scratchy connection. It was the first time he'd heard his voice in fifteen years. He said he was coming back to America, to Pasadena, to visit Dorothy. He was asking Matthew to fly from Hartford and meet him. It would be like old times. Matthew woke up in a panic. When his head cleared, he realized his sleeping mind had produced a credible excuse to physically meet with Dr. Batiste. He would have to lie – tell her this call actually happened. The made-up crisis would be sufficiently removed from his established source of despair. There would be a lot of new material for him and Dr. Batiste to talk about, and because it was Saturday, there would be no clock – no beginning, no scheduled time to end.

In his kitchen drinking an espresso, he waited until nine o'clock to call.

"I hope you took some aspirin before you went to bed," she said after he apologized.

He took a deep breath.

"Dr. Batiste, would it be possible to meet today? Something has come up."

"Oh? What, can you tell me?"

"My father called me last night. Totally out of the blue."

"Is this why you were drinking?"

"Well, yes, now since you mention it," he lied some more.

"Can it wait until Monday?"

Matthew let out a long sigh. "I never got back to sleep. I'm a bit of a mess. It would be much better if we could do it today. I'm kind of, I don't know…"

There was a pause and he could hear her fumbling with something.

"Come to my house. Bradley's at a playdate. How about three o'clock?"

Not expecting the affirmative reply, he was for a moment speechless and his heart was racing.

"Matthew?"

"I'm checking," he said, as if he had anything going on. "Mid-afternoon works."

She gave him her address. And then she said, "Bring me one of your little trinkets, will you?"

Dr. Batiste lived on the western edge of Hartford in a gated community, which required him to announce himself at the entrance. The houses sat back from the street on big, snowy lots with towering beech and oak trees. The Batiste residence was a sprawling one-level ranch. As he pulled up her driveway he wondered if it was just her and the boy.

She greeted him at the front door dressed in a white turtleneck sweater and jeans. Her glasses were pushed up on top of her head. She was holding a steaming mug of tea.

"I thought you'd be driving a cute little sports car, eligible young man such as yourself," she said as he walked up the stone path that had just been shoveled.

"She's my most trusted companion," Matthew said, looking over his shoulder at his ten-year-old Volvo wagon. "Other than my dog, of course." He was carrying a small box that contained a faux filigreed nut dish he'd recently finished.

Inside, she took his coat, hung it in the closet, and led him to the back of the house to an open kitchen. He followed her through a hallway lined with photos. There were several studio portraits of nuns, and one of a convent. There were at least a dozen pictures of her and Bradley: on the beach, posing in ski gear in front of a snowy mountain, on a cable car in San Francisco; on a beach before turquoise waters in what had to be the Caribbean. There was no picture of a man who might be the boy's father, or a husband.

In the kitchen, she went to a massive cook's stove where a kettle was steaming.

"I'm making tea. Would you like some?"

"I'll have water please," he said.

She gestured toward the couch.

"Let's sit here. This is where we live."

The room ran the entire width of the back of the house. On the north end was a massive stone walk-in hearth that could have held a cauldron of stew, or a spit for a roasting pig. Oak beams ran the length of the ceiling, adding to the colonial motif.

"I can see why," Matthew said, surveying the entire space with all its thoughtful appointments.

She made her tea and poured him a glass of mineral water, executing each task with grace and efficiency that demonstrated how comfortable she was in the privacy of her own home. Now the false circumstances he'd created, the bald-faced lie waiting to be told in detail, had him sweating. She sat down while he continued standing. He commented on her art and mentioned in passing the Picasso exhibit he was planning to attend the next day. He began to comment on the weather and she cut him off.

"Please sit," she said. Her feet were tucked under her as she leaned back into the corner of the couch.

"So, tell me."

Matthew sat with his water. He scanned the room, still studying her art. She was no slouch in the culture department. On a far wall, a signed Frank Stella lithograph hung beneath a gallery lamp, its vibrant colors dominating the end of the room with a dazzling constellation of geometric patterns. Placed on shelves and corner tables she had positioned some exquisite sculptures and figurines of bronze and pewter, several quite valuable he guessed, mixed with some serious replicas. Together her *objets d' art* evinced not only an eclectic sense of style but also a trained eye.

He finally began in a whisper, unspooling a longer version of his past as it related to his father, most of which she already knew. But for effect, he repeated his explanation of the sudden departure, the total break, how there was no communication for years. He added an exaggerated account of his mother's downfall, and the devastating toll his father's disappearance had on her. He finished his soliloquy by saying he'd managed to forget his father was even alive. And then, the phone call, out of the wild blue.

"Were you drinking when the call came?" she asked.

"Maybe a little."

She was looking him over, more thoroughly now, her mind obviously weighing all of this carefully.

"Where is this all going, Matthew? We've already discussed most of this."

Matthew took a sip of water. He gave Dr. Batiste his best look of gloom.

"Now he wants to come back," he said, looking up from the floor, "like nothing ever happened."

Dr. Batiste said nothing. He looked for her reaction. She was staring at him with disturbing intensity, different from what he'd become accustomed to. Beyond the vast picture window, a light snow had begun to fall.

"Matthew?"

The room was deathly quiet.

"Did you make this up?"

Matthew cleared his throat. He had come here assuming she would buy this. She'd seen through it like a pane of glass. He put his face in his hands.

"Matthew?"

"I can't lie," he finally said in a whisper.

"You just did," she said. "That whole story. What's going on?"

Matthew stood and walked to the broad picture window looking out across the back. The scene was from a Christmas card. In the corner of the acre lot, marked by a split rail fence, the bows of the spruce trees were heavy with snow. Directly in front of him, a tiny wren house with its tiny hole hung from the limb of a bare fruit tree. In the opposite corner stood a snowman with charcoal eyes and a carrot nose. The snow was coming heavier now.

"I'm such an idiot," he said under his breath, his back to her. "I'm sorry to waste your time," he said louder as he turned to face her.

"So I'm right, this has nothing to do with your father."

"It was a dream. Honest. I just wanted to see you."

Her eyes narrowed.

"Dreams can be telling," she said as if trying to ease his discomfort. "But the fact that you made this up, with elaborate deception, well, now we're headed into uncharted waters," she said.

"Uncharted waters?"

Dr. Batiste put her mug on the table and leaned back into the cushions.

"Since I'm supposed to be the responsible one –" she paused to gather her thoughts. "Since I'm demanding honesty, I need to tell you something."

Matthew stared at her, unable to guess what she was about to say.

"I've had certain feelings for you," she said flatly. She was staring at him with remarkable calm.

The blood drained from Matthew's face. He walked to the couch and sat down at the opposite end.

"In all honesty," she continued, "I am confused, and frankly a little shocked. But I know one thing for certain. I cannot continue as your therapist."

Matthew looked at her.

"What will you tell Holmes?" he said, hoping she hadn't thought of that.

"That I've done all I can do. He'll let it go."

Matthew frowned. This was suddenly very confusing for him too.

"We need to stop seeing each other altogether," she said.

"Why?"

"You know why. There's too much to lose – my job, your job. Our reputations."

"I don't care what people think," Matthew said. "I don't care about my job."

"You should. You have a bright future there."

Her face grew more solemn.

"Matthew, we need to go our separate ways, plain and simple. This was never supposed to happen."

He was speechless, staring at her. She was even prettier in her distress. He headed toward the door.

"Let me get your coat," she called out behind him, rising from the couch.

"I can find it," he said from the hallway.

"What about your box?"

"It's just a dish. Put it on your shelf with the other ones."

He put on his coat and now she was behind him at the door.

"I'm so sorry," she said.

"I'm the one that screwed up," Matthew said.

He opened the door and she grabbed his arm.

"This was entirely unexpected," she said. "I didn't see it coming."

"Do we ever see these things coming?"

She looked sad and then stood on her toes and kissed his cheek. Her lips were warm and her lipstick smelled divine, like a raspberry *chouquette* fresh from the oven. He turned toward her, and in a move so quick she couldn't avoid it, put his mouth on hers. She didn't resist right away but straightened, and now he was levitating, looking down on the two of them connected. She pulled away. He looked at her desperately. She was looking beyond him at nothing, stunned. He stepped outside. In the driveway, through a veil of driving snow, his car was encased in white, a frozen sculpture of hardened ice.

∗ ∗ ∗

Matthew arrived the next day as the doors opened. The East Hartford Gallery was a community art museum that housed traveling exhibits. The literature they were handing out explained that Picasso took up ceramics late in his career yet managed to produce hundreds of pieces; eighty-five were in this traveling collection. They ranged from colorful platters to pitchers and vases and bowls whose shapes were as bizarrely imagined as the painted images fired onto them. They were arranged on a series of plinths, encased in plexiglass viewing boxes, positioned around the room like giant chess pieces.

He paid the five-dollar contribution and made his way to the pottery collection. There was one pitcher that caught his immediate attention, a fish painted tan and black with a handle running from nose to tail. It was a simple, frivolous design, child-like in its affect. He pulled a pad from his pocket and made a quick sketch and continued through the displays, stopping at each plinth, and by the time he'd viewed most of the pieces, there was the low roar of visitors echoing off the high-pitched ceiling. The museum had suddenly filled.

He first saw her at the entrance as he was preparing to leave. Dr. Batiste was standing at the door, waiting to pay. She wore a full-length puffy black down coat, with a red scarf and high black boots. He immediately panicked, feeling the need to escape, and pivoted to face the opposite direction. He looked to the far wall for an exit sign, his mind racing. There was none. He pretended to browse the exhibits, his back to the entrance. Minutes later, debating his next move, with his back still to the door, he caught her scent, the distinct whiff of persimmon, and turned to face her.

Chapter 14

They called it the dead of winter for obvious reasons. The grey, bitter cold days of New England ran seamlessly together, into and through one another like an overlapping string of monochromatic post-cards. The only distinction came during the weekends, when Matthew's world shifted to a more acute version of a lonely middle-aged widower, a man with nothing to do and nowhere to go. He managed through these days the best he could, determined to find a kernel of value in his dreary life, which inevitably became an analysis of his job. Even though it was soul-crushing, it was his life now, like it or not and it was paying the bills. While at work, instead of trying to find ways to intersect with Dr. Batiste, he was looking to avoid her. They had no shared projects that would bring them together in a meeting; she had cancelled their Friday sessions, and Matthew took the extreme measure of delaying his daily lunch time to the last possible moment, just before they closed down the steam tables, knowing she was always in the cafeteria when it opened at eleven-thirty. He had reluctantly accepted they could not be together and was, infuriatingly, unable to shed a stubborn longing to be with her.

His weekends were mostly spent in the studio, throwing random pots and making small mammals and other curios. Occasionally, just to get out of the house, he'd have a drink next door with Hughes. But winter had its icy grip on everyone he saw, whether at work or in the corner store or on the sidewalks along Elm Street. It was evident in the puffiness of added pounds, the listless expression on their pallid faces. Next door, Hughes was drinking more than normal, out of boredom he claimed, and from missing his new love, Peter. Matthew wondered how his health would hold up under the barrage of abuse but realized that for him this was nothing new.

There had been several conversations with his mother. If she was making any progress, it wasn't apparent. She claimed she was still sober, and given her rigid environment, he had to believe it was true. But her behavior was still erratic. One day, clear and calm in her thinking and elocution, she'd storm into tirades about her misfortune and bad luck two days later. Above all, she was still a deeply bitter woman, and sobriety didn't appear to be setting her free. On one call she targeted him, lashing out for being so far away, adding her roommate Percy said he was nothing more than an 'ungrateful son.'

The stories Matthew had gathered about Percy were as alarming as they were unbelievable. He knew of this band she was in, the Meteors. Perseid was the lead singer and widely known in the rock world as someone who modelled herself after Janis Joplin. Everything he'd heard about her and the band had to do with hedonism, drug abuse, and destruction. It would have been better for Dorothy to room with a fellow mad housewife; they'd probably have more to talk about. But God willing, she'd be released in late February and would be ready for the halfway house. She didn't let up on the requests for Matthew to come out, if only for the transition between facilities, and he was stalling her, for reasons different than before. The obsession with Dr. Batiste had been replaced by a simple desire to stay home by himself, either sitting by the fire with his book or freezing in the basement, coaxing his fingers to work the cold, wet clay.

It was the middle of the morning, a week to the day before Dorothy Banks was to be released, that spelled the end of her journey. Her wing at the clinic was quiet, with nearly all patients out of their rooms, in Yoga class or attending meetings. Dorothy Banks, patient number 1351, was alone in her room, drunk. On the verge of passing out, she stumbled into the hallway and fell hard on her face. The sound of her head hitting the floor, a distinct *thud* not unlike that of a bowling ball hitting the tile, filled the hallway. A woman from two doors down rushed out and screamed her name. There was an alarm on the wall and she flipped the switch. The siren, like an air raid horn, began blaring. The staff doctor and two nurses came running. The doctor turned her over and checked for a pulse. He immediately tried to resuscitate her. Dorothy Banks lay sprawled on the floor turning blue, a trickle of blood oozing from her right ear. The doctor compressed her chest while a nurse applied mouth-to-mouth. Ten minutes later she was dead.

Matthew got the call as he was leaving for work. When he was able to talk, all he could utter was, "But she wasn't drinking."

The doctor explained. Matthew was standing in his kitchen preparing Bella's food, half asleep after a night of tossing.

"Mr. Banks, may I suggest you travel here as soon as you can to make the final arrangements."

Matthew stood holding the phone, frozen in disbelief.

"I'm sorry for your loss, Mr. Banks."

He hung up and looked out to the quiet street. A school bus pulled up in the early morning twilight and stopped and two children carrying lunch pails climbed on and it drove off with a low growl, white exhaust puffing out the back.

His first thought was to call Dorothy's sister Betty in Seattle, even though they'd been out of touch for decades. But he had no number or address. There were no other immediate relatives to contact. He felt no obligation or reason to call his father. He sat at the kitchen table and stared into space while Bella lapped up her food. He could hear the blood coursing in his ears. The furnace below kicked on, sending a quiver through the house. He looked next door and saw Hughes moving behind the sheer curtain in his kitchen, still in his bathrobe. He appeared to be making coffee.

"Hi neighbor," Hughes said as Matthew stood outside his door, coatless. He studied him for several seconds and Matthew stepped inside without speaking. He was moving robotically as Hughes stood gaping at him, alarmed. It was an odd time for his neighbor to pop over.

"What's happened?" Hughes put his good arm around Matthew's shoulder and guided him into the living room and onto the couch.

Matthew explained in low, labored tones. Hughes, stone sober and clear-eyed, listened intently.

"I can watch the dog," he said when Matthew stopped talking. "When you need to go."

Matthew sat on the couch saying nothing, staring out the window. Hughes got up to make him some toast and poured him a cup of coffee. Matthew remained on the couch, his mind now churning with a million different things to consider, to weigh, to plan. The practical was stifled by the emotional. His mother's last words to him: *Please come.* But no, he wouldn't, didn't, come. All for a selfish desire to wallow in his new chapter of loneliness. And, if he really looked deep, to secretly remain close to a therapist who'd spurned him. How was his mother's lapse allowed to happen? Did she relapse because she felt abandoned? Did her crazy roommate have anything to do with it? If he had heeded her request, would she still be alive?

Hughes said as he came in with a tray, "Peter sent this wild blueberry jam a neighbor made. It's divine."

Matthew took the coffee, ignoring the food.

"When do you need to go?"

"I don't know."

"Soon?"

"I guess so."

"Is there anything I can do to help?" Hughes said.

"Bella."

Matthew remained in a trance the remainder of the morning. He needed to call into work, tell them he'd be gone for a while, maybe two weeks or longer. He recalled Dr. Batiste offering to procure a leave of absence, that he would be paid to help his mother, and it wouldn't count as vacation. But this was before she died. Was this worse? His thoughts turned to how he'd made a dunce of himself in her living room the last time he saw her, and she said they must not meet again. Would this change anything?

He made an espresso and tried to figure out what to do next, what the proper order of events should be. He was struck by the mystery of how she died, and figured he'd know soon enough. The caffeine made him squirrely; his thoughts came and went without registering, and then in the middle of all this noise he had an idea that was so bizarre, so counter to his current reality, it could not be ignored. Now was the perfect time to go for a long run. Take advantage of the warmer day, get some air. Thirty minutes outside, breathing hard, would surely clear his head.

He put his espresso cup in the sink and went upstairs, where he changed into his running suit. Out the front window, he could see last night's rain had left frozen puddles on the sidewalk, bubbled over with a thin pane of ice. He laced up his shoes and stepped out the back door. The sun was bright and there was a slight breeze. He bent to grab his ankles, breathing in the cold air while his hamstrings and tendons eased. Between his legs he could see Hughes on his front porch, eyeing him.

He began jogging at a lazy pace. The air stung his cheeks and as his limbs loosened he fell into a rhythm, his strides synchronized with his breathing. Ten minutes further on, with the edge of town behind him, he felt strong and confident; his head was indeed clearing. His thoughts shifted from his mother to his surroundings: brown fields, flattened from the melted snow; a breeze caught up in the trees; black cinders heaped on the sides of the road. He was running over a rise and saw an animal lying on the edge of the asphalt. Twenty yards away he could see it was a deer, a fawn, its pure white underbelly contrasting its dappled coat. The animal was pawing at the air with her foreleg, the rest of her body still. Matthew slowed to a walk as he approached. Now he could see the little deer's hind legs were broken; one stuck out at a right angle at the elbow, the other jammed flat in the wrong direction. Her big brown eyes rolled up and were staring at him. Foam had gathered along her thin black lower lip. She was laboring to breathe. On her flank, her coat had been ripped away, baring a swatch of flesh the size and color of a baked ham. He tried to remember Bella's vet's name. He could run home and come back with his car, but it was unlikely the animal would survive long enough. He looked down the length of the country road. It was empty and quiet. The only sound was the rattling of frozen branches above him. His breath, slower now, clouded in the frigid air. One hundred feet away, he saw a pile of rocks stacked beneath a new utility pole. He jogged over and picked up a chunk of granite the size of a football. Heavier than it looked, he waddled back to the injured animal with it held to his waist. The deer's eyes opened wider. The rock was slipping and he looked for the best place to release it on her head, a fatal blow that would end her misery. Just then, a pick-up truck pulled up from behind and parked on the shoulder, coming to a stop ten yards away. A farmer climbed out with the engine running.

"She dead?" he said.

He was a ruddy-faced man wearing a stained baseball cap and canvas jacket. Dried manure and straw were stuck to his boots.

Matthew shook his head no.

The farmer looked at the rock in Matthew's hands, and then at him.

"Gonna kill 'er?"

Matthew raised his eyebrows. He was bent at the waist now, the rock resting against his thighs. The farmer trudged up to the deer and squatted to get a closer look. He turned to Matthew, now shivering in his nylon suit. Then he walked to his truck where he reached beneath the seat and returned with a pistol. In one easy motion he lifted the gun and shot the fawn precisely between her eyes. The sharp crack made Matthew jump. The deer's legs straightened for a second and went lax. The sound rolled across the countryside. Three crows lifted from a wire, flying off in a loud chorus. Matthew looked off toward the horizon. He turned back to the dead animal. Still, there was no blood, even where the bullet entered. The farmer stood with the gun at his side and began lecturing. What he'd just done could be illegal, but the animal was in misery and would have died. The game warden, a friend of his, would look the other way. Then he began talking in a more neighborly way about how tender young venison is, how sweet it could be. He'd take this carcass home and dress it, and the missus would make some of her stew, unless he, Matthew, wanted it, because it was really his deer. Sharing it was the right thing to do. Do you want some, he said?

Matthew was hearing a small part of this as he stared blankly across the field. The farmer waited a while for him to reply and hearing nothing stuffed the pistol into his belt. Then he picked up the animal by its four hooves and walked to his truck, heaving her into the bed like a bale of hay. After climbing into the cab he pulled up beside Matthew.

"You need a ride?"

Matthew shook his head no.

"There's a cold front comin'. I'd put some clothes on, if I was you," he said through the half-open window.

✷ ✷ ✷

The alarming death of the fawn, on the heels of his mother's, had Matthew on the verge of emotional collapse, and one sign was the measuring of his own mortality. Now he feared for his life, for his mental state was in a more delicate place than ever, and he felt the need to do something, anything, to move toward normalcy. Taking a shortcut on the run home, thinking very clearly now, he decided a personal visit to Dr. Batiste could be justified. He had a full-fledged, honest to God crisis on his hands! But he'd have to see her today, and so he would show up at her office unannounced, eliminating the chance of her saying no.

He arrived at *Connecticut Life*, still wearing his running suit, and sprinted up the stairs to her office where she was reviewing some reports.

"What are you doing?" she asked, startled, assessing his outfit as he stood at her door.

Matthew took a seat in front of her desk, his hands gripping the arm rests.

"My mother is gone," he said, looking out the window with a blank stare.

"Gone?"

"Dead."

Dr. Batiste stood and walked around her desk and closed the door. She sat down beside him and waited. Matthew's face was frozen in a rictus gaze, focusing on some object beyond the window. Both feet were flat to the floor. She sat with him for several moments until he spoke.

"How am I supposed to feel, Dr. Batiste?" he said. "My mind has turned to mush."

Dr. Batiste leaned into him and saw his eyes filling with tears.

"You are in shock now Matthew. You aren't supposed to feel any certain way beyond sad, and of course somewhat disoriented. Tell me more. Was she still at the facility?"

"She fell and hit her head. Somehow, she got a bottle of rubbing alcohol. Can you believe that? I'm an orphan! Just like you! How do you like that? We now have something in common."

She put her hand on his arm, then removed it.

"Matthew, try to gather yourself," she said softly. "Technically, you're not an orphan. I can see how you might feel that way."

"I don't have anyone to talk to." He was looking now at the credenza and Bradley's picture.

"You have me."

"But we can't anymore. You made that clear at the Picasso exhibit."

She suddenly stood and picked up a leather satchel from her desk.

"I'm sorry Matthew. I'm late for a meeting with Lawrence and a board member."

Matthew shot a look at her, shocked.

121

"And I'm tied up all afternoon," she said. "I suppose you will fly out soon?"

"Tomorrow or the next day," he said.

"Then we still have time to talk," she said. "Again, I'm so sorry for your loss."

Sorry for your loss? The clerk at the grocery store might say something like that. He realized the discussion was over and stood to go. But he wanted to tell her about the deer! Her detached behavior wasn't so much of a surprise, but he'd hoped, without thinking, the meeting would last longer. He rose to leave.

And then she said, "Would you like to meet later? I'll set Bradley up with the neighbors. I can come to your side of town, if that's easier."

What? Now his mind was shattered. He had come with news of his mother's death, using tragedy as a foil, and the situation had arced like an electrical current to an a different but even more appealing opportunity. He didn't know what to say.

She said, "I think I have your number but give it to me just in case. I'll call you when I get home."

He scribbled down his number on some note paper and handed it to her, then continued standing idly by her desk.

"Thanks Dr. Batiste."

She made her way around him and walked to the door.

"Matthew," she said, "I think it's time you called me Madeleine."

∗ ∗ ∗

She arrived at Rico's at the precise time agreed. Matthew was already seated in a booth with a glass of whiskey. He rose to greet her, abstaining from any show of affection.

"Thank you for coming, *Madeleine*," he said in pointed response to her request. She slid out of her puffy coat and dropped it in the corner beside him. She looked at him sternly and then nodded to his drink.

"You need to keep a clear head," she said. "I can't stress that enough."

"Just a shot of courage," he said.

"You've got plenty of courage." And then, "On the other hand, I will have a glass of wine."

He called to Alec for a glass of Chardonnay.

"You mustn't take this the wrong way," she said as they sat assessing one another. "I've been thinking of nothing else since you came to my office. This is a highly specific situation. You are vulnerable and in a delicate place. I consider you an at risk employee. Of course, you feel like an orphan, and that's a painful and lonely sense of dislocation. But somewhere out there your father is living his life. That's what I meant when I said you aren't an orphan. Keep that in mind."

Matthew looked up from his empty glass.

"He's dead to me," Matthew said. "I won't see him again."

"But odds are you will. And those odds would improve if you try. You could track him down, if you had to."

He grimaced. She changed the subject to herself.

"I never found out who my parents were, or if they were even still alive." She let this sink in. "Nor did I know the whereabouts of my sister, beyond the fact that she was consigned to a convent in another state. I was forced to grow up very quickly. I was really never a child."

She finished her glass of wine and now Matthew sensed her mood sinking. He signaled to Alec for another round. The drinks were delivered and he drank most of his immediately, leaving one small sip.

"But you turned it around, you built a life," he said after the break in their discussion.

"Maybe so, but I will never get back those years. Honestly, I think this is one reason I was interested in you," she said without looking up. "That's something I've given a lot of thought to."

"But I wasn't an orphan, until today."

"I'm trying to make a larger point."

Matthew sensed the core of their relationship morphing, moving to a new place, more even ground. They were both damaged in their own parallel way. Now it occurred to him this meeting was more than just providing a sounding board for his grief; she wanted him to feel less alone but was enjoying the company.

They began talking about life's frightening randomness, the fear of what sort of tragedy might hit next, the challenge to remain hopeful. For the first time, she opened up about her own insecurities, her own struggles, at one point becoming teary talking about motherhood.

"I don't know where I'd be without Bradley," she said as she wiped her eyes. "He defines me. He keeps me sane."

"Maybe I should find a child. Adopt some abandoned kid," Matthew said, trying to lighten the mood.

She looked at him with a sadness he'd never seen. She had finished her second glass of wine.

"Do you remember the night we met? At the party?" she said.

"No, I'm sorry. It's all pretty vague."

"Do you remember what you said to me after we danced?"

"I've forgotten we danced. I'd rather not know."

She sat beside him staring intently and the silence grew awkward.

"I should go," she said abruptly, moving to the edge of the booth. "I'm sorry."

"But we haven't –"

"You'll be fine. I debated whether or not to do this, but decided it was my professional duty. I feel better now."

"How about me? You're confusing me."

"Think about what we discussed. And don't ever feel alone. Because if you do, it's your own doing."

She rose and lifted her coat and he stood and pulled it over her shoulders.

"I'll walk you out," he said.

Alec winked when he paid at the bar. Matthew escorted Madeleine to the door.

Outside the night was sharply cold and clear. A skyful of stars was also winking from deep in the dark, indigo universe. He took her arm and they walked to the Mercedes parked beside his dirty Volvo. A lone streetlamp cast a dim glow over the empty parking lot. When she reached to open the door he turned her toward him and kissed her forcefully. She didn't respond, her surprise evident in her unmoving lips, but then she pulled him into her as she leaned back against the car and returned the embrace. He could feel the warmth of her body through her open coat and now her lips were welcoming him.

Two bar patrons came through the door and they pulled apart.

"My house is a mile from here," Matthew whispered.

"I'll follow you."

He couldn't remember the precise sequence of events, such was the sheer incandescence of their coming together that night. Everything became one thrilling blur. Naked beneath the duvet, they both acted out their repressed desires, having their own way with one another until their rhythm synched and they were one and they climaxed in a shuddering, shouting finish. They rolled apart in the darkness, out of breath, damp with sweat, and lay for some time without speaking. One thing would, in time, become clear: he had no clue how their three hours together would forever change him, and the trajectory of his life.

Afterwards, Madeleine had remained curled against him until nearly midnight, when she awoke with a start and dressed in a hurry in the freezing room. He put on a bathrobe and walked her downstairs and they held one another at the half-opened door. She made him promise to take care of himself and try to forgive his mother. It was alright to be angry that she failed in her last attempt to get sober, but in time this would soften and he would miss her, and further on, someday, the thought of her would bring a smile to his face. He should try to find his father, if for no other reason than to prove he was not an orphan. It wasn't impossible to build an entirely new relationship. Be the bigger person! This all made Matthew bristle, such as he could in the aftermath of their lovemaking. She said nothing about staying in touch but asked how long he'd be gone. Unclear, he said. Maybe he'd take a sabbatical. Stay out west for a while.

He walked her to her car, oblivious to his stinging bare feet on the icy driveway, and when she was settled and had her seat belt on she lowered the window. He bent down and kissed her again, a deep, more knowing kiss, and she started her car. As he turned to go inside, he could see Hughes standing in his robe behind his living room drapes, peering across the divide.

✳ ✳ ✳

The next morning, Hughes greeted Matthew in the driveway as he was picking up his newspaper.

"Dipping the pen in company ink last night?" Hughes said.

Matthew dismissed him with a wave of the hand and said nothing. The odd concurrence of emotions had his mind blazing: on the one hand mourning his mother's bizarre death; the other soaring, vivid recollections of Madeleine moving beneath him. He preferred to focus on the latter, a fantastical dream finally acted out, surreal, sublime. And rather than feeling as though he'd made a conquest, as he sometimes did in his youth, he felt he was fulfilling his role in a preordained coming together, sanctioned by a higher power. He wanted to shout it from the rooftops.

"Well good for you," Hughes said. "Maybe that will lift you up a little. When do you leave?"

"Tomorrow."

"I'm going north to see Peter for a few days," Hughes said. "I can take Bella if you'd like. I told you I would watch her. I'm a man of my word."

Matthew thanked him, and Hughes promised to pick her up, with all her food and trinkets, later that evening.

In the stillness of the house, Matthew came face to face with his strange new life. He walked by the table by the front door where his mother's Christmas card still sat unopened. On the wall in the kitchen, he glanced at a phone that would never again ring with her call. Could the space his mother once occupied in his day-to-day thoughts be replaced by this outrageously exciting but confusing former therapist? No, that's a ridiculous thought, he said to himself; the woman who gave him life versus another who gave him some advice and one night in bed.

He found himself talking to Bella as he sat at the kitchen table. Tonight she would go with Hughes for a while, he said. Her ears perked up. Tomorrow, he would land in Los Angeles. And catch a taxi to the abandoned family estate in Pasadena and walk into another empty house, a mausoleum of memories. And then there would be the annoying details – identifying the body, signing the papers, the cemetery plot he'd need to arrange. When he stopped talking, Bella continued looking straight up at him with her deep brown eyes, soulful, seeming to understand and accept exactly everything he said. Then she nestled her snout on his lap and let out a long sigh.

PART II

Pasadena

Chapter 15

"I'm not exactly sure of the directions. It's been a while," Matthew told the taxi driver. "The address is three-forty-five Santa Teresa Way."

The sun was a red beach ball hanging low in the haze over the Los Angeles basin. Matthew was traveling northeast in a cab from the LA Airport, headed to Pasadena. He was bracing for whatever awaited him at his mother's house, fearful of the traces of her broken life left lying around recklessly, unattended to before heading to rehab. He counted the years since he last visited *Las Palmas*. It was his Junior year in college, Christmas of 1992. His grandfather Harry had just died, and Dorothy's mother was only partially present – semi *compos mentis* – essentially senile yet still living unassisted in the house. Between Dorothy's chronic drinking and Granny Blevins' dementia, it was like being in a fun house at an amusement park, without the fun. What was up was down, and vice versa.

As the cab neared the house the neighborhood began to look familiar. Harry Blevins was the visionary behind the entire development, buying the first and largest lot and building a big house. Others soon followed, all on two- or three-acre plots, and the grand structures, mostly Spanish style, sat majestically back from the street with towering palms and eucalyptus trees and manicured gardens with fountains. Back then, long shiny cars cruised the neighborhood streets lazily. Neighbors were spread out but friendly, some with tennis courts and pools that often hosted group gatherings. Matthew closed his eyes and recalled pedaling down the street with Billy Rooney, on a sparkling summer day, with a pocket full of change his grandfather gave him for candy.

As the taxi pulled into the long driveway, Matthew saw a car parked by the garage, a compact Japanese model. As he got closer he saw a rental sticker on the back bumper. He paid the driver, pulled his suitcase from the trunk, and walked to the massive wooden front door. The outdoor lights were on, wrought iron Spanish lanterns on either side, yellow bulbs casting a soft glow over the shadowed entrance. Matthew set his suitcase on the step. There was movement in the back of the house, in the kitchen. He looked under a statuette of Don Quixote, where they historically hid the key. It wasn't there, and now he saw the front door wasn't fully closed.

"It's open," a voice said from within.

Matthew recoiled. He couldn't make out the face, but the voice was unmistakably his father's, the same steady tone that woke him for school each morning, taught him the Lord's Prayer, explained how to shape his first bowl. The man who came to the foyer was smiling devilishly in the shadow of the entrance.

"How are you, my son?"

Matthew froze. *What?* The man who pulled the vanishing act fifteen years ago suddenly materialized before him, talking like he left yesterday. Unable to find any words, Matthew's first impulse was to belt him.

"What the hell?" he finally gasped. His anger could be heard in the growl, and his father moved back a step.

"Stan Morris tracked me down the day your mother died," he said, referring to their longtime family lawyer. "I caught the next direct flight from Paris."

"Step out here where I can see you," Matthew said.

Under the amber glow, Albert Banks was leaner than his son remembered, and better looking in late middle age. He wore a chambray shirt and linen trousers–which were baggy and reached right above his ankles–leather sandals and aviator sunglasses, even in the waning light. He looked like he just stepped out of a French art film.

"You sound like a cop," Albert said.

"You're acting like a thug, sneaking in here wearing those stupid sunglasses. You have no right to be in this house."

"The key was in the same place." He was rubbing his hands together as if to warm them.

"I should call the cops," Matthew said.

"That's awfully harsh, don't you think? We haven't seen each other for this long, and you talk to me like this?"

"What did you expect? You show up like – like a vulture, ready to pick your ex-wife's remains. You expect a happy reunion?"

Albert Banks shifted his stance and looked out to the evening sky.

"That's not fair, son. I came to see you. You've lost your mother. It's a terrible thing."

"A terrible thing? You really feel that way?"

"Of course. She died too soon."

"And what do you know about that?"

"Only what Stan told me. She was in a bad place."

"Yeah – you might say that. She died before I could get here."

"That's unfortunate."

"What's unfortunate is that she died alone."

"Why weren't you here?" Albert asked.

"I was planning to visit at some point," Matthew said, his rage mounting. "She asked me to wait until she was released, not that it's any of your business."

"You don't have to explain, son. No one is judging you."

Like hell. Matthew's head was about to blow apart. The torrent of emotions was taking him over, nearly impossible to control, and he felt like he might do something violent.

"Can we talk inside?" his father asked calmly.

Matthew stepped into the foyer, his chest heaving. Albert's bags were on the first step leading upstairs, a leather satchel and a backpack.

"What makes you think you can stay here?" Matthew asked.

"I assumed…"

"Don't assume *anything*," Matthew said. "I'm sure they have a room at the Skylark."

"What are the plans for the funeral?"

"There aren't any. I haven't even been to the hospital yet. I just got here for Christ's sake."

"I can take you there tomorrow, if you'd like."

Matthew took a deep breath and tried to get a handle on what was happening. His anger had plateaued. His harsh tone had become surprising even to himself. Never, ever had he talked to his father in this way.

"Look," Matthew said. "As far as I'm concerned, you're a guest who showed up for the funeral. Get a room."

"Grampa would have welcomed me here."

"Would he?"

"I was going to move into the old bedroom I used to share with your mother," Albert said.

Matthew's face was crimson.

"Not a chance!"

Albert Banks studied his son, slowly shaking his head. A hush fell over the darkened foyer. He walked to the stairs, picked up his bags, and went out the front door. As he headed to his rental car, his shoulders slumped by the weight, Matthew noticed his father had grown a small ponytail.

✳ ✳ ✳

Las Palmas was a wreck inside and out. Curtains were torn, windows were cracked, the floors were filthy and scraped, the walls and ceilings needed painting. Artwork hung askew. The kitchen, a grand room in the back where the family used to gather, with its double gas stoves, massive butcher block, and wooden dining table, smelled of rotten food and sour milk. The clock was exactly an hour off. The porcelain sink was filled with dirty dishes. Matthew was reminded this was the home of a shut-in alcoholic. He could also smell a hint of his mother's lifelong perfume – Chanel No. 5, from the seventies, sickeningly, over-laying the odor. He suddenly wondered if he'd made a huge mistake in coming. His mother's arrangements could have been made remotely, in Hartford, maybe with Madeleine providing personal and professional help. But with Albert here, he realized his presence was a stroke of good fortune. There was no telling what he'd try to pull if Matthew wasn't on site to prevent it.

As dusk descended, he stepped into the garage. It was the only space in its original condition. Old man Blevins' huge Cadillac was still parked in its own bay, covered with a cloth shroud. It was the same car Matthew had ridden in to get ice cream, go to the beach, go anywhere, all those years ago. His grandfather would put the convertible top down, fill the car with neighborhood kids, and off they'd go. When was the car last driven? He would find a way to get it going and it would be his principal mode of transportation.

He found a can of soup in a corner cupboard, and there was a loaf of garlic bread in the freezer. He ate at the kitchen table beneath the single hanging lamp and listened to the sounds of the old house as nighttime fell. He considered opening a bottle of whiskey he found under the sink and reconsidered. Exhausted from the time change, the travel, the confrontation with his father, and everything else that was churning in the middle of his soul, Matthew decided to cut his losses and go to bed. He climbed to the third floor, his childhood bedroom, a converted garret-like room called "The Crow's Nest," with windows on all sides and views of the entire lot. During his summer visits, when his grandparents took him for a month to give Dorothy and Albert a break, he'd spent countless hours up here. Often, when family gatherings became too loud and boisterous, he'd withdraw to this quiet perch at top of the house to read or draw pictures or just look out his bedside window to the back gardens overflowing with colorful flowers. The Crow's Nest became his own private retreat, and the family respected it as such. His grandfather even put a brass nameplate on the door: "This Crow's Nest is Property of *Matthew Blevins Banks*".

He rose at dawn and waited for the corner gas station to open at 7:00 am to call for service. A kid dressed in blue overalls and a Dodger's cap, looking like he should be in school, showed up and attached jumper cables and sprayed something into the carburetor. He was able to get the big white Cadillac running with a minimum of coaxing. It sputtered to life, belching blue clouds of smoke from the tail pipe, filling the driveway with noxious fumes of older models that the EPA banned years ago. When the humongous vehicle settled into a quiet idle, the mechanic assured Matthew it would be okay after a few miles on the road.

"I can't believe how frigging big this thing is," the mechanic said as Matthew wrote him a check.

It was indeed immense. It appeared to be the length of a city block, with gleaming chrome bumpers and sleek fins running to the back and a steering wheel the size of a manhole cover. Matthew put the top down, backed her out slowly onto the street, and made a quick loop through the neighborhood. She ran smooth and low to the ground. The neighbor across the street picking up his newspaper from the driveway waved tentatively, squinting as he tried to identify the driver.

✶ ✶ ✶

"You'll need to sign these papers," said the woman behind the broad hospital counter as she slid a file toward Matthew. "Customary release forms. One copy is for the Funeral Home."

Matthew forced himself to go to Pasadena General Hospital that afternoon. He'd learned the undertaker, some guy named Luigi Visconti, would pick up the body and prepare it for burial in two days. He declined the option of an autopsy. His mother had hit her head and hemorrhaged. There were surely other things going on in her tired body that could have killed her – failed liver, kidney damage, but none of that amounted to anything now.

"You will need to confirm her identity," the woman said. She was stern and overdressed and had her hair done up with pins.

"I'd rather not," he said.

"Is there anyone else who can do it?" she said.

Matthew thought about Paulina and quickly decided there was no one but his father, and there was no way he was going to afford him that opportunity.

"I'll do it."

138

He waited in the visitor's lounge to be taken downstairs, where the morgue covered the entire level. A frivolous pop tune played overhead.

"Please follow me," the man named Arturo said as he approached. He looked like a defensive end dressed as a male nurse. He led Matthew to the elevator, where they descended three levels to the bowels of the building. The doors slid open and immediately he was hit with the sharp scent of disinfectant and formaldehyde. As they headed down the hall Matthew saw everything glistening in its sterility, the pale green subway ceramic tile covering the floor, walls, and ceiling. They came to a door marked *Pathology* and entered a space that could be the changing room in a gym. The cadaver lockers ran the length of the wall on their right. Near the end, they found the door with a tab labeled "D. Banks". The male nurse stopped and turned to Matthew.

"Do you need a minute?"

"No."

Arturo unlocked the door and Matthew first saw his mother's feet in the shadow. Her heels were together and her feet pointed away from each other in a "V". A tag was looped over her big toe, identifying her. *Just like in crime shows,* Matthew thought. Arturo looked at Matthew once again and Matthew nodded to proceed. He rolled the gurney out, its metal bearings tinkling inside the little wheels, and now he could see the silhouette of his mother's physique pressing up through the shroud. The nurse pulled back the sheet to her waist. Dorothy's hands rested evenly beside her hips; her breasts drooped to each side. Her stomach was concave. She couldn't have lost that much weight, he thought to himself. But it was her face that startled him – how youthful she looked, at peace, an ever so slight smile on her lips. Her eyes weren't fully closed, as if in a dream state. Matthew wondered if maybe she died thinking happy thoughts.

"Is this Dorothy Blevins Banks?" the nurse said, holding the sheet up. Matthew nodded, unable to look away from a face he'd never seen so tranquil. He looked into her partially opened eyes for a glimmer of light, maybe a reflection that would allow him to pretend she could hear.

"You suffered mother," he said under his breath. "I always loved you. I'm sorry I was too much of a coward to tell you. I will regret that until the day I die."

Two days later, Matthew heard from Luigi Visconti that his mother was prepared for burial and they were awaiting instructions. The body was missing organs, the director said, and they were obligated by law to tell him this. When Matthew asked why somewhat outraged, the director said she signed a release at the rehab center that offered specific body parts to be harvested for research, in the unlikely event of death while on the premises.

"At least they didn't take her brain," Matthew said.

The funeral director started to say something and stopped.

"What?" Matthew said

"They did, actually."

Chapter 16

"How's our boy Banks doing?" Lawrence Holmes asked Madeleine, popping into her office one morning. She was at her computer with her back to him. Without turning around, she gave a brief update, simply saying that Matthew was taking a sabbatical.

"So your sessions are over?" Holmes said.

"That's right."

"Who cleared the sabbatical?"

"I did," she said, swiveling around to face her inquisitor.

"He's not going to do anything crazy, is he?"

"I hope not," she said.

Holmes said, "You need to be very clear with him as to when he's expected back."

She smiled indicating she already knew that.

"He'll be of little help around here," Holmes said, "but get him back in twenty-one days anyway. No more than that." He disappeared as quickly as he came.

Since that night in his bed she'd had reoccurring visions of their three hours together, thrilling but tarnished by regret and self-reprimand. To say what she did was inappropriate didn't come close to capturing the depth of her transgression. She had violated strict, time-honored professional codes – not to mention state laws– and it was entirely irreversible. The subject involved was not only a patient; he was a co-worker under her direct supervision, vulnerable and in danger of deepening emotional duress. She had opened herself up to harassment charges in the workplace, but far worse than that put her professional status, her career, in extreme jeopardy. Surely she had helped him by giving his self-esteem a much-needed lift, she tried to assure herself. Or did she merely make his life more complicated? If any part of their affair were to be exposed, she would at the very least be summarily fired, and if the company chose to turn her in, her license would be reviewed by the state board and likely revoked. She had acted in a way that fed her own wanting ego, a recklessness wholly uncharacteristic of her. But those three hours spent with him had so thoroughly inflamed her passion for Matthew Banks, she wondered now if she might have gone slightly insane.

There was another less complicated reason she wasn't going to forget the visit to Matthew's bed. She'd forgotten her gold necklace, left on his nightstand, a cross with four tiny pearls, one on each tip. It was a graduation gift from the sisters at St. Agatha's, a cherished token of faith and love from the women who'd nurtured her and prepared her spiritually, academically and nearly every other way for the life before her. She had depended on this steady icon of faith ever since leaving the convent. And now she felt naked and vulnerable without it, and she needed to find a way to get it back.

✴ ✴ ✴

Albert Banks was getting little sleep at the Skylark, the drive-up motel two miles from *Las Palmas*. The bed was like a bench and the cinder block walls provided little insulation from the sounds of inhabitants on either side. One couple was apparently going for a Guinness record on orgasms tallied in one night. He was startled awake repeatedly by cycles of piercing shrieks and bellowing moans. He called the front desk to complain. The night manager wasn't much help.

"Put a pillow over your head," he suggested.

His insomnia was only made worse by the shocking reception he'd received from his son. Matthew acted like a stranger, or worse, his enemy. After three nights at the Skylark, Albert was considering a return, another attempt at some kind of *détente*. He was not optimistic but decided to call his son one evening to take a reading on his current frame of mind.

"What do you want?" Matthew said when he picked up the call.

"How'd you know it was me?"

"Your number. You better have an international calling plan or your rates are going to bankrupt you. Maybe that's already happened."

"I don't know about my plan, actually. That's a good point," Albert said, trying to deflect the harsh tone.

There was a long pause.

"What are you after?" Matthew asked.

"I'm wondering if you've been to the hospital."

"She's in the funeral home now."

"Can I see her?"

"Of course, you can. You have a car."

"I turned in the rental. Could you take me?"

Matthew sighed. "I don't want to see her again."

"Please?"

"I'll think about it," Matthew finally said.

"What is there to think about?"

"Seeing my dead mother once was enough."

There was another long pause. Matthew was too tired to argue.

"I'll pick you up tomorrow," he said, suddenly surrendering.

At the base of it, Matthew was having trouble accepting his father in the flesh, as the pitiable, penniless vagabond, a deserter, a total loser. After all, he'd written him out of his life, any thoughts or emotions, years ago. He'd convinced himself their estrangement was not so abnormal, and he thought he'd found peace around it. But now, somewhere in his heart, he knew this was wishful thinking. He had come west expecting to deal with the complicated and sad void left behind by his mother, and instead found the other half of his parentage – a man he considered no longer his father, waiting at the house. That Albert had supplied half of his DNA was causing this odd push-pull dynamic that had him studying their physical and behavioral idiosyncrasies, little ticks, and gestures they shared, such as the way they buttered their toast, or how they rubbed their hands together when talking about uncomfortable issues. He didn't like what he was seeing, and still the temptation to compare was irresistible.

Matthew pulled into the pothole-strewn parking lot of the Skylark the next morning and nosed the big white Cadillac up to room 18. It was a perfect February day in southern California, and he had the top down and seat back. The car sat growling as it idled; the muffler had sprung a small leak.

"Oh boy!" Albert said as he opened the broad car door and climbed in. "Now *this* brings back memories!"

Matthew said nothing and pulled onto the highway. This may have been a big mistake, he thought to himself. He could have paid for a taxi to take him to the funeral home on his own and he would have to put up with this charade.

"Why did you turn in the rental?" he asked his father.

"They came to the Skylark and took it. Apparently, my French driver's license expired. It's just as well. The daily rate was more than I could afford."

"How do you plan to get around?"

Albert held out his hands toward the massive car transporting them, raising his eyebrows as if it were obvious.

Matthew was too incensed to answer. He accelerated and moved into the passing lane.

"What's with the sunglasses, anyway?" he said.

"I left my other ones on the plane."

"Figures."

The Visconti Funeral Home, a three-generation family business on the north edge of Pasadena, occupied an entire city block, its architecture low and dark with heavily cloaked windows and a semi-circle driveway that ran beneath a portico. The building was surrounded by Magnolia trees that put the entire structure in deep shadow, and two black hearses were waiting on the west side. Matthew introduced them at the front desk.

"I'm the son. This is her ex-husband," he said.

Mr. Visconti, a short balding man with hair so black it had to be dyed, came from behind a curtain and shook their hands. He didn't waste any time reminding Matthew he needed a credit card for the services performed and upcoming.

"We'll keep it on file until all the necessary details and procedures are accounted for," he said.

Matthew said alright and looked to his father to weigh his level of involvement and quickly dismissed any hope that he would help pay. Albert's failed financial state was clearly the only reason he'd come to Pasadena; the funeral was merely a foil. Matthew produced his Visa card and Mr. Visconti disappeared behind the curtain and left them standing alone. They stood studying the grim surroundings, and when Albert decided to sit down, Mr. Visconti reappeared.

"Let's go see the old gal," he said with a wink.

Matthew and his father exchanged a look of mild shock, the first time they'd aligned themselves in any way in over fifteen years, and followed Visconti to the back of the building.

She had been moved to an empty parlor and the casket was on a pedestal. The room was set up for a wake, with chairs grouped in two sections with an aisle up the middle. Behind the casket was a statuette of the Virgin Mary. The lid was open, propped up with a hinged support arm, and as they approached Matthew started to wonder if they had the wrong corpse. The body in the casket vaguely resembled Dorothy Banks. Albert seemed unfazed; Matthew was stunned.

"What did you do to her?" Matthew asked the director, who stood by, beaming at his handiwork.

"She had a bruise on her forehead, so we changed her complexion."

She looked like she'd just spent a month at the beach.

"And what about this?" Matthew asked, pointing to her eyes. "The eye make-up? She never wore thick mascara."

"It keeps the lids closed."

Matthew stepped back and looked at his father.

"What do *you* think?" he said to Albert.

Albert arched his eyebrows.

"She's certainly not looking her best. But all things considered, not too bad."

All things considered? Not too bad? Matthew walked to a corner chair, sat down, and put his face in his hands. For twenty-five hundred bucks, which had just been charged to his credit card, Visconti Funeral Home created a rendering of his mother that wouldn't pass in a wax museum. Why did he bother? His father was acting like a neighbor who tagged along for the hell of it. Matthew stared into space, exhausted of all commentary and emotion, and rose to leave. His father stood by the casket looking sheepishly down at his very tan and dead ex-wife.

"I'd like some time with her," Albert said.

Matthew ignored the comment and turned to the funeral home director.

"How much time do we have?"

"You mean now? As much as you want," Visconti said.

"No – before we need to get her out of here."

"You have thirty days, and if you haven't moved her by then she'll be cremated."

"And I guess there's an extra charge for that," Matthew said.

"Twelve hundred dollars. I can put it on the card on file. There's the cold storage fee included in that."

Matthew shook his head and looked to his father, who remained quiet, standing by the casket.

"I'll be in the car," he said, and walked out of the room.

Driving back to the Skylark, Albert asked Matthew what he was doing for lunch.

"Is that Mexican place still on the corner?" he said.

Matthew stared ahead, trying to come to terms with the macabre, bizarre morning, dominated by this odd relationship unfolding with his remaining living parent. He'd suspected Albert was there to take what he could get and then go on his way. A less cynical voice in his head said maybe he really did want back in the family, or what was left of it.

"There's food back at the house," he said.

They pulled into the driveway and Albert commented on the abandoned gardens, the crabgrass growing wild.

"The place has gone to hell."

Matthew stopped the car abruptly and jammed it into *PARK*.

"What did you expect? Matthew said. "Mother never cared about keeping things up."

"We won't speak poorly of her now, Matt."

"I'm just saying she wasn't the neatest person. And I didn't say anything at the funeral home, but I think we'll just let that jerk Visconti cremate her. I can't deal with the body right now," Matthew said.

"I think that's something we should talk about," Albert said.

"What's to talk about? Ashes to ashes."

"And where will we bury her?" Albert said.

"There's a family plot over on Poppy Hill," Matthew said. "If we cremate her, we could put her in the back yard."

"Hmmm," was all Albert said.

They went into the house and Albert continued with his criticism of the place, pointing out the cracked walls, the shabby furniture. They were in the kitchen where Matthew was mixing up some tuna.

"I guess we're going to have to put some money into the old homestead," Albert said.

"I beg your pardon? We?" Matthew said. And then, "And where were you planning to get the money from?"

"I'm in the will too," Albert said.

"No—no you are not."

"That's what Stan told me."

"Stan's smoking dope. Mother made it clear before rehab, everything goes to me. Why would she leave anything to you?"

Albert was sitting at the table, wearing the same clothes he had arrived in, the baggy linen pants, the light blue work shirt, his aviators.

"*Before rehab* doesn't help me believe she was in her right mind. Is this going to be a problem?" Albert asked.

"Let me talk to Stan," Matthew said. "I'll set him straight."

They sat eating sandwiches in silence. Matthew was trying to remember where his mother kept her papers. Last he knew there was a box in her closet. A copy of her last will and testament would be in there.

"Regardless, Matthew, you and I have some catching up to do. I have a fifteen-year blank slate when I try to envision your life up to now. For instance, I heard you were married, but I don't know anything about your wife or what happened."

"That's personal. Not something I care to talk about," Matthew said.

"I'm no expert in marriage, but I know things change, people change. Is that what happened?"

"I've got to take you back now," Matthew said, carrying his plate to the sink. "As you have so brilliantly pointed out, there's a lot to be done around here."

Albert sat watching his son while he stood at the counter. From the back, he looked more like his mother's side of the family–broad shoulders, high waist. And he was proving to have the Blevins stubborn temperament too, narrow-minded often unswayable.

"Are you thinking we'll sell the place then?" Albert said.

"How many times do I have to say it? There is no *we* in this equation. You have no ownership. I am inheriting this entire goddam mess. I can figure it out on my own. I don't want or need your help."

They walked outside to the car. Matthew was done talking. By refusing to engage any further, he gave the man no power. They drove to the Skylark in silence. As they turned into the parking lot Albert began singing his sorry song.

"I have three-hundred dollars of cash in my pocket. It's the last of my money. I'm paying this fleabag motel with my last traveler's checks.

I have no credit. I came over on a one-way ticket. It was all I could do. I have nothing back in France."

Matthew turned and stared at his father. Pathetic or what? To an outsider, this would simply be sad.

"I'm sure you'll figure something out," Matthew said. "Like when you left, and you assumed mom and I would figure something out."

Albert's forlorn expression suddenly turned desperate. He swung his legs out of the car and sat with his feet on the cracked asphalt with his back to his son.

"I was hoping you'd turn out better than me."

Chapter 17

"How's Bella?" Matthew said to Hughes. He was calling to check in.

"She misses you. She walks around the house with that old sock of yours in her mouth."

"I'm calling about your friend the lawyer," Matthew said.

"Goldman? Why?"

"I need him to take a look at my mother's will."

Matthew had remembered the night before, as he lay tangled in his sweaty sheets, a comment Hughes made one night about a college roommate who'd gone on to be a wildly successful Hollywood lawyer. Mel Goldman had won settlements for more than a few named film stars. Dorothy's will was indeed in her closet, and after reading it over there were several vague references to her parents' estate, with Albert's name appearing in several places.

"You'd be taking a howitzer to a knife fight," Hughes said. "He'll destroy your father. And he's probably the most expensive lawyer in Tinseltown."

"My father's like a dog with a bone. He's not letting go."

"Let me call him before you do anything," Hughes said. "I'll make the introduction, ask for the friends and family discount."

✳ ✳ ✳

Matthew was spending his days cleaning up *Las Palmas,* going from room to room removing old clothing and furniture, tossing out frayed rugs. With no definitive plan, he was preparing the house for whatever its next life would be, either with a new family, through a sale, or if he decided to keep it in the Blevins trust and perhaps rent it out. In any case, it lifted his spirit to see the old homestead come back to life.

He called in an industrial cleaning company to scour the floors and walls, take down the dusty curtains and wash the windows, and wax and buff the tile floors, all of which made an astonishing difference. He assembled a pile of broken-down furniture and appliances in the garage, including a cache of his father's painting supplies from years past: a wooden easel, some pallets, and tubes of oil paints. Years of collected household items his grandparents had acquired and held onto, for one reason or another, soon filled one of the spaces in the three-car garage, ready to be whisked away by a hauling company. He called St. Vincent de Paul to remove most of the ratty but useable furniture and sent the good carpets to the cleaners. He threw away cupboards of decayed pots and pans, old condiments and boxed processed foods, boxes of knick-knacks, and scrubbed all the cupboard surfaces, covering them with liner paper. With each passing day, traces of his mother were disappearing. It was only a faint hint of her favorite perfume now, still hanging in the air, that kept her present.

In lighter moments, he envisioned his pottery studio. He'd forgotten how certain rooms of the house were saturated with diffuse light from all directions, especially the solarium in the back corner, and the family room that fed into the kitchen. His grandfather had positioned the house to receive maximum sun in all seasons, and Matthew began thinking about the best place he could set up, if by some chance he ever lived there.

In the early evenings, he would back the big white Cadillac out of the garage and if it was warm enough, put the top down and head south. It was an hour to the coast where he picked up Highway 1 and cruised beside the beach watching the sun drop toward the wide-open expanse of the sea, its fire intensifying as it neared the horizon. He liked to think of it as riding along the edge of the world. Driving so close to the water, the organic aromas of kelp beds and beached sea creatures wafted over the highway smelling like the beginning of life itself. The waves came steadily, like white foam rollers, the soft *whissh* allowing him to think in an uncluttered way about where and who he was, and how he wound up in this bizarre set of circumstances. He thought of Madeleine, about how she convincingly fended off his attraction but then succumbed and suddenly acted out her own desires. That they both had such powerful feelings for one another only partly explained the eruption of passion that first (and last) night together, the blissful sleep that came after, the sense that what transpired was not only thrilling but predestined and numinous. Where things were going with her was anyone's guess, but for now, he was happy to bask in the warm afterglow of the memory.

His father's intrusion was an entirely different matter. Equally complex and difficult to parse, Albert had been the focus of much discussion with Madeleine, specifically how Matthew felt about him when he was a boy. That he still so stubbornly refused to even acknowledge his father was a source of concern. Madeleine had tactfully encouraged him to consider his father the larger and more daunting threat to his emotional health, understanding how he had become a distant stranger when he used to be a role model, a hero even. Picturing him now at the Skylark, with its cinder block walls and cheesy swimming pool hard against the highway, the last of his money running out like sand in an hourglass, made that extremely difficult.

✳ ✳ ✳

Madeleine reached out to Matthew two weeks later when she still hadn't heard from him. Matthew saw her number on his cell phone and his stomach tensed.

"Can you talk?" she said. It was early evening in Hartford. Her voice wavered as if she were either shivering, or nervous.

"Of course. It's just me and Dorothy's ghost bouncing around the old hacienda," Matthew said.

"You could call *me* some time, you know. Or are you the 'love them and leave them' type?"

"I haven't talked to *anyone,* Madeleine. Except for my lunatic father. I'm not out here having fun, you know."

"What?"

"He showed up. He wants his part of the estate."

There was a pause.

"Oh shit," she said.

He'd never heard her swear.

"How does that make you feel?"

"Shit is right," Matthew said. "Out of the blue and pretending he's still my father. Paging Dr. Freud."

"Ha!" Madeleine laughed. "I could use a few sessions with old Sigmund myself. Should we channel him and try couples therapy?"

Her joke fell flat. She asked about where his father was staying and whether they were even talking, trying to get a sense of the state of their reunion. Matthew declined to go into it and changed the topic to the weather.

"How are your plans coming along?" she said. "When is the funeral?"

He explained the situation. There was no pressure to have any service. His mother's sister in Seattle was unreachable. He'd lost touch with old family friends, some of whom had been calling, leaving messages on her machine, but he wasn't returning any. He declined an offer by the paper to run an obituary.

"You remember our talks about closure," Madeleine said.

"Let's talk about something else," Matthew said. "Do you ever think about us?" he said boldly.

She let out a long sigh.

"I can still feel you inside me," she said. "I want to feel you forever."

Matthew tensed. Thoughts of her these past weeks had been a comforting, dreamy place to go, but he'd warned himself not to get too cozy with the idea.

"It was a little crazy," he whispered. "But I'd like another night with you, too."

He heard Madeleine take a sip of wine.

"We would need to be in the same location," she said. "Preferably in the same bed. That reminds me, Lawrence Holmes wants you back here by the end of the month."

"You really know how to kill the mood," he said. "Tell Lawrence he needs to relax."

"He's serious. He asked me to make you aware."

"And if I don't come back by then?"

"It'll probably cost you your job. You know how he operates."

She told him it was time to put Bradley to bed. Think about returning to Hartford, she said.

"I understand you need to deal with your father," she added. "You may need more time. I'll try to get Lawrence to come around. And remember, no matter how awful he was to you, Albert's still your father."

Matthew hung up and stared out the kitchen window at the gathering dusk. There was nothing he wanted more right now than to go back to Hartford and be with Madeleine in the same bed. If they were to continue, he would need to quit *Connecticut Life and Casualty,* for it would eventually become public knowledge. She had much more at stake than him, and with his inheritance, which was still far from certain but definitely significant, he could certainly afford to take a year or two off. Before falling asleep, his thoughts were about how crazy life could be, how new opportunities can arise in the wake of disaster. One door closes, another opens. Madeleine once told him it was the way of the universe.

Chapter 18

"This must stop. Now."

Ira Cummins was an elite psychoanalyst whose list of patients included fellow therapists with the self-awareness to seek another opinion when it came to their own personal mental health. He was also a tenured professor at Trinity College and participated in the doctoral candidate's mandatory analysis program. Madeleine had met him at an American Psychotherapy seminar in New York City several years before. She came to him in confidence, with her deeply conflicted conscience, and explained the entire dilemma concerning Matthew.

"You'll lose your license," he added, "Guaranteed. In fact, by law, I should report you. Do you realize you've put me in a very precarious spot here?"

"But we have doctor-patient confidentiality!" she said desperately.

"It's not even a grey area. I think we should stop talking about it immediately. I have written nothing down, and will not do so going forward."

Dr. Cummins stacked some papers on his desk.

"Let's talk about Bradley," he said curtly.

Madeleine sat upright in her chair facing the broad oak desk. Dr. Cummins looked nothing like a psychiatrist, more of a financier. He wore expensive custom shirts with double cuffs. The silver links were monogrammed. His tie was Hermes, his half-glasses were light, tortoise shell Polo frames he wore halfway down his nose. His long silver hair was swept back off his broad forehead. For a man of sixty, he was strikingly handsome.

"He's doing well," Madeleine said. "He still hasn't asked about his father. I'll need to share the story with him, eventually."

"Bradley's old enough now. Have you talked with him about drugs?"

"Ira, he's only eight."

"There are ten-year-old junkies down the street shooting up right now, I can promise you."

Madeleine stared out the side window of the doctor's twentieth-story office. It was a grey winter afternoon in New England and everything in the frame was one drab color: The sky, the concrete buildings, the hills in the distance. She had come seeking advice about her impossible situation with Matthew, her lapse in self-discipline, her egregious mistake. But Dr. Cummins was not having any of it. He would only talk about the safer subject of Bradley's predisposition for drug abuse, behavioral signs she needed to look for, genetic probabilities passed down from his father. She'd spent years trying to forget these genetic flaws, and the horrible last months with Adam, but now they were alive again in her memory. If summoned, she could remember so clearly the day Adam Rich collapsed in the operating room halfway through conducting a knee reconstruction. Her immediate world, that of her young marriage, her bright-eyed three-year-old son, and her private psychotherapy practice, came to a gut-wrenching halt. Adam had been dependent on opioids for years to control his own knee pain, chronic inflammation from repeated college hockey injuries, which had led to his addiction and uncontrolled abuse. The morning he overdosed, his addiction became public. His partners in the private clinic they had formed, highly regarded throughout New England for treating professional football and basketball players, threw him into rehab. He made it three weeks clean but escaped through an unlocked door one night. He hadn't been seen or heard from in fourteen months.

"I'll ask about his friends, whether he sees any pot," she said.

"That's a good place to start."

She looked at her watch and realized their time was up.

"You're vulnerable, Madeleine," he said as she stood to leave. "Don't throw your career away. Turn your attention to Bradley. Say goodbye to this character, Banks."

"He's not a character," was all she said.

She left his office and rode the elevator to the basement garage. Her Mercedes sat parked in a dark corner, its usual bright red finish barely detectable beneath the layer of winter grime. As she drove through town toward the western suburbs, a pinkish band stretched across the grey horizon. The days were getting longer. It was the middle of February; Lent was coming, and then Easter. The purple and yellow crocuses would be popping up in her front lawn flower beds any day now, and she longed for color, any kind of relief from this dreary existence.

As she pulled into her driveway a different kind of dread came over her. She was facing a weekend alone with no plans. Her neighbor friends were vacationing in the Caribbean, on an island she had recommended. Bradley had quit hockey, and baseball season was six weeks away. Tonight he had a birthday party and a sleepover. He was spending more time out of the house with friends, showing more independence every day, and she could swear she heard his voice break that morning. It wouldn't be long before he was growing hair under his arms, and everywhere else, and she'd need to have *that* talk with him, a harder one than drugs. Even with all her training, the idea was daunting. This was her only child, her progeny, her legacy. It was all now up to her, and she felt the pressure and loneliness of her responsibilities bearing down on her. Life was charging ahead for everyone but her, and nobody had the time to give a damn about Madeleine Batiste's situation. Dr. Cummins was right. She was in a very vulnerable place.

As she pulled into the garage, the idea to call Adam's brother popped into her head. Dooley lived in rural Vermont. He had initially stayed in touch with her and Bradley, ashamed of his brother's failings. But over time his calls had fallen off, and despite this, Madeleine knew he was the only family support she could summon. Both Adam's parents were dead, his father succumbing to a brain tumor at sixty-eight and his mother, crushed by the loss of her husband, and then Adam's disappearance, lived only two years longer. But Dooley still took her calls, and she would ask him to have the man-to-man talk with Bradley. It wasn't merely that she was intimidated; he was the perfect influence to explain his father's addiction and the need to stay away from drugs, as Ira Cummins had reminded her. The sex talk could wait.

Dooley's life as a naturalist, living alone among the rushing streams in the deep forest of the White Mountains, had turned him into a recluse. He'd built his own one-room cabin using spruce trees felled on his 40-acre property, and now had limited contact with the outside world, beyond the modest business of teaching fly fishing to enthusiasts who came from all across New England. He was widely known as a skilled instructor and it supported his simple life that had few demands. Certainly, Madeleine thought, he could take the time to counsel his only nephew.

So it was pure coincidence when, on the morning she planned to call him, the phone rang and Dooley was on the other end.

"I was just thinking of you!" Madeleine said. It sounded like he was running through the woods.

"Hold that thought. I need to tell you something first."

His voice was hurried, out of breath.

"Adam was arrested in New Haven. I'm hiking to my car. I should be able to bail him out in a few hours."

Every muscle in Madeleine's body froze. Of all the possible scenarios, this was her single greatest fear. It had been years. She had given him up for dead.

"I can't go with you," she said after gathering herself.

"I'm not asking you to. I'm just letting you know. I'll call tomorrow, after I get him released. I've found a clinic that will take him."

Madeleine pictured Adam being led into a facility in a straitjacket.

"What made you think of me? Is everything else alright?" Dooley asked.

"It can wait," she said.

Chapter 19

Matthew was pulling into *Las Palmas* after an edge-of-the-world evening cruise. The sun had set in its usual golden display, and a silhouette of the grand hacienda in the twilight cast a majestic image. From the driveway, he saw a light on inside, a lamp he never used. He pulled the car into the garage and went around to the front door. The Don Quixote statuette by the entrance had been moved. The door was unlocked. He could hear someone inside rummaging in the kitchen. He walked inside and went to the back where he found his father standing at the open refrigerator.

"Got anything to snack on?" he asked.

"What are you doing here?"

"I was evicted from the Skylark. They got tired of my excuses."

Tired? Matthew was beyond tired, especially of his father and his vain, Euro look, his demeanor, the way he continued to force himself like a sniveling beggar. He had on the same peasant bohemian clothes he was wearing when he arrived, the ridiculous sunglasses. His straw planter's hat sat on the counter. He had become something like a cartoon character in a very unfunny movie.

"You think you can just drive over and let yourself in?"

"You seem to forget. I used to be a member of this family, and this home. I'm not robbing the place, for crying out loud. By the way, do you know where the will is? We need Stan to read it."

"You're right about one thing," Matthew said. "You *used* to be a member of this family. Stan's not going to have anything to do with the will. He can't represent either of us. He's conflicted."

"Who do you have in mind?" Albert said.

"I have a guy."

Albert gave his son a concerned and confused look.

"I've put my things in the help's quarters downstairs," he said.

Matthew took a step back. He could hear Madeleine's therapist voice. *He's your father.* He took a calming breath.

"There's a kitchen down there," Matthew said. "If you have to sleep here, I'd rather you stay below. And you can get your own damn food."

He turned and went to the stairs and listened as his father took the ingredients for a sandwich from the refrigerator and descended the basement steps to his new quarters.

***

Matthew went to bed that night feeling on the verge of insanity, his nerves raw, jangled, like he might do something stupid. It was the way one feels standing on the edge of a bottomless precipice, thinking a jump would be easy, and fast. He wondered: was he ever in control? He'd certainly made progress. These past few weeks had been productive and therapeutic. He'd been working around *Las Palmas*, sleeping in the Crow's Nest, and the rich memories of his childhood had steadily comforted him. He was sheltered and loved all those years ago, and now he could fully appreciate how Harry and Eleanor Blevins had quietly but earnestly gone about their job as surrogate parents. They wrapped him in affection and encouragement, allowing him to separate himself from the calamity unfolding in his own home, never once shedding light on the shortcomings of his parents.

If he was honest, the thought of evicting his father was unsettling, and Madeleine's advice couldn't be silenced. But the man hadn't done himself any favors. The way he appeared unannounced and made such outrageous assumptions. And it had all come on so fast! He was just getting used to the idea that Albert was *alive*, and now he was maneuvering to rid his life of the man, make him feel like a villain, ex-communicated from the family. To do this he would have to summon the cold, take no prisoners approach of this Hollywood attorney named Goldman.

* * *

In the days that followed, Matthew continued to focus on restoring *Las Palmas*. He turned his attention now to the grounds. The flower beds had grown over, now just shaping indentations in the lawn with ugly weeds and crabgrass. He pulled some tools and a wheelbarrow from the shed and began the monotonous work of digging them out, replacing much of the sod with fresh soil and peat moss. He'd hire a gardener to replant it all, and he tried to remember the various plants and flowering shrubs his grandfather had chosen so meticulously. Some trees needed attention, a stand of shaggy eucalyptus in the northwest corner that was messy needed to be trimmed; four towering palm trees at each corner of the three-acre lot had retained their majesty but were in desperate need of pruning. All this work progressed without a scintilla of involvement by his father, who was either hiding or hibernating in the basement (he wasn't sure which) making his way through Grampa Blevins' library of Raymond Chandler crime novels. It was unclear what the man was eating, and Matthew figured there had to be cupboards containing canned foods; he remembered the freezer was always stocked with cuts of meat and pizzas his mother kept on hand for emergencies. Occasionally, he smelled something cooking; more frequently the distinct scent of baking made its way upstairs, yeast and dough, delicious smells, rich and buttery. He could have been living above a French *patisserie*.

Matthew's own diet was sparse and lacked imagination. He was living on instant soup and pasta with oil and garlic. Each night he'd take his plate and a glass of wine onto the back Oval, a flagstone patio with a fire pit in the center where the family used to gather to roast marshmallows and sing songs. On cool nights he'd fill the fire pit with seasoned mesquite, flames quickly shooting skyward in a brilliant orange glow, and he'd watch for a long time the grey ash rush into the clear dark night.

One morning, Matthew came downstairs to a new smell. It wasn't of baking bread, which he'd come to expect, but a sharp, chemical aroma. With the mnemonic power of a distinct odor, he was instantly back in his childhood basement in Pasadena. The smell of linseed oil and paint was unmistakable. He spontaneously yelled downstairs.

"What are you doing down there?"

He heard some fumbling and Albert came to the bottom of the stairs wearing a paint-splattered smock over his usual clothes.

"I'd forgotten about the supplies I kept here. They were in the garage with the trash. I wish you would have checked with me before throwing them out."

Matthew made his way down the stairs, his first visit since Albert moved in. In the room where he now lived, the easel from the garage was standing beneath a line of windows running along the ceiling, capturing what little natural light coming in. A decades-old canvas had been painted over and a new image was taking form. Matthew could see the outline of *Las Palmas*

"What else am I going to do while we get this sorted out?" Albert said. "I've always wanted to paint this place." His eyes were turned to his unfinished work. On the table beside him was a black and white photo of the house taken in the 1960s.

Matthew shook his head. By the day, by the hour, he could see it was becoming less likely he'd uproot the man. Albert Banks had begun making *Las Palmas* a place of his own, and Matthew knew how an artist's studio, which was exactly what his father was building, could anchor someone to any given location. He said nothing and turned to go.

"I'll have hot baguettes later, if you're interested," Albert said.

★ ★ ★

Mel Goldman's office was on Hollywood Boulevard amidst the most shimmering district of Los Angeles. Entering the deco era building in the late afternoon, Matthew took the elevator to the tenth floor of the law building and walked to the end of a long hallway where his offices were situated. The attractive receptionist told him to take a seat. He sat on a plush leather couch and took in the photos on the walls surrounding him. Dozens of well-known Hollywood actors appeared in studio portraits, past and present clients Goldman represented. It was an impressive roster, and all Matthew could think about was the cost of what he was getting himself into. Minutes later, a tall young man in alligator loafers and no socks walked him back to the inner offices.

"Relax, Matthew B," Mel Goldman said without getting up, glancing down at a file. "We'll get this sorted out to your satisfaction *tout suite.*"

He was absurdly tan, as only someone living on the beach in Malibu can be. He wore his white hair like Julius Caesar, with bangs cut straight high on his forehead. Both wrists were thick with bracelets and his shirt was open to the middle of his deeply brown chest, white fur spilling out.

The Hollywood lawyer immediately began firing off awkward questions. None of them seemed pertinent to his case. Had his father ever abused him, physically or otherwise? Did his father have a criminal record? Did he ever abuse his mother when they were living together? What did he do for a living?

Matthew shifted in his chair, groping for answers before replying.

"I ask you these things because there are two ways we can go about this," Goldman said. "We can contest the will, which I can't speculate about until I read it, or we can take your father down, get him on something that will break him."

He pulled out a copy of the document Matthew had given him.

"I'm assuming he knows something about the will that you don't. We need some dirt on him. We need to play hard ball Matt, break him in two, and from what you've said, you're okay doing that, right?"

Goldman was leaning back in his tilting chair, far enough to cross his beefy legs, his hands clasped behind his head. Matthew remained silent. Goldman continued eyeing the quiet young man.

"So, you have the *cojones*?" he said.

Matthew winced.

"*Balls*?" Goldman said.

"I know what you mean," Matthew said. "I don't have anything that would be criminal," Matthew said. "He was a lawyer – I think he followed the law. He never abused us, unless you consider abandonment abusive."

"It depends."

There was a pause. Matthew looked at the wall behind Goldman. One picture was him standing with Frank Sinatra, both in tuxedos, bent over laughing. Sinatra was holding a trophy, maybe an Emmy.

"I'll have my team do some digging," Goldman said. "But I'll tell you this, it was pretty damn stupid of you to let him move in."

No shit Sherlock, Matthew thought to himself. He was beginning to dislike this man.

"How are your finances?" Goldman said. "Hughes said you were coming into some money."

"You tell me." Matthew nodded at the will. "Hughes mentioned the possibility of a friends and family' discount."

Goldman began chuckling. The chuckle swelled into hysterical, choking laughter.

"Now that's *funny*!" he gasped. "A friends and family discount!" He was laughing so hard, his face had reddened beneath his tan.

As Matthew rose to leave, Goldman stood for the first time.

"Don't worry chief," he said with a wink. "Hughes has your back. And before I forget, I need Albert's social security number."

* * *

Outside, Matthew forgot where he had parked. Normally the big white Cadillac stuck out like an historical monument, but his mind was so cluttered with reflections of his father in the basement standing by his easel and Goldman's guerilla-like style, he was having trouble

168

remembering what he did five seconds ago. Just when he started thinking it had been stolen, he spotted the long white beast of a car behind a panel van.

He drove the car out of the lot and headed for the freeway, dreading his return to *Las Palmas*, now shared with the bohemian squatter who called himself his father, who Mel Goldman said they would break in two. Rather than head east on the 10 Freeway, he got onto Hwy 1 and headed south. As evening descended, and the big car rambled effortlessly down the Pacific Coast Highway, high above the waves lapping steadily onto the beach, he immediately felt the calming effect of the open sea, the noisy city behind him replaced by the quiet hush of the ocean. It was the perfect escape. As the sun lowered near the horizon, it cast the coastline in a rosy glow. The air was beginning to cool.

He pulled into a rest stop and parked the car, its nose pointed to the water like the prow of an ocean liner. He flicked the button and the convertible top whined as it climbed toward the sky and came flopping down, enclosing him in a hushed cocoon. It was good to stop moving, and he sat with the stillness. He put the seat back and leaned into the headrest, closed his eyes, and took long, measured breaths. His mind lifted above the rumble and chaos of his life, drinking in his peaceful surroundings, and as he rose, looking down now like a sea bird soaring in the wind, the white beaches stretched as far as he could see in either direction, the vast body of the Pacific now deep purple in the diminishing light. Absolutely, he could imagine himself living in Southern California again. But if it turned out his father was by some chance included in the will, his options would be severely limited. They would sell the property and he'd return to Hartford. By that time, he assumed, he would be fired from *Connecticut Life*, but his finances would be secure. Would he stay in Hartford? For a while. Let things settle. Get to work on some important projects in his basement studio. And if he wanted her, Madeleine was there to be with, and perhaps to love.

The other scenario was growing in its appeal. If he could rid himself of his father and assume ownership of *Las Palmas,* admittedly he would walk into a massive project. But he would do it forthrightly and with a tremendous amount of pride, for it would please his grandfather, would be a noble act of gratitude for all Matthew had been given as a child. His mind bounced back to Madeleine. Was he ready to leave her back east? She was special, that is if his instincts were right. But his instincts had come up short in the past. He would need to spend more time with her, then if he wanted, persuade her to move west, with her son, which would be complicated. His thoughts ambled along for an indeterminate length of time, and he drifted off into a light sleep.

A knock came on the window. He sat up with a start and saw a weathered old man standing beside the car. He appeared homeless, maybe a beach bum. He motioned for Matthew to lower the window.

"Got a light, friend?"

The man's voice was as harsh as his face, his hair a greyish blond, hanging to his shoulders, loose shorts falling off him, and a frayed luau shirt. *He must be cold*, was Matthews first thought. He leaned forward and pushed in the car's lighter. It popped out and he nimbly passed the red-hot cylinder to the man, who took it and put it to his hand-rolled cigarette.

"Thank you, friend," he said, handing back the lighter, and then exhaling a plume of white smoke. He looked out to the water.

"Say, did you catch the green flash tonight?"

He had watery blue eyes like miniature jellyfish, eyebrows that were tiny tumbleweeds. Matthew nodded. He had indeed seen the emerald burst spark above the waterline, just as the sun disappeared into the ocean. It hadn't registered.

"You know," said the old man, "that signals a shift in the universe, that exact moment." He was leaning down now with his head nearly inside the car, his leathery hand gripping the door. Matthew could smell the stale tobacco and feel, as he continued to stare straight ahead, the man's eyes boring into him and it was becoming uncomfortable.

"But you already knew about that," the man said, standing back. And then, "Son, you look troubled."

Matthew tried to ignore the man's forwardness and kept staring out to sea. From the corner of his eye, he saw the man's cigarette flare in its loose construction as he took a deep drag.

"I'm fine," Matthew finally said.

"I know what 'fine' looks like," the man said. "I'm not seeing that right now."

Matthew took a deep breath. *Come on, dude.*

"What do you know, anyway?" Matthew shouted, turning toward him. "And what do you care? Maybe you should worry more about your own damn problems."

The man took one last drag of his cigarette and dropped it to the pavement, crushing it with his bare heel. He was still studying Matthew with his penetrating stare.

"Walk?" he finally said.

"*Jesus!*" Matthew cried from his seat. He leaned forward to start the car.

"Wait." The man nodded toward the beach.

"There's a spot I want to show you. *Por favor.* You'll be glad, *amigo.*"

Amigo? His voice was neither pleading nor threatening. It had a beneficent, all-knowing resonance, as if he understood more about Matthew than Matthew himself. Without thinking, he climbed from the Cadillac.

"This way," the old man motioned with his head.

They walked south in the sand along the waterline until they came to an inlet where the beach reached into a stand of locust trees. A small fire smoldered in a pit beside a lean-to tent. A wooden crate held assorted items that Matthew assumed were his worldly belongings.

"*Bienvenido*," the old man said as he lowered himself and sat cross-legged in the sand. "*Mi casa es su casa*." He motioned for him to sit down, lifted a bottle from the crate, and removed the cork.

"*De mi hermano en Oaxaca*." He raised his crazy eyebrows. "*Mescalito*." He handed it to Matthew.

Matthew studied the bottle. The label had a rudimentary illustration of an agave plant, its leaves sharp tongues darting up like flames. He drank freely, ignoring the rank flavor; its harshness reminded him of something he couldn't quite place.

The two strangers sat, trading drinks silently in the gathering dusk, pinpricks of light green stars beginning to appear above in a pale blue field. A quarter moon hung in the southwest like a yellow cuticle. Matthew sensed the day's grip ease as the strong liquor flooded his brain.

"Feel like talking?" the man said.

"What?"

"Your family, your life."

"How do you know anything about my life? Why would you care?"

"Your energy – when you handed me the lighter. It came through me."

Matthew eyed the sea. *Oh boy*, he thought.

"My name is Kanakis," the old man said. "My friends call me Cosimo."

Matthew took a longer drink from the bottle. *Creosote.* That was what it tasted like.

The old man went silent.

Without pretense or wondering why, Matthew began talking about his mother.

"I came out here late," he whispered. "She'd already died."

Matthew spoke flowingly about his failures. The company holiday party, the cheating wife, the beating he took from her lover. He became too upset to get into his father. He put his face in his hands and wept.

Cosimo said, "Pull yourself together son. Come on now. It was your mother's time. You must flow with this, like a river through the crease of a canyon. Today, tomorrow, and on and on. It's your time. You have things to do here."

They were leaning back against large smooth boulders that still held the warmth of the day. Cosimo dropped more wood onto the fire. The wind kicked up and it caught flame, cracking, snapping as it blew sideways. Matthew watched as one flare shot away in a gust, its orange plume an asteroid flash blinding his field of vision. He turned to the old man and watched his face melt. He jerked his head, snapping the image back into clarity.

They finished the mescal and now Matthew was talking about his father. He continued, until night had officially fallen and Cosimo was listening as he stared out to the black sea. He asked no questions. Matthew rambled on.

When he finally stopped, Cosimo said, "The man is seeking atonement. You are of his seed. Read the scriptures. We must forgive our fathers, and the penitent. Sometimes the son is the father to the man."

"I don't want to be the goddam father," Matthew said tersely. "And he's not asking for forgiveness. He's already assumed it."

A few minutes passed and Matthew calmed down. The two men stared out to the open sea for a while. Then Matthew opened up about Julia, his spurned love. The more he spoke, the louder he became again, until he was shouting. This was a different loss, he yelled, a betrayal, more of life's ugliness! He railed into the night, Demosthenes' voice carrying above the wind. Cosimo sat silent and motionless. When Matthew's railing finally ceased, Cosimo lifted a necklace over his head and held it out for Matthew to see. It was a sun-bleached sand dollar the size of a poker chip with a hole drilled through it with a loop of rawhide. He dropped it over Matthew's head and palmed the white medallion against his sternum.

"Accept my token of serenity, son. Wear this in peace. It will bathe you in humility and grace, and in time bring forgiveness."

There was dead silence now, but for the soothing metronomic *whish* of the tiny waves folding just beyond their feet. A lone tern cried from above.

It was Cosimo's turn to speak.

"Now, this new woman," he said. "You will open your heart to her, and all that she brings."

Matthew squinted. "I never mentioned a new woman."

Cosimo smiled. He stood and looked out to sea. Then he stepped out of his clothes and walked into the waves. He motioned for Matthew to follow. Matthew wanted desperately to sleep. The powerful mescal was pulling him down to the beach. His spirit, his consciousness teetered on some invisible precipice. The naked, wrinkled old man stood waiting for him.

"Come, my son."

He managed to rise, shed his clothes, and follow the man's footsteps into the dark glistening water. The ocean felt surprisingly warm. Brilliant jade-colored flecks of phosphorus fizzed around his ankles.

Cosimo advanced and disappeared into the darkness. Matthew went in up to his chest and splashed like a child. He exhaled sharply and filled his lungs once, twice, and dove further out. He swam down, down, and set his bare bottom on the ocean floor. His mind emptied. Bubbles fluttered above as he exhaled. He heard his name. The sea was calling him. There was a rock outcropping. Kelp waved to him, swaying in the current like Geisha girls. Glancing up to the surface, the moon was a slash of maize, the color of corn. He felt no hurry. *I've got you,* he heard his father say. But in an instant his father was gone. The current wrapped a strand of kelp around his ankle. He swiped at it and moved toward the rocks, scrabbling like a crab. Barnacles scored his skin and he pushed himself away. Embedded in the rock was his mother's face. *Come inside. It's getting late.* At the surface now, a van Gogh painting – a murky mélange of colors running together with the scythe-shaped moon. The ocean continued to talk to him. *This can be your world, your eternity. It's time you joined our universe! Swim beside loving creatures mammoth and small, inhabit the seven seas!* The current shoved him in another direction. The water was deeper, colder. His lungs raged. He drifted toward the black void. A balloon-shaped fish nosed up to him, its dime-sized eyes ogling. Matthew cupped its round head and the fish burbled. *Meet my family.* There were two smaller fish, smiling. He remembered a poem: *The ocean has its silent waves, deep, quiet, and alone; though there be fury on the waves, beneath them there is none.* Madeleine's face appeared. *Come home.* A fish jumped directly above, the plunk of its reentry disturbing the tableau that was his new sky. He screamed, letting go another cloud of bubbles. He must breathe now or sink. He remembered Cosimo: *You have things to do here.* It was now, or forever be one with the sea. He crouched to a squat and pushed off, arms flat to his sides like the fins of a rocket, shooting up to the van Gogh sky.

His head broke the surface and he filled his lungs with the sweet sea air, treading water, scanning the horizon. Cosimo was gone.

He paddled ashore. A slab of magenta ran along the top of the eastern range where the new day was beginning to show. He climbed from the water and sat on the beach looking out to the flat grey expanse, fingering his necklace. A breeze came up. The air was warming. He picked up his clothes from the sand and got dressed, tucking the necklace beneath his T-shirt. Near the trees beside the burned-out fire, the naked Cosimo was curled beneath the canvas lean-to. Matthew draped the flannel shirt he was carrying across the sleeping man's shoulders. In the sand beside him, he wrote with a stick:

THANK U

Chapter 20

As the days grew longer, Matthew continued his work around the grounds of *Las Palmas*. His father remained aloof, spending most of his waking hours in the basement painting or reading, and Matthew left him alone, constantly bracing for his sudden, unwelcome appearance. He was less certain than ever as to how to treat the man. Cosimo's entreaty that night on the beach, suggesting Matthew 'forgive the penitent', had stayed with him, although he had no clue which scriptures he was quoting, or if he actually believed it.

Among the disposable artifacts Matthew had amassed in the garage was a surfboard, a classic seven-footer his grandfather gave him for his sixteenth birthday. When he first came across it, he passed it off as something he'd grown out of. He couldn't remember the last time he caught a wave but could easily recall the joy he found in his trips to the beach as a teenager. Whenever he needed to separate himself from his warring parents, the Pacific ocean offered a welcome refuge that welcomed him unconditionally, no matter how big or small the waves were. It was the one place he found solace and peace and hope.

He pulled the board from the rubble and leaned it against the wall. It was in remarkably good shape. He found a can of wax and after an hour of polishing it looked like the last time he'd used it. He grew more excited as he planned his first trip to the coast. Tomorrow, he would stand it up in the back of the convertible and spend the day at the beach.

When he awoke at six o'clock, Matthew had second thoughts about jumping into the cold Pacific just to find out if he could still ride a wave. But he roused himself from bed, made a pot of coffee, and went into the garage where he loaded the surfboard vertically behind the front seat and went back inside to retrieve his wetsuit and other necessities.

It was a damp, cool morning and he had to pull on a jacket as he cruised down the Pacific Coast Highway. People eyed the convertible with its top down, a great white shark slicing through the traffic with the board jutting straight up like a dorsal fin. He'd hoped to beat the morning surfer rush, but by seven o'clock the beach was filling up. Carpenters, stockbrokers, mechanics, lawyers, all with a love of surfing had heard the report: four-to-seven-foot waves on the outgoing tide. Each enthusiast had come early to stake out an area and take on the challenging waves, and Matthew quickly realized this wasn't the best day to reintroduce surfing to his life. Only surfers deeply experienced and serious would be in the water today. It was better to find a quieter spot, and he remembered a place around the point.

The area indeed had fewer people, and he dipped his foot in the water. It was icy cold and he congratulated himself for bringing his wetsuit. There was a pod of about five surfers catching waves just down the way, where they were larger and more challenging. Matthew picked out one in particular, who was clearly the most skilled. Whichever wave he chose, the young man got the most out of it, riding it out for extended lengths until it completely dissipated. On the taller waves, he was able to turn back into it and flip the board upward into a 180, catching the wave on the way down, crouching effortlessly, keeping his balance from any angle. Each time the young man displayed his impressive talent, a piercing whistle came from the beach, and he followed the sound up to where a young woman in a yellow bikini sat on a towel. The skill of this surfer, thin, tanned, and probably in his early 20s, was intimidating, but at the same time inspired him to get on the water. He'd made it look so easy, as professionals tend to do. And the whistle, what a creative idea. It added an interesting dimension, as had the girl.

Paddling out on his stomach, the first wave came head-on over the board slapping him in the face, which served to fully awaken him. Thirty yards from shore, a perfect smaller wave rolled to him and he caught it easily, crouching into it as he gained speed, gliding across the surface in a smooth, graceful ride until suddenly the wave collapsed and he fell with it. He'd forgotten how quickly a simple wipeout could come but was encouraged that he had been able to get up in a move that was somewhat athletic. He soon realized it was beginner's luck, as the next four waves either tumbled him into the water straight away or slid ahead of him, out of reach. He was reminded of the ocean's command, its brusque absence of concern for any thrill-seeking humans audacious enough to expect a free ride.

After thirty minutes the waves began to change, growing taller, and he saw one rising well above the rest. It was easily the biggest yet today, and he assessed the risk as the sea began to swell beneath him. His board began to rise and he was sliding toward the beach now, feeling the tectonic energy of the water gather below him. He considered back-paddling but held his position. Quickly the board was teetering on the wave's crest and he instinctively jumped into his crouch. The board soared like a stone skipping across the water, with the force of the tide and currents that moved mountains, lifting him higher, swooshing him across the surface. He gained speed by the millisecond, the beach rushing at him now, and he caught brief glimpses of umbrellas in the sand, people pulling on wetsuits. The wave began to curl and he knew as long as he stayed upright and on the forward edge, his traversing momentum would thrust him onward, preventing him from catapulting into the boiling water. He rode the wave for what seemed forever but suddenly it folded on itself, jettisoning him headfirst to the ocean floor, and instantly the weight of the Pacific ocean was jamming him down and holding him under, his face skipping along the pebbly bottom. He scrabbled to gain purchase, and after summersaulting for what seemed like minutes he came to rest, prone on the beach and dead still. The sea drew back, and he remained stretched out like a six-foot flounder. Gulls overhead cried. He felt the water come back and touch his feet, then heard it pull back again. His mouth hurt. His nose was filled with sand, his eyes clouded with salt water. He could sense people standing over him.

"Dude – you alright?"

It was the surfer he'd been watching earlier, his silhouette casting a shadow over him. Beside him stood the young woman in the yellow bikini with the whistle around her neck.

Matthew coughed and spat out phlegm and seawater. He wiped his face and saw blood. His forehead and nose were bleeding, bright red rivulets of water dripping off his jaw. He was dazed, semi-conscious, and managed to sit up. He looked up and down the beach. He looked at the couple, squinting into the sun. He'd obviously twisted his neck; a cramp ran down through his spine. He was having trouble turning his head.

"I'm alright," he mumbled.

"Dude, that was *nasty*," the surfer said. "You should chill here for a while." And then, "Where do you usually surf? Are you even *from* here?"

Matthew considered the question.

"I'm from Connecticut," he said.

"See?" the man said, looking to his girlfriend. "I told you he wasn't from here."

He looked back down at Matthew.

"Try the inlet on the other side. It's more your speed."

The two turned and walked away hand in hand. Matthew wanted to tell them he surfed here all the time as a young boy and never had a problem, but it was too late.

✶ ✶ ✶

"Lawrence is asking after you."

Madeleine had caught him in the bathroom tending to his scraped-up face. He considered not taking her call but changed his mind. It had been a week since they last spoke. He'd purposely avoided her, taking some time to see how he felt about her after not talking for a while.

"Tell him to worry about something important," he said. He'd put her on speakerphone and was dabbing some ointment on his nose while looking into the mirror.

"He was hoping you'd be back last week. He's talking about taking you off the payroll."

There was a pause.

"I'm not coming back for a while," he said. "My father shows no sign of leaving. I've been advised by a lawyer to stay here."

"You're okay not getting paid?"

"I've got my mother's checking account."

"In that case, I have a favor to ask," Madeleine said.

"What?"

"I left my necklace on your bedside table. It's very special to me. I feel lost without it."

"I could ask Hughes to let you in."

"Do I know Hughes?"

Matthew explained.

"He also has Bella. Tell him I'm thinking about asking him to put her on a plane. I miss her like you miss your necklace."

He said he'd give her phone number to Hughes and suggested the two make their own arrangements. Of course, Hughes would be more than amused to meet the woman he'd seen through the curtains that night. To be given the chance to assist in the retrieval of her jewelry left by his bed would add more drama to the man's life than he'd seen since Camden.

"I miss you," Madeleine said.

Matthew didn't respond. He was stuck on the image of her hurrying up the stairs, shedding her clothes as she went, while he was already undressed and under the covers. He remembered she'd said something about her conscience as she took off her necklace.

"Matthew? Did you hear me?"

"Yes," he said, returning to the present. "You too."

The next morning, he came downstairs to find his father sitting at the kitchen table, the coffee maker gurgling beside the sink. He'd seen him only once in the past week when Albert left by way of the servants' entrance to walk to the store.

"What's going on with your lawyer?" Albert asked.

Matthew hesitated, not sure if he should say anything.

"He's submitted the will to the court," he said. "It's being reviewed. I see you've helped yourself." Matthew nodded toward the coffee.

Albert turned to him.

"It's time we stop this nonsense," Albert said.

"As soon as we get a ruling, it will all be very clear," Matthew said.

"You and I have a lot of work to do, son. I mean catching up. I don't want this to go on any longer."

"I don't know how you make up for fifteen years," Matthew said.

"We can try."

"Don't get your hopes up," Matthew said as he poured himself a cup.

"We can start by putting this inheritance business behind us. I've asked Stan to get involved."

"I told you – that's not necessary," Matthew said.

"He's representing me. You have no further say in the matter, son."

How dare he call him *son*? The man was nothing more than a poseur, an interloper, a parasite, a hanger-on. Forget that he was once his mother's husband or his genetic sponsor, or that he was now an eccentric bohemian artist who'd been traipsing through western Europe for the past fifteen years. He had no right calling him *son*.

"We'll see about that," Matthew said.

✶ ✶ ✶

"I bought Bella a one-way ticket, non-stop leaving next Friday," Matthew said to Hughes, who was at home, polishing silver after being stuck inside for forty-eight hours during a snowstorm. He immediately pushed back.

"Please Matthew, think twice about this," Hughes said. "Pets die in cargo holds all the time."

"I want my dog! I've already spoken with the airline. Aren't you tired of her by now, all that crap to clean up?"

"She's been a model guest," Hughes said. "We have our routine down with military precision. Maybe I should accompany her. I'd love to get out of this bloody weather."

"Just get her to the airport. The paid ticket will be waiting."

He went on to explain Madeleine's necklace and provided her details. Hughes pried for more information. Matthew cut him off, citing she was only a friend.

"She's the friend at work with benefits?" Hughes asked before Matthew hung up.

Chapter 21

Matthew was spending more time at the beach. He could sense his upper body bulking up from all the paddling, and his legs were stronger, better able to react quickly to the quixotic movement of the waves and the board beneath him. He'd made some new friends too, among them the young couple that came to him after the first day's wipeout. His name was Bo ("like Bo Diddley," he said) and she was April, a taciturn, lovely girl from a small town north of the Mexico border. As they surfed, she spent most of her time on the beach sunning in the smallest bikini ever made, and occasionally she sat up and watched. Matthew's skills had advanced to the point where he could keep up with him, but they spent a lot of time just sitting on their boards drifting offshore, talking, and waiting for the good waves, and then, when they were good, waiting to hear April blow her whistle. Matthew wished she would blow it for him, but that hadn't happened yet.

At home, ambitious projects were moving ahead. A roofing company was replacing tiles and several windows were getting reframed. The grounds were shaping up too after the Blevins' former landscaper stopped at the house when he spotted Matthew in the yard. He'd finished clearing and shaping the flower beds and replanted several exotic plants, including Birds of Paradise and flowering cacti. All the palm trees on the lot had been pruned, the yellow fronds cut away to reveal the green in perfect geometrical parasols, and the grass had regained its deep lush thickness after the gardener applied weed killer and fertilizer.

Despite all the work and obvious improvements, Albert continued with his lackadaisical attitude, never complimenting Matthew on what he was doing or even acknowledging how improved the old place was looking. The simple addition of Matthew's favorite companion, Bella, would transform this place into a home, and provide much needed moral support. But Hughes was still pleading with Matthew to not put her on a plane, even getting a vet's opinion, who agreed it was too risky considering her age. The flight Matthew had scheduled came and went, prompting him to scold Hughes for squelching on the deal, insisting he pay the non-refundable ticket.

"I never promised anything," Hughes told him. "I'm only hoping this will convince you to come home."

"Not likely, neighbor," Matthew said. "I'm trusting you to care for her until we work something out."

"By the way," Hughes interjected. "I wanted to comment on your friend Madeleine. Quite a striking lady. I let her in your house and she ran upstairs like she owned the place. Not the least bit shy, that one. Cool as a cucumber. When she came back down, she noticed the painting I'd given you on the mantel. We ended up having a lively discussion about art. It turns out she's quite educated. Apparently, she has some pieces that complement my collection, several Mondrian's. When I offered to help estimate their value for insurance she invited me over for coffee. I thought I'd ask you before accepting."

Matthew sat silently shaking his head, reminded of the last woman Hughes lured into his web with his art. He wondered if another secret alliance might be forming, and if he was once again just an unsuspecting bystander.

"Hughes, do me a favor. Nix the coffee with her." He hung up without further comment.

One evening after dinner Matthew was sitting on the oval, enjoying the peaceful nighttime air. He'd been in Pasadena exactly eight weeks. California was beginning to feel like home again, which came as something of a surprise. Was it the persistent, hopeful sun? The salty, primordial scent of the nearby Pacific? The relative warmth, felt even in February? Whatever, it was a welcome, regenerative feeling. When he thought back to Hartford, his mood sank. Sure, he missed the excitement Madeleine had brought to his life, first as Dr. Batiste, then as a brief but intoxicating lover. But oddly, the intensity of that spark was diminishing. He told himself that when he finally resolved the issues with his mother's will– which Mel Goldman insisted would happen, he'd be free to pursue his next chapter, live out his life, right here if he wished, and watch the sunset from this very spot, a glass of wine in hand. Whether it included Madeleine was uncertain, but in the larger picture not critical. His fear of living a life Thoreau warned of, one in quiet desperation, seemed to have been replaced with a whole new *joie de vivre*.

The next day, as he scraped peeling paint from window frame in the late afternoon, his phone buzzed in his pocket.

"I have some important news."

Matthew looked at his watch. It was 8:00 pm in the east. The last time Madeleine called and skipped the greeting it didn't go too well. He descended two rungs from the ladder and stood near its base, waiting for her to continue.

"This is going to be very hard for you to hear," she said. Her voice was tense, clipped. "Are you sitting down?"

"What is it?" Matthew said. He was watching his neighbor across the street throwing a ball for his dog.

"I just left the doctor's office. I'm pregnant."

Matthew froze and continued staring across the street without blinking.

"I don't think I heard you," he said.

"You heard me."

His gaze shifted to the ground, two feet beneath him. He had his free hand resting on the back of his head like a yarmulke.

"After one night?"

"It's been known to happen."

Teetering on the rung, he grabbed at the ladder to keep from falling.

"Has this ever happened before?" Matthew said. "You're sure it's me?"

"Don't insult me. I'm not a slut."

Slut? Was this street language supposed to make her sound tough? A pair of jackdaws in a eucalyptus tree above him were trading insults. He looked to the horizon. The sun was ablaze in the orange LA haze just above the basin. He said the first thing that came to mind.

"I assume you're planning to have this taken care of?"

Another long pause.

"It's not that simple, Matthew," she said. "Abortion is a primary sin. I spent eight years in a convent, you may recall."

He'd stepped to the ground and was walking in a circle, phone jammed to his ear.

"Matthew?"

After balancing the phone on a rung, he walked inside, pulled a bottle of bourbon from the cupboard, poured a glass, and drank it down. A few seconds later he poured another, emptied it, and went back outside, hoping she and this nightmare were gone. He could hear her squawking, her voice sounding like it was coming from a cheap transistor radio. The phone vibrated off the ladder and fell into the grass. He looked around the yard and smelled the jasmine. The temperature was cooling. Birds of many species were noisily feeding in the twilight. A lone bat swooped above his head. He stared upwards and spotted the first star, the North Star. He remembered the axis of the earth pointed at it precisely, and for this, it was called the *Polestar*, Ursa Minor, the brightest star in the constellation. If Madeleine were looking up at the sky right now, she'd find it in the same place, providing the same coordinates, the same point of reference for the entire hemisphere. His thoughts shifted to his mother as a teenager. How did she tell her boyfriend, Albert Banks, she was pregnant? Over the phone? In a letter? It was the early 1970's and she was only nineteen. Abortion was illegal. Did Albert tell her to get rid of it? – *of him!* It was so risky then, with unlicensed gynecologists performing D-and-C's in back-alley walk-ups. Thank God, he thought, it was so much easier now. Unless you were raised in a convent.

Chapter 22

Mel Goldman called the next morning.

"I've got some dirt on the old man. It should be enough to make him go away."

He was calling from his convertible. The top was down and it sounded like he was on the tarmac beside a jet plane. Matthew, his stomach still knotted from Madeleine's news, asked him to speak up.

"When he went to France he tapped into the retirement fund from his law firm. He lived off that the whole time. Never paid a dime in US or state tax. He owes thousands. That's a felony."

"How do I tell him?"

"Don't. Let the court do the talking."

Matthew said he would need time to think about it.

"What is there to think about?" Goldman said.

He spent the night awake in bed, staring into the blackness, his thoughts ricocheting inside his skull like a ping pong ball. To say Madeleine's pregnancy made things more complicated was a bit of an understatement. Jesus, it would change everything: who he was, the course of his life, for now, and all time. And if she was so committed to having the baby, would she make him marry her? She couldn't do that.

190

But, and this was a big *but*, was he ready to be a father? He hadn't even sorted out how to be a son! She had every right to refuse an abortion, no matter how fiercely he protested. It was her body. He rose from bed and went into the bathroom and threw up.

As the first sign of dawn appeared beneath his window shade, he surrendered. He went down to the kitchen and made coffee and and gathered his wetsuit and surfboard and loaded them into the back of the big white Cadillac. The surf report was calling for a four-to-five-foot swell, and he'd need to get there early if he wanted his usual spot.

When he arrived at the parking lot, the sun was breaking through the marine layer and the air was balmy. He saw Bo and April climbing out of the old, faded Land Cruiser. She had a cooler and towels. Bo was pulling the boards off the roof. She came over and said good morning.

"Connecticut guy!" she said in her coquettish way. "I've been meaning to ask you. Where's the girlfriend?"

He looked at her, mildly annoyed.

"There is no girlfriend."

"That's a bummer," she said. "A stud like you? I can introduce you around if you want." She walked by with her arms loaded with the day's supplies.

He shrugged and watched her find a spot and lay down the towels. She was young and nubile, and he realized part of her sexiness came from her innocence, the opposite of Madeleine. He could teach her some things, given the chance, he thought as he sat on the bumper of his car. He finished putting on his wetsuit, snugger now with his added bulk, and he briefly wondered if this had prompted her compliment. Bo was thin as a wire, tall and bony, not much to look at with that big nose. Other than his permanent tan, streaked hair and surfing prowess, he was not much of a catch. Despite all the heavy news from Hartford, he managed a grin as he walked to the water's edge with the board under his arm, looking out at the coming waves. The wind was picking up, and soon they would double in size. It would be a perfect set of conditions. But he'd grown to expect this now, just another southern California morning at the beach. As he paddled out to meet them head on, he remembered April's comment: Why *was* he alone?

The surfing that morning was average, as it turned out, with waves closely spaced and capping with a minimal break. But for the time, it took his mind off Madeleine. He stayed in the water for almost two hours, spending much of it straddling his board just beyond the swell, talking to April and Bo and several others who had gathered in anticipation of better waves. Each set of gentle swells presented a different opportunity – or in this case, disappointment– but it was the anticipation of what might yet come that held their excitement. These idle moments of board-sitting had a certain Zen-like effect. With only the sound of the sea and wheeling birds crying overhead, the rhythm of the ocean beneath him as the tide gently tugged the board toward shore, he had time to absorb the astonishing news from Madeleine.

As the sun climbed into the sky, Matthew rode one last wave and came onto the beach where he stripped off his wetsuit and sat on the sand, facing the water, allowing the sun and the light breeze to dry him. He thought about the day ahead: he would call Goldman and tell him to move forward with whatever he had to do to make Albert leave. It was extortion, essentially, which on the face of it seemed harsh, and possibly illegal. But it would move that problem off the table. Now, a far more chilling fear had taken hold of him. With every passing hour, he felt the urgent need to call her, maybe find another way to talk her into terminating the pregnancy, free him of this unthinkable curse.

★★★

"I'm using your address at Santa Teresa," Goldman said when Matthew spoke with him the next day. "There will be a summons for him to appear in court at a specified date. My neighbor is a judge at the District Court. I'll know the day it's being served. Believe me, he's going to get the message."

Matthew was sitting on his bed, staring out the window after hanging up with Goldman. He reminded himself what exactly that message was: Albert must leave the house immediately, and not contest the will. Mel had identified some vague language that Albert and his lawyer Stan might try to leverage. But there would be no funds to pay for a defense unless Stan were to front it, and Goldman was guessing the case wasn't strong enough for him to take that risk. Either way, this was a line of demarcation and the message would be clear. Albert had been hiding in the basement apartment for several days straight with no communication. Matthew had an alarming thought that he might harm himself. Cosimo's voice whispered to him: *He is your father. Read the scriptures.*

Chapter 23

Madeleine got the call late one afternoon in her office.

"Adam will be in rehab for at least six weeks," Dooley was saying. "Let's just hope they can hold him."

Madeleine shuddered.

"Did you see him?" she asked.

"You wouldn't recognize my brother," Dooley said.

She shuddered at the thought of a man once so gifted, so vital, now homeless and craving a fix.

"You might consider visiting him," Dooley said. He gave her the name of the treatment facility. Madeleine thought about it for a few moments.

"That could backfire. It might make him more anxious," she said. "Or desperate."

"Maddie, we've got nothing to lose," Dooley said before hanging up. "The man is a walking corpse."

She rose to close her door and sat back down behind the desk, put her head down and began quietly weeping. Her surging hormones had put her on an emotional roller coaster, but even on a good day this was more than she could bear. The news about Adam came from nowhere, just like the pregnancy. She figured Adam Rich, if he got clean, would likely want to reestablish a relationship with Bradley, as thorny as that could be. Since they weren't yet legally divorced, her status with him was vague. If that weren't enough, she had not heard a thing from Matthew. He hadn't returned her calls since their last argument, a long shouting match in which she refused to back down. It was looking highly likely she would face this predicament alone, and deep inside her body was a fleeting yet palpable feeling of a complicated pregnancy. Her training, combined with acute maternal instinct, was telling her something wasn't right. The doctor had called her back for more tests; there was an anomaly in the ultrasound. And things at home weren't going well. Bradley had gotten into a fight at school and was generally misbehaving, which she attributed to her recent distractions and the lack of attention she'd given him. But she did not see that changing anytime soon.

She picked her head up off the desk and tried calling Matthew again. She was shocked when he answered.

"Accept your responsibility," she said. "Engage in adult dialogue with me," she said, spitting out her words. She could hear him breathing into the phone and waited for his response.

"I'm having trouble just talking to you," he finally said. "For all I know, you aren't even pregnant." He knew it was a ludicrous comment but said it anyway.

She gasped.

"*Why* would I make this up?" She was shouting again. "I can send you the test results! Better yet, I'll send you a urine sample and you can do the test yourself!"

"What a quaint idea."

"When are you coming back?" She said, "When are you going to grow up?"

She was so worked up he half hoped this might put her into labor and end the whole thing.

195

"I have no plans," he said.

He could hear her breathing, slower now as she tried to calm herself.

"You're off the payroll the first of the month," she said. "Lawrence told me today."

"I'm surprised he kept me on this long."

"You can thank me for that." And then, having regained her composure, "Matthew, I'd like you to come meet with my doctor. He's recommended some genetic counseling. There are some things we need to discuss."

Matthew was ready to hang up. Now she had his ear.

"What kinds of things?"

"Your family history. There's an anomaly in the ultrasound, something with my uterus too complicated to explain."

"Aren't we getting ahead of ourselves? And has it occurred to you that I am not interested in being a father? My idea of fathers right now is pretty messed up."

"Matthew! I'm twelve weeks pregnant. It's almost May. I *absolutely* will not have an abortion and I'm not having this baby alone!"

The hiss of the distance between them filled the silence.

"God help me," Matthew whispered.

"No! Matthew, God only helps those who help themselves. Act like a man!"

Madeleine ended the call by saying she had another doctor's appointment in two days and would have more information. She was no longer sad or weepy.

Of course, she was angry with Matthew, but more so with herself. For a graduate of the convent, a woman of divine faith, schooled by sacred, revered institutions, devoted to her dual practice in therapy and administration, she accused herself of nothing short of blatant blasphemy. She stared out her window that overlooked the woods behind the building, working her fingers over the gold cross she'd retrieved. Then she gathered her things and left for the day.

She took him to his favorite burger place and sat him in a back booth. He ordered the signature triple cheeseburger with onions and a strawberry milkshake. Madeleine settled for a glass of water.

"Honey, there's something I want to explain," she said as the waiter walked away. "It's about your father."

The milkshake arrived and Bradley immediately began the intense sucking required to pull the ice cream through a straw. Without looking up he said, "I thought he was dead."

"No, honey, he's alive, living not too far away. Your uncle Dooley found him."

Bradley lifted his head from the straw and looked across the Formica table at his mother.

"Can I meet him?"

Madeleine reached across the table and took his hand.

"He's in a special place that helps people get better."

"A hospital?

"Like a hospital."

She talked about his illness, that it started after they were married, and was at first due to injuries he'd suffered when he was a star quarterback in college. Bradley wanted to know all about his sports achievements, as this was something new, and seemed excited to finally meet his father until he asked the toughest question of all.

"Why did he leave?" he said.

Madeleine paused and looked tenderly at her son.

"If I understood why, darling, I would tell you. He loved you. I thought he loved me. But his sickness made him forget about what is important, his family, and it took over his life. It's a miracle he didn't die." Then she told him she would visit him soon and would have more information.

Bradley quickly changed the subject and asked for a sundae. The two sat a while longer as he emptied the goblet. On the way to the car, Bradley, holding his mother's hand, brought up his father again.

"Can I go with you?"

She told him no children were allowed, but hopefully in a month or so he'd be out, and then they could all spend some time together.

"Maybe he can teach me to throw a football," he said. "That would be really cool."

✶ ✶ ✶

Matthew returned home to find Albert sitting at the kitchen table, unshaven and pale, his bare legs sticking out of his bathrobe like an ostrich.

Matthew asked what he was doing.

"I'd like to move my studio upstairs," he said sheepishly. "The light down there is horrible. I was thinking you could set up a wheel and find a used kiln. We could create some art together, like we used to. It might be just what we need, what the doctor ordered."

"Ha! What doctor is that?" he said, scrambling for words. He stared at the man in disbelief. What he had just proposed was so far from the reality of the current situation as to be comical.

Albert stood from the table as if to address a jury.

"I'd like to stay here with you. I can't fight this thing with the will. Stan said it will be a drawn-out legal battle that will cost too much money, money I obviously don't have. I'm willing to let you have the house if you let me live here."

Matthew tried to absorb the preposterous request.

"For how long?"

Albert's eyes shifted up to the ceiling, as if seeking divine guidance.

"As long as I want?"

As soon as the words left his mouth he doubled over and cried out.

"What's wrong? Are you alright?" Matthew said.

He shook his head no, remaining doubled over.

"My stomach does this every so often." He straightened up and took a seat, breathing deeply.

Matthew said nothing. The man's wishes were complicated, especially the part about making art together. Matthew would never share with him how desperately he missed his pottery and sculpting, an impassioned love of art they obviously shared. His cold, dimly lit studio in Hartford was about the only thing pulling him back in that direction. He'd tentatively selected a spot for his new studio in *Las Palmas*, in the corner of the back solarium, where the south-facing windows rose from the floor to ceiling and filled the room with natural light for much of the day. There was little doubt his father had espied the same space, and to set up, side by side, as they worked all those years ago, was simply a surreal notion. He wondered if this stomach issue was merely an act.

"Whatever it is, with your stomach, you should get it checked," Matthew said.

"It's a bug I picked up in Marseilles," Albert said. "It'll pass. And I have no insurance."

With his father slumped over in his chair, gaunt and dejected, Matthew for the first time felt something akin to pity for the man. He thought about the court order, which Goldman had promised was imminent. He'd ask him to postpone it for a while.

"You might try eating something," Matthew said.

✶ ✶ ✶

"I'm bringing her to you, special delivery," Hughes said. He was calling a week later to tell Matthew about his latest plan. He and Peter would set out sometime in the coming weeks, with Bella, to drive across the continent. They would not be taking the African Queen, but rather Peter's larger and sturdier Land Rover.

"Isn't that a capital idea?" Hughes said.

"You have no idea how big this country is," Matthew said. He was thinking back to when he towed a U-Haul trailer from Hanover, New Hampshire to Pasadena after college, a trip he thought would never end.

"Peter hasn't been west of Indianapolis," Hughes said. "It will be a good test of our compatibility."

"If you have any hope for preserving your relationship, I would, by all means, kill this idea," Matthew said. But then he realized it may be the most expedient way to get Bella out west.

"But if you insist, pick up some Dramamine. She gets car sick."

Hughes began thanking him for seeing the light and promised all necessary precautions would be taken with the dog. Matthew asked for an arrival date. Hughes said it would likely be June.

"The weather will be warmer," Matthew said. "And Albert should be gone. There's plenty of room at *Las Palmas*."

They ended the call and Matthew looked out his bedroom window, down to the Oval where today his father was sunning himself in his boxer shorts. His color was better, and he seemingly had bounced back from whatever stomach issue he picked up in Marseilles. But still, the man appeared unwell. Maybe it was because he had given up on his plan to gain ownership, or more devastating, occupancy. Or he could merely be depressed, a condition for which Matthew refused to claim responsibility.

Mel Goldman had been badgering Matthew to move ahead with the summons, threatening to drop the matter altogether if he didn't act soon. Matthew had unconsciously put it from his thoughts, not wanting to deal with something that could wait longer. Matthew asked him to sit tight. Whatever the case, it was looking more like he'd be in Pasadena for a while. Word that his dog – his truest, most loyal companion, would soon be at his side, was the best news he could imagine.

Matthew's diligent efforts around *Las Palmas* were really beginning to show. The tile roof had been scrubbed clean and now glistened brick red in the sun; the adobe walls were white again and the dark wooden beams beneath the windows were sanded and refinished. The grounds had grown back greener and with more vibrant color, as the expansive flower beds were all in bloom, and the towering palm trees were all manicured and majestic, standing high and nobly marking the ample lot. Neighbors were stopping in their cars to congratulate Matthew and he was beginning to feel like the rightful heir to this memory-filled edifice. Even Paulina, Dorothy's friend who had helped in her final days, stopped by. She asked how he'd get along in a place so large.

In fact, as big as it was, it no longer felt lonely or austere. And the validation he was now receiving from his efforts, sparse as it was, had lifted Matthew's sense of himself and restored a degree of pride in his heritage that had been sorely missing. Madeleine might well continue with her harsh demands to have the baby and for him to return, but day by day his attachment to *Las Palmas*, and the beach, was deepening.

Springtime brought consistently higher temperatures and longer days, and now Matthew spent nearly every morning by the shoreline at his favorite surf spot. He'd been accepted among a small legion of seasoned locals, convincing them, with the help of Bo Diddley and April, that he was a legitimate Californian. They still teased him as the guy from the east coast, clinging to the sarcastic nickname "Connecticut guy", but he'd accepted it as part of his initiation dues.

One morning, he arrived early and came upon April, alone, dressed in sweatpants and a thick poncho. There was an early morning chill, with heavy overcast skies.

"Hey, Connecticut guy!"

Matthew approached and saw she'd brought two coffees and some doughnuts.

"I got you some breakfast," she said. "Figured you'd be here."

"Where's Bo?" Matthew said.

"Having one of his fits. He needs to chill. He weirds out sometimes."

She explained he was probably bipolar and his moods were unpredictable. He refused to take any medication.

"The drugs make him impotent, which means he can't be the world's greatest stud."

"So you two are an item? Matthew said.

"He'd like to think so. I can't live with him. We hang out, but that's it."

The sun began to break through the dense fog, brightening the beach and putting a sparkle on the water. She squinted up at Matthew with her cute smile.

"So, like, tell me, Connecticut guy – are you gay?"

Matthew sat down beside her, holding his wetsuit. He'd never before had the chance to speak with her one-on-one.

"I was married," he said.

"Oh, you're part of the sixty percent of marriages that die."

Matthew shook his head no.

He explained as simply as he could. April edged her way next to him and handed him a doughnut. He took it and stared out at the waves. An onshore breeze was gathering. They would soon be worth riding.

"I'm sorry," she said with a frown. And then, after a long pause, "So, should I call you Matt or Matthew?"

"Call me whatever you want," he said.

April stood up and peeled off her outer layer. She was wearing a new bikini, so revealing it was no more than an afterthought, and he was having trouble taking his eyes off her. Her skin was a darker now, maybe more of a cappuccino, and her shoulders looked stronger from all her recent surfing sessions. She bent over to pick up her board and the top of her suit fell away and he made no effort to look away.

"Last one to catch a wave is a wimp!" She said, sprinting toward the water, board under her arm. Matthew ditched his wet suit and in a flash caught up with her and leapt onto his flattened board, skimming headfirst into the oncoming waves and gliding twenty yards past her. He looked over his shoulder to see her struggling to stand.

"Okay, you win!" She yelled. "Wait – I stepped on something!"

Matthew went to her. She was standing on one leg with her other foot across her knee. Blood was dripping into the water. Matthew shoved both of their boards up onto the sand.

"It's a piece of glass," she said, picking at her heel. She held out her foot for him to examine and he immediately saw a gash in her arch the size of a lemon wedge. The blood began coming more heavily.

"Can you walk?" He said.

She looked at him with a fearful grimace and he lifted her arm around his shoulder and carried her onto the beach where they had left their things. He had a bag with a bandana inside and tied it tightly around her foot to staunch the flow.

"I'm taking you to the ER. This needs stitches."

He scooped her up and scurried across the broad beach, gathering her sweatshirt and leaving their boards and bags behind. By the time they got to the big white Cadillac the blood from her foot had saturated the bandana. He pulled a plastic bag from the glove compartment and slid it over her foot, and as they drove to the entrance of the parking lot they spotted Bo Diddley's Land Cruiser turning in. He recognized them immediately and swerved in front of Matthew's car to block his exit.

"What the fuck?" Bo said, climbing out, agitated.

She explained the situation.

Bo looked at Matthew, his face reddening, a vein bulging down the middle of his forehead.

"Bullshit. I'll take you. Get in the jeep, April."

Matthew assessed Bo's attitude but was in no mood to argue. He slowly edged the big white Cadillac closer and tried to reason with him.

"Dude – chill," Matthew said. "I've got this."

Bo began walking toward the car and Matthew punched the gas and swerved around the Land Cruiser, barely fitting between it and the guard rail, his tires spinning on the sandy asphalt and forcing Bo to jump aside.

"I'll be back!" April yelled, smiling innocently as they passed him by. In the mirror, Matthew could see Bo violently pumping his fist and yelling something vulgar.

Chapter 24

Brother's Keeper, a full-service, medium-security rehabilitation center, was located on the Connecticut River fifty miles southeast of Hartford. It could treat a maximum number of seventy-five patients, most of whom were there for alcoholism or opioid addiction. They were typically paired in double rooms according to age and the substance they abused. The staff included three full-time GP's, six licensed Psychologists, and a dozen trained nurses. It had the reputation of being a "country club" rehab center, partly because it was housed in a converted Victorian mansion up on a hill. It also happened to be by far the most expensive facility in the state. Adam's former partners had leaned on their connections and status as the state's foremost orthopedic surgeons to get him in and had all assumed financial responsibility. The facility was always full, with a waiting list, but they had talked the chief administrator into allowing their former partner to be their seventy-sixth patient. The day Madeleine drove down to visit, he'd been there exactly three weeks, half of his prescribed stay.

It was a sunny spring-like day filled with promise, the elm and oak trees along Route 9 in bud, about to unfurl to create a dense green corridor leading south. Random daffodils in vivid yellow were scattered along the side of the road in clumps or singles as if they'd fallen off a truck, a lovely contrast to the grey landscape this time of year. In the hush of her luxury sedan, Madeleine's thoughts shifted from her own condition as a middle-aged pregnant woman entering her second trimester to that of her imperiled husband, confined against his will and battling a deadly addiction. Did he really want to live? How much permanent damage had been done to this once nearly perfect human specimen? Would there be anything left of the man she married? Worrying he'd detect her pregnancy, she covered herself with a loose-fitting cardigan. How would he react to her showing up? Adam's counselor, who had first insisted she wait until the end of his program, gave in and allowed her to come after she had used her own psychiatric *bona fides* to convince him it was the right thing.

A few miles north of the facility she realized the most vexing question now concerned her objective: what did she hope to accomplish today? She told herself it was solely for the benefit of Bradley; if Adam and his estranged son could find a way to salvage something like a loving relationship, Bradley would be on far firmer ground as he entered the tricky years of puberty. And, if she were truthful, all anger and bitterness aside, she still cared for Adam Rich, and fervently wished he would get clean and healthy and resume his brilliant career. Her son needed a father, and the world needed his extraordinary talent.

As she drove up the long entrance to the converted mansion sitting atop twenty acres of manicured grounds, she petitioned her higher power: *God grant me the serenity to accept the things I cannot change; the courage to change the things I can; and the wisdom to know the difference.*

"You will have twenty minutes of supervised time, Dr. Batiste."

The admitting nurse was a stern elderly woman who, after checking Madeleine's credentials, asked her to sign a waiver guaranteeing she was bringing no drugs, firearms, or communication devices into the building.

"You'll need to walk through the metal detector," she added. "On your way out, stop back here." And then, "How should we identify you?"

"Please just tell him a family member is here."

Madeleine was greeted by her escort, a handsome middle-aged man with intensely blue eyes. His badge read "Paul" and he asked her to follow him to the back of the building where the visitation lounge was situated. They walked down a linoleum-tiled hallway, their shoes squeaking on the polished surface, and Paul said nothing until they approached the room.

"They're bringing him up now," he said.

As they entered the room she saw several groups positioned in clusters, each huddled in their private *tête-à-tête*. The room was furnished in period antiques with heavy, flowered drapes and upholstery and fine Oriental rugs covering the polished oak floor. The area was silent except for low whispers, the tenor of the room sullen and without a single break of laughter. Madeleine now felt the full weight of her decision. Paul seated her in a far corner with two facing wing-back chairs, a small settee placed in between. He asked if she would like a cup of coffee and she declined. She looked up and saw a man – who she took to be another staff member– approaching. He had a short beard and wore a crew neck sweater, khakis, and a pair of greasy running shoes. It was only when he came within five feet that she recognized his deep-set, piercing eyes. She looked twice to make sure it was him. Adam stopped several paces from where she stood. They stared at one another, each aghast in their own kind of shock, and neither spoke.

Paul finally stepped in.

"Maybe you'd like to sit," he said.

They each took a chair and continued staring with disbelieving eyes. Madeleine could see what Dooley meant. She would not know this man on the street. He was gaunt; his eyes were still blue but otherwise dim and lifeless. His skin had a tallow tinge, not quite yellow. On his forehead, an angry purple scar arched above his left eye, mimicking the brow.

"Why are you here," Adam finally said, his voice a hoarse whisper.

She could see he was missing a tooth. His once slender hands were scabbed over and bony. His left thumbnail was missing. She looked down to the small table between them where Paul had placed two glasses of water without being asked. She took a sip and thought carefully about her response.

"Dooley said he'd found you. This was his idea, that I come. At first I said no. But Adam I don't have the right to keep you and Bradley apart, and I figured this was at least a start."

Adam absorbed her words and searched her eyes.

"How old is Bradley now?" he said, openly anguished by not knowing. His clenched hands, resting in his lap, trembled slightly.

Madeleine's face softened.

"He's eight. Precocious, sweet... looks like you. I've never told him that." She immediately regretted saying this.

Adam's face went slack, and then the start of a smile, as if imagining his son.

"Do you have a picture?" he whispered.

Madeleine rifled through her purse and pulled out Bradley's Little League photo.

"He's an amazing pitcher," she said, handing it to him. Her voice was shaking now. "No surprise."

Again, she regretted giving information that would only make him feel worse.

Adam took the photo in his unsteady hands and stared for what seemed a long time until his eyes began to fill with tears. Paul leaned forward and took Adam's arm.

"Adam, let's give the picture back."

Now Adam's entire upper body was convulsing as he pulled the photo closer to his chest and he leaned forward, stomping the floor in a tantrum. His eyes closed tightly and tears ran down his face. Paul reached over and gently pulled the photo from Adam's hands and gave it back to Madeleine.

"That's going to be all for today, Mrs. Batiste," he said.

"But –" Madeleine began and stopped.

She remained in her seat, studying the father of her child: diminished, skeletal, his wrists and ankles like sticks that could snap. She thought back to their honeymoon, of him diving in the Aegean for sponges that he collected and gave to a local shop in trade for fresh fish. He had been perfectly muscled, like a Greek statue, blessed with a physique matched only by his razor-sharp intellect. Now she couldn't decide which was more upsetting– his shattered emotional state, so ashamed he couldn't look at her, or his ravaged body.

She rose from her chair.

"Goodbye, Adam," she said in a whisper, leaning down to him as he sat weeping. "Have faith."

Chapter 25

In the weeks that followed, Matthew was beginning to crack under the weight of reality, of what appeared to be his inevitable fatherhood, trying but failing to accept the hard facts. As he went through his days, whether working around *Las Palmas* or gliding over the tops of waves, he thought of nothing else. The chances of Madeleine terminating the pregnancy were nil; his only possible way out would be some kind of life-threatening prenatal condition. They had spoken just once in the past two weeks, when she called to tell him she resigned from *Connecticut Life*. She had reached him that day as he sat in the beach parking lot, waiting for the morning tide to turn and the waves to come up. He immediately noticed her all-business demeanor.

"You could call me once in a while, you know," she said.

"I needed time to think. What's going on?" he said.

"I had to quit," she said. "*Connecticut Life* has now lost *two* valuable employees."

"Couldn't happen to a nicer bunch of crooks," he said. He peered over the hood of the big white Cadillac, feeling slightly better since their discussions were more controlled now, their emotions tempered. But nothing else had changed.

"You act like this is all my fault," he said. "If I remember right, you couldn't get into my bed fast enough that night."

"Are you going to go there *again?* That's beside the point," Madeleine said.

"What *is* the point?"

"If you don't know by now, your cognitive assessment tests must have been taken by someone else."

"You pulled my files?"

She didn't reply.

"And you still agreed to work with me?" he said with a short laugh.

"We're getting off-topic," she said. "When are you coming back? You've left Bella with Hughes for so long. I thought you said you missed her."

"I haven't told you. He's bringing her out by car. He won't let me put her on a plane."

There was a pause.

"Speaking of planes, I'm grounded," she finally said. "Doctor's orders. Otherwise, I'd bring her myself."

Her pleasant attitude was making Matthew nervous, so he took the opportunity to remind her of his position.

"Madeleine, I'm not coming back anytime soon. You need to accept that."

Another pause, longer.

"Why are you so against me having this baby? What are you afraid of? We don't have to get married. If you come back to Hartford, we can raise her together. She'll add so much to your life. You know better than most the importance of a father's presence, and the damage that can be done by one who refuses to engage."

"Did you say *her?*"

There was a pause. She wasn't planning to share this.

"The last ultrasound showed the missing penis."

The missing penis? He tried to downplay any possible Freudian overtones. But the full weight of this new detail was like an anvil on his chest. And then, why did this make things more complicated, knowing he would have a daughter?

"Why are you grounded?" he said. "Are you sick?"

She cleared her throat. "My blood pressure gets dangerously high. It's called preeclampsia."

"I must have the same thing," Matthew said. "I'm constantly dizzy."

"Matthew get serious!"

They ended the call no closer to an agreement. When he hung up his first thought: *Thank God she can't fly.*

Albert was spending more time upstairs now, and the two were even sharing the odd meal together. There was no more talk about kicking him out. After repeated soul searching, Matthew sometimes felt like a disrespectful scumbag. Mel Goldman, who had quickly turned into a pain in the ass, had chastised him for not moving forward with the summons, telling him he knew Matthew didn't have the *cojones.* Matthew responded forcefully, insisting he'd make his own choices, thank you very much, especially those concerning immediate family. He made a mental note to refuse the Hollywood lawyer's calls going forward. He'd come to realize this case with his father was far more complicated than a fancy lawyer or any third party could resolve, and he could no longer avoid holding himself accountable. He'd be better off without Goldman, and his extravagant fees, although, oddly, he had yet to see a bill for his services.

Nor could Matthew ignore his growing resentment. Since when was it up to him to support his father? He knew some cultures honor older generations, recognizing the value of their wisdom and sage advice. But the irony of Matthew stepping into a parental role, emerging from the ashes of a family riddled with dysfunction, was not lost on him. He kept reflecting on the night with Cosimo, whose assessment had placed Matthew at a lofty, beneficent station. He had suggested to Matthew that his position was actually enviable, that he was special, and had important things to do, making it all sound so providential. *And there was a woman,* he had mysteriously said, who would be of help to him. This idea of a higher calling should surely be a sign of hope, something he could hold onto, a welcome change from his persistent self-excoriation. Madeleine often gave him similar optimistic possibilities, a "sky's the limit" kind of encouragement, if he would only let his father atone for his mistakes. He agreed to a point; if the two could at least reach *detente,* he might have more energy to tend to the other various catastrophes in his life.

Matthew's occasional rendezvous with the lovely young April soon became the highlight of his week. Bo Diddley had faded away and was rarely seen. Whenever the skinny surfer did show up at the beach, Matthew and April acted like they barely knew one another. But the day they raced to the emergency room proved to be just the start of regular hook-ups.

They'd left the Urgent Care Center after she had been stitched up that day and went back to pick up their boards. Unable to drive, April had Matthew drop her at the bungalow on the beach a few miles south. She asked him in and they sat and talked for two hours and then she cooked him dinner, fresh pan-fried snapper, and plantains. Although the girl was short on intellectual curiosity, she had a breezy, come what may approach he found refreshing. He drank her rum until it got late, and without too much convincing she coaxed him into bed. Now, it was a given he'd spend Tuesday evenings at her bungalow (she had the Wednesdays off) and Matthew considered the ongoing tryst with obvious casualness, careful not to make any formal commitment and asking none from her. Above all, he would pay strict attention to making damn sure she didn't get pregnant.

Darkening all this sexual frivolousness was a nagging question: was he cheating on Madeleine? He'd never been in a position where he had to ask himself this question. His acquaintance with her was tied to their professional connection; the personal bit had been a flash in the pan (albeit wildly exciting.) Now, the inconvenient new twist was that she was carrying his child. He would continue to wrestle with this murky question of morality, whether there were relationship type strings attached to a freak pregnancy, a conception some might call miraculous.

* * *

One morning Albert asked to borrow the Cadillac. He needed some supplies, and to drop some letters at the post office. Matthew thought it over for a moment and handed him the keys, realizing it would be nice to get him out of the house, even for a little while. Plus, he'd been looking for an opportunity to go downstairs to see what he was up to, check out his work. Albert had been diligently working away these past weeks and had been quiet about it. How had his father's style evolved over the years, if at all? More modern, or in the other direction?

As soon as the car disappeared down the street, Matthew was in the basement looking at three paintings of different sizes and styles, each in various stages of completion. One was sitting on an easel, the others lined up against the wall. On the easel sat a garish three-by-four-foot canvas of *Las Palmas*, which he had seen in its very early development. His father had employed bright, brash colors with wild strokes reminiscent of a contemporary sports painter, and it was contrary to any Spanish style he'd ever seen. Leaning against the wall was a horizontal format of a landscape which he assumed to be southwest France. A field of wildflowers, geraniums and honeysuckle, stretched before a backdrop of jagged, snowcapped mountains. It showed bright but natural colors of summer and was a more traditional composition, with a deep, authentic perspective. The third painting was simpler. It was of Matthew, standing on the beach with his surfboard stuck in the sand, a rich blue ocean behind, dappled with white caps and blurred images of surfers and swimmers. He was deeply tan, his hair sun-streaked and whipped by the wind. His father had managed to make him look carefree, without a worry in the world. To anyone who knew Matthew Banks, it would be a flattering depiction. He had to admit the paintings were the work of an accomplished artist; his father's talent had deepened through the years. His eye, as expressed through his brush, seemed more confident and encompassing. An odd sensation gripped him, a tug on his conscience, a whisper for him to go a little easier on the old man. The unnerving fact was, Albert had made something of his time on his own, even if it was at his family's expense. If Matthew could separate himself from all the noise and hostility, perhaps there was a path to some kind of peace. If not, well, that would only be what he expected in the first place.

Matthew returned upstairs and walked into the solarium. So much brighter and alive than the basement, the light here was dense and even through the whole of the day, an artist's dream. He began envisioning where his pottery equipment would fit. But he feared once he started constructing the studio his father would insert himself and try to join in. It would be another confrontation, calling for another frank assessment of just what his father meant to him now, and then, asking: What is the trajectory of their relationship going forward?

He took a seat in a corner chair and thought back to their early years together in the first basement studio in the old house. What impressed him then was how prolific his father was. He'd produced hundreds – maybe thousands, of paintings. Where were they? There were a few here in *Las Palmas*, in fact one was hanging on the far wall of the solarium, a small watercolor that had been there for as long as he could remember. It was one of his grandfather's favorites, a simple composition of two mules standing side by side in a corral, heads drooping over a split rail fence, their big brown eyes empty and forlorn.

Chapter 26

The second dreaded call from Dooley also reached Madeleine in her office.

"Don't freak out," he said over the phone. "Adam escaped." Dooley was calling from his cabin in Vermont.

It had been one week since Madeleine visited *Brother's Keeper.* She was sitting at her desk preparing for a busy day with the audit committee. She closed the file she'd been reviewing and stared out the window trying to stay collected.

"They've posted a bulletin in New Haven," he said. "That's probably where he's headed, but I'm more worried about something he said to me a few days ago."

She felt tears coming on and was so tense she was beginning to shake.

"What did he say?" she asked. "You saw him?"

"No, we were on the phone. He said Bradley needed his father. And he needed Bradley. Then he began raving. He sounded like a lunatic, Madeleine."

Madeleine rose from her desk and shut the door.

"What if he comes here?" she whispered, trying to gather herself. "I can't let Bradley see him."

There was a pause while Dooley thought over the question.

"You could bring Bradley up to me. But there's the chance Adam might come here."

"I have to keep him in school. I could leave him with the Conway's." Tommy Conway was Bradley's best friend down the street. The family had virtually adopted Bradley, taking him when Madeleine was called away on business, and often including them at holiday meals.

"I would arrange that Maddie– like *pronto*," Dooley said.

Madeleine hung up and immediately reached her neighbor.

Her next call was to Matthew, ignoring that it wasn't yet 5:00 am in Pasadena. As he slowly came around, she explained Adam's status.

"Good for him," Matthew said.

"No – he broke out!" She burst into tears.

Matthew sat up and turned on the light.

"This is no time to panic," he said. "Tell me what's going on."

He heard her sigh as she gathered herself.

"I saw him last week at the facility. I showed him Bradley's baseball photo."

"Can I ask – why are you calling me?"

"I thought you should know."

Matthew cleared his throat and swung his feet to the floor. He realized Madeleine needed to talk.

"Okay, okay," he said. "You're not going to do anything drastic, right? Like, come out here?"

There was a long pause.

"I don't know *what* to do Matthew. Visiting him at Brother's Keeper was a big mistake."

"I could have told you that. But it's water over the bridge, or – you know what I mean."

"Matthew get serious! I need you here!" Madeleine said, her voice quivering.

"Please don't put this on me," Matthew said. "I don't have a dog in this fight. I've got enough on my hands."

Madeleine let out a loud *aaarrrrgggghhhh.*

"I can't understand why you need to stay out there! she yelled. "You're running away. Did it ever occur to you that I might need you?"

Matthew didn't answer. The familiar hiss of three thousand miles between them suddenly got louder. Then she hung up.

He got back in bed and turned off the light and lay staring at the black ceiling. Madeleine was absolutely panicking. She used to be such a model of composure. She had shared very little about Adam and his illness, and now Matthew was getting a sense of the severity of the situation. Bradley was the real victim here, poor kid. From the sound of it, he was about to get a double dose of reality.

Later that morning Madeleine called the New Haven Police Department. After explaining she was a doctor assigned to Adam's case, she got the officer talking.

"We have an all-points bulletin out on him," the policeman said. "You can check back later." He took her phone number. The rehab center, he added, had yet to send a picture for the APB.

"Do you have one we can use?" he said.

"Not one that looks anything like him now."

It was all arranged for Bradley to go to the neighbors, but she hadn't yet given him a reason. The days of dropping him off without saying why were long gone; he'd demand an explanation. She would figure something out and tell him in the car, after picking him up at school. Suddenly a vision: Adam, in his ratty sweater and greasy running shoes, lurking on the school grounds, high on street drugs, waiting for his son to come out. Then she realized it was unlikely he would know where his school was.

She called Dooley next. He had some news. A likely match was spotted in Middletown, halfway to Hartford. That would rule out the hypothesis that Adam was going to New Haven. She shuddered, thinking he could be coming north to Hartford.

Bradley was standing by the corner stop sign, hair hanging in his eyes, leaning under the weight of a backpack full of books. The tall eight-year-old showed no emotion as Madeleine approached.

"What's up?" he said, dropping his backpack in the backseat, surprised by the unusual early pick-up.

"I'm taking you for a snack," she said.

"Am I in trouble?"

She shook her head no.

At the burger place, they ordered strawberry shakes from counter stools. As he was taking his first long sip, she began.

"You're going to stay at Tommy's for a few days."

"Where are you going?"

"I've been called out of town on business."

"But you can't fly, you said so, your doctor gave you orders."

"We're making an exception. It's very important, and it's not a long flight."

Three lies in one. She never lied to her son, or anyone, for that matter. It hurt her inside to say the words. But Bradley had to remain apart from these latest developments. Knowing of his father's escape would fill him with confusion and fear of the unknown. Dooley had suggested they get out of the house, and he was probably right. But where could she go? Although she'd given her notice to leave *Connecticut Life*, she agreed to stay until early June, which was over a month away.

Lawrence Holmes knew she was forbidden to fly. The best plan, she decided, was to take some personal time, book a spa stay. She knew of a place in the Berkshires in western Massachusetts.

"Tommy can help me with my Spanish!" Bradley said excitedly. "He's so much smarter."

Madeleine patted his hand.

"Tommy is not smarter than you, honey," she said, relieved he was not only buying the story but had also found something good about it.

At home, Madeleine was packing Bradley's clothes. He sat at his desk beside her, doing homework.

"Have you heard from him?" he asked, startling her. She put down a stack of shirts and sat on the bed.

"Not since I saw him two weeks ago," she said.

"Do you think he's better now?" Bradley said.

Madeleine took his hands and held them softly in hers. "Your father is not all better yet. Maybe someday, my love."

She looked at her sweet, innocent boy. He knew nothing about his parents' busted marriage, his father's hideous illness, the slim chance he'd pull it together enough to rejoin society. But someday, after Bradley had lived through one or two of life's harsh eventualities, those experiences that change you forever, he might be able to handle it. For now, she vowed to protect him with the ferocity of a mother bear fending for her cub.

Chapter 27

"I was hoping to set up there," Albert said as he came upstairs one morning. Matthew was in the southeast corner of the solarium, putting together a wooden sideboard for drying bowls and vases. A heavy cast iron kiln sat beside it; a potter's wheel, unassembled, was still in its box.

"I saw your paintings," Matthew said. "It looks like you're doing just fine downstairs."

"You went downstairs?"

Matthew shook his head as he tightened the screws on the last leg.

"Well?" Albert said.

Matthew put down the screwdriver and turned to his father.

"I'd prefer the privacy of my own studio," he said. "You should stay down there."

"I'm asking what you think of my paintings."

Matthew looked to the ceiling.

"They're good. I mean, not exactly my taste, but they're fine."

He turned back to the table.

"Why do you want to move up here?"

"Are you joking? The light in here is superb!" Albert said. "Have you forgotten how well we worked together, how – come on! We used to push each other, inspire..." He'd become very animated, his arms waving furiously. "Plus –"

Matthew interrupted him. "I didn't forget. It was a different time."

Matthew slid the finished table into the corner. He could feel his father's eyes drilling into him.

"Buy some floor lamps if you need more light," Matthew said, his back still turned. "I'll lend you the money."

Despite this latest interruption, Matthew felt alive again, reconnected with his craft. He understood better than ever the importance of having a studio, a sanctuary where he could escape to perform a task as simple as putting his hands to the smooth, wet clay. In all honesty, even with his father in the basement creating his art, even in this toxic environment, there had developed a peculiar new motivation. And although he loathed the idea of again working beside the man, he couldn't deny the obvious: his own innate talent, and likely his passion was borne of their shared DNA. Albert's love of art was infectious, as it always had been, and Matthew was once again excited to begin creating. This time, however, it would be on his own terms.

The studio was completed that week and he began working, mostly at night, to avoid interruptions. His new supplies included spatulas and shaping tools and a box of wet clay that contained two twenty-five-pound bricks. It felt so good to get back to work. To start, he was easy on himself, throwing small soup bowls and the like, finding his touch, awakening the pressure points in his fingers and thumbs. He moved quickly onto vases, far more challenging. When not satisfied with the end result, they simply were balled up, rehydrated and used for another project. But the initial indications were encouraging; his fingers were confident, his mind automatically in a calmer, more reasonable place.

✷ ✷ ✷

"You showed such promise as a youngster, a real prodigy."

His father stood at the doorway of the solarium one morning, now a fully functioning studio replete with the smell of damp earthen material and baked clay, studying several of Matthew's pieces. Matthew didn't hear him enter; he was engrossed in shaping a new vase.

"Athenian or Etruscan?" Albert asked.

Matthew turned around and looked at him with what had become a fixed show of antipathy.

"I'm not sure I know the difference?"

"It looks Athenian," Albert said. "But without any illustrations – soldiers with helmets, and spears, it could be anything else."

"Whatever," Matthew said, turning back to his work.

"I could paint some on," Albert said excitedly. "It would make it more authentic."

"No thanks."

Albert continued watching as Matthew smoothed the bottom of the vessel.

"Anyhow, I like where you're going with it. When you're finished, at least let me cut some poppies for it and we can place it in the kitchen."

It had become automatic, Matthew's dismissive response to his father's random comments, passing them off as offensive and patronizing. This whole ethos had become the energy flowing through the cavernous house. Contrasted with this: his lack of ability to manage his thoughts of Madeleine, not only her condition, but now the added threat of Adam, whose whereabouts were still unknown. In their last conversation, she'd explained her plan for what she'd do with Bradley until Adam was apprehended. It concerned him that the boy had asked to go along on her "business" trip. He was clearly smart enough to sense something was up. She had promised he would stay at his friend's for no longer than three nights, putting more pressure on her to come up with yet another plan if Adam wasn't apprehended during that time. She explained to Matthew she would be heading to the Berkshires by herself, spending a night, maybe two at the spa, and then she'd figure out her next move.

"What are you going to do if Adam doesn't turn up?" he asked her.

She had no answer.

Chapter 28

"You didn't tell me about any aunt in Cleveland," Hughes said, bristling. "I'd really prefer not to stop in that godforsaken town."

Hughes and Peter were an hour out of Hartford when they began arguing. Peter, behind the wheel of his massive Range Rover, stared straight down the highway.

"She lives in a suburb," he said. "Horse country. You might be surprised. And what do you know about Cleveland anyhow?"

"They had a river catch on fire."

"That was thirty years ago. It's no longer a steel town," Peter said.

"And you absolutely promised we'd stop?"

"We'll be there in time for cocktails. Aunt Marie is putting us in the Carriage House in the back. It's lovely."

Hughes glared out his window at the wet, grey morning. They'd left in a thunderstorm and now, as they passed through the heart of the cold front in upstate New York, a hard rain pelted the windshield.

"Does she know we have a dog?"

"She adores dogs," Peter said.

Hughes turned around in his seat and reached back to pet Bella, quiet and stretched out on her favorite blanket in the plush back seat. She lifted her head and licked his hand, giving him a questioning look, and promptly going back to sleep. The cargo space behind the back seat was packed with suitcases, surfcasting gear, and a cooler full of sandwiches and wine. There also was a trunk lashed to the roof. Peter never traveled without at least twice the amount of clothes needed, even though he and Hughes wore the exact same size and had taken to trading outfits.

Hughes' and Peter's two-day stopover in Cleveland was pleasant but uneventful. Peter's aunt, who owned a horse farm in a wealthy eastern suburb, welcomed them, fed them, and gave them horses to ride, even fitting Hughes with a prosthetic bridle designed for handicapped riders. They spent one day cantering through the forests and polo fields of the beautiful valley, bisected by a rushing, trout-filled river. Hughes was indeed pleasantly surprised by its beauty and commented on how friendly the Midwesterners were. They stopped at a tavern called The Red Fox, complete with a hitching post out front, tied up their horses, and ate kidney pie with cornbread and a mug of ale. Peter felt validated when Hughes finally admitted there were other places worth living beyond Hartford.

The visit would represent a nice break in their eight-day journey, preparing them for the grueling stretch across the rest of the country. When Hughes and Peter left the lovely estate behind early one morning and made their way to the interstate, they would begin a deadhead drive due west, each driving six-hour shifts and stopping at cheap roadside motels for a few hours of sleep and a shower. There were no more planned layovers.

Somewhere west of Rawlins, Wyoming, the Range Rover's red warning light came on. It was just past midnight. Hughes was behind the wheel and reached over to jostle Peter awake.

"There's something the matter," Hughes said, his prosthetic hand locked onto the wheel.

Peter jerked awake. "Pull over," he said hoarsely.

They were on a desolate, dark stretch of highway with no lights and low, heavy cloud cover. Hughes pulled over and put on his emergency flashers and Peter got out to check the vehicle. Steam was rolling from under the hood as he came around the front. He told Hughes to slide over.

"Didn't you see the temperature gauge?" Peter said, peering into the dash. "This engine is way overheated." The car was equipped with a satellite on-call service device and, in minutes, a disembodied feminine voice came over the speaker above.

"Good evening Mr. Carver. My, you're a long way from home. How may I help you?"

Peter explained he needed a tow to the nearest dealership.

"That would be Salt Lake, Mr. Carver," the voice said. "It's about four and a half hours away. Are you parked in a safe place?"

The voice said she'd be happy to find a local tow. Peter and Hughes relaxed in the quiet of the SUV, Bella asleep in the back. Every few minutes a car or truck would roll by with a *whhhisssh*, the red taillights disappearing into the desert blackness beyond.

As nighttime gave way to dawn, the massive semi-sized tow truck pulled alongside, dwarfing the Range Rover. The truck looked old and out of service. A whiskered man looking more like a rodeo contestant than a mechanic climbed out.

"Howdy!" he said, sticking his head in the driver's side window. He had on a shirt with *Lou* stamped on a patch above a pocket holding several pens and a tire gauge. He surveyed the front, looking beyond Peter to see Hughes with his yellow sweater and Nantucket red pants, and checking the back seat where Bella was snoozing. He stepped away and went to the front of the vehicle. Steam rose from under the hood. He came back to the window.

"You really need to go all the way to Salt Lake?"

Peter explained he needed a qualified dealer, not just any mechanic. He asked about the cost. The man paused and squinted into Peter's eyes.

"I can try to fix it here if you want," the man said.

"I prefer a factory-trained mechanic," Peter said.

"I need to call my boss," the driver said. "Don't normally make runs that far." He went back to his truck and returned in two minutes.

"Damn! It's not as expensive as you might think," he said. "Five hundred dollars. Four-fifty if you got cash."

Peter sat back in his seat and drew a breath. The truck looked like it might not make it that far. He tried to negotiate a lower price.

"The way I see it," the man said. "You ain't got much choice. He was peering into the car and said, "There a lotta gays in Maine?"

Peter took another deep breath and gathered himself.

"Why?"

"Just curious. Never been that far east, is all," the man said.

"What does that have to do with getting us to Salt Lake?" Peter said.

"Homos aren't too welcome there. Them are Mormons. Just thought you might want to know."

Peter smiled patiently.

He again attempted to negotiate a price, based on the condition of the truck, and the man held fast, insisting it was fully operational. In minutes, he had the truck positioned in front of the Range Rover and the driver was lowering the tow sling.

"These new SUVs and their so-called bumpers," he said, maneuvering the device toward the undercarriage. Hughes was standing on the shoulder. Traffic was picking up as the sun edged above the eastern range of the Laramie Mountains. The winch's electric motor switched on and the operator stood holding the lever for the hydraulic lift. As the front of the vehicle began to rise, the lever popped out of place and slammed down, pinning the man's hands against the bed of the truck. The front of the Range Rover slammed down onto the asphalt.

"Goddammit!" the driver cried out. "Somebody pull this goddamn thing off!"

Peter ran to the back of the truck and took stock what had happened.

"Hughes, get the jack handle out of the Rover," he said calmly. He gave explicit instructions where it was located and Hughes pulled it straight out and brought it to where the man was grunting in pain, his eyes squeezed shut. It looked like at least one of his hands had been crushed. Peter jammed the handle beneath the hydraulic lever and forced it up, freeing the operator's hands. He slowly lifted his hands off the bed of the truck and turned them over. His right hand was covered with blood. One finger was bent sideways at ninety degrees.

"Hughes get my bag," Peter called out. The man gave him the frightened look of a rabbit with his paw in a trap.

"I'm a physician," he said to the man.

"What kind?" The man asked.

"The kind you want. Today is your lucky day."

He was gently palpating the man's fingers, causing him to cry out every few seconds. "Hughes," he yelled, "Call 911. Lou won't be driving anymore today."

After several minutes of further examination, he cleaned the man's hands with alcohol and positioned them on the top of the fender.

"You have a dislocated finger and a fractured thumb. Those lacerations on your palm all need stitches. I'll splint what I can and put some butterfly bandages on the wounds. It'll get you back to Rawlins but go to an urgent care center there. Do it today. Do you understand?"

Lou grimaced and said, "Yeah."

In minutes, an EMS vehicle pulled over behind them and the Lou was taken off to a local hospital, leaving behind the old hauler. In another thirty minutes a newer backup truck came, contacted by the local Highway Patrol, and this time it easily lifted the Range Rover and in ten minutes they were on their way to Salt Lake City.

Peter and Hughes were squeezed together on the broad bench seat of the big tractor, knees angled to the door. As the driver, dressed in a clean uniform, shifted vigorously, Bella sat on the floor staring at them, panting her hot breath. The diesel engine growled through the gears as they headed southwest toward the darkened horizon. Peter and Hughes dozed off, Hughes' head on Peter's shoulder, and they slept most of the way, when the harsh sound of hail rattling on the cab's roof startled them awake.

Chapter 29

A violent spring storm was sweeping across western Massachusetts as Madeleine arrived at the Mountain Spa and Resort outside Pittsfield. She had reserved one of several detached cabins set amidst a stand of mature spruce trees. Limbs and debris were scattered over the property and a maintenance crew had been deployed to clean up the lot. Although nearly May, it was cold and there were patches of snow from a late April blizzard.

By the time she got settled she need to step out for her three o'clock massage. She pulled the waistband of her elastic yoga pants over her bulge, looking sideways at her profile in the mirror. It was a still a shocking reminder of her condition, but also one that elicited a mother's instinctual love. She was carrying a child, fathered by a man she barely knew. There were strong feelings for both. The father's status was unclear, but how could she not love this child? Still, a new, darker concern troubled her: could carry this baby full term?

As she hurried off to her appointment, which would end just in time for her pedicure, her mood was surprisingly gay. The spa services scheduled were a gift to herself, for all she had endured these past months. As she walked among the fragrant balsam grove, a fresh wind blew through the pines and the sun was high, a harbinger of the coming spring.

Her plan was to stay two nights, hoping Adam would be found by then. Assuming he would be readmitted to rehab, under tighter security, she could bring Bradley home and their lives could return to some semblance of normalcy. As long as her sweet innocent son was kept apart from any encounter, she felt sure he would be alright. Eventually, father and son would need to be reintroduced, but that would be carefully controlled, and she would have time to prepare for that.

Sitting in her room beside a fire that evening, admiring her bright red toes, she had a cup of tea while waiting for dinner to be delivered. Just as a knock came she remembered to call Dooley. When the waiter had set up her table and left, she dialed his number.

"I faxed his photo to New Haven," he told her. "They're checking it against some video from a convenience store. I'm waiting to hear back."

Madeleine gave him the land line number in the cabin, worried the cell phone coverage would be unreliable, and hung up with the sinking feeling she and her son were not yet out of danger. She picked at her salad, tried to watch a movie, and quickly fell asleep with the plate on her lap. She awoke at midnight and crawled into bed and didn't move until early the next morning when the cabin phone began to ring.

"The Hartford police department just called," Dooley said as she pulled herself from sleep. "He's been spotted in the bus station. He's wearing a Yankees hat I gave him. There's no question, Madeleine."

Madeleine hung up, jumped from the bed and wrapped herself in a plush spa robe. She pulled back the curtains and the bright spring sun blasted into the room.

"I've got to get Bradley out of town. As quickly as humanly possible," she whispered to herself.

She continued talking out loud, mostly in prayer, as she prepared to leave. She needed to bolster her courage, gird for a rough day. She made a cup of coffee to go and was on the highway heading south in less than a half-hour.

Driving through the rolling mountains, the budding trees shimmering green against a clear blue sky, she frantically tried to devise an escape plan. She would need to lie to Bradley, again, about the business trip being cancelled, then come up with an alternate reason for the both of them to leave town. If she didn't make any stops, she could arrive at Bradley's school just as he broke for lunch.

✶ ✶ ✶

Matthew was pulling into *Las Palmas* after spending most of the day at the beach. On this perfect southern California afternoon, with light winds and an unseasonably warm sea air, he and April had surfed intermittently for nearly five hours. They took a break to visit her bungalow where they had tacos and Mexican beers and a siesta and then went back to the beach. It was actually hot in the afternoon, and they had lingered in the water, catching the fat and plentiful waves coming off a gentle but formidable western swell.

Climbing from his car, his thighs quivering, he wondered if it was the hours of surfing or the particularly lively romp in April's bed, deciding it was probably both. The first thing he saw was Bella, sitting on the front step, staring blankly out to the street, sniffing the air. She didn't recognize him at first, but suddenly let out a whimper and then a screeching bark and ran to him as he got closer to the house. Nearly knocking him down, her tail wagging furiously, yapping and nipping at his ankles, she turned in circles and they danced and played on the grass for a minute until Albert appeared at the front door.

"Now that's a happy pooch!" he said from the step. "Your friends went to get supplies."

Matthew rubbed Bella's ears and told her what a good dog she was over and over until she finally began to settle down.

"Wait till I get you to the beach!" he told her as he pulled his board from the car and walked to the garage. He entered the kitchen from the back door and showed her the bowls he'd set out and she went straight for them and began attacking the food. Albert came in and sat at the table.

"That Hughes character is interesting," he said, as they both watched the dog devour her food.

"He's a good neighbor. You'll learn to like him," Matthew said.

"Can't get a weather report out of the other one."

"Peter doesn't mince words, or suffer fools," Matthew said, smiling as he realized his best friend Bella was finally in the house. "Did you put them in the east bedroom?"

"I wasn't sure where you wanted them."

Matthew walked into the foyer and saw the heap of bags and suitcases.

"Jesus Christ. How long are they here for?" he said.

"I thought you would have made that clear when you invited them," Albert said with a smirk.

Matthew was shaking his head. "Why does everyone think they can just move in here? Is there a sign out front saying *Vacancy* or something?"

The two bantered like this now with some frequency, speaking in simple, phatic terms to communicate in the most efficient manner possible. But there was markedly less vitriol, and sometimes their back and forth sounded almost like friendly jousting. They were slowly uncovering an established familiarity, albeit one that now carried a new sense of wariness. The easy father-son rapport of years past was gone, but to hear them talk it was clear they shared more than a trace of DNA. The raspy timbre of their voices, the intonation, the syntax were uncannily alike.

Albert's fawning over his son, however, continued unabated. He heaped praise on Matthew's work, suggesting the hours he'd isolated in his studio in Hartford had brought a higher level of understanding and execution, further evidence of what he'd always claimed: Matthew's was a divine, God given talent. Matthew sloughed it off, taking it as nothing more than part of his strategy. In every other sense, Albert was a self-absorbed, singularly focused artist, living hand to mouth downstairs, offering no help around *Las Palmas* and taking whatever he could get. He never missed the opportunity to remind Matthew the solarium was plenty large enough to house a studio for two, going so far as to promise he would keep to himself and refrain from distractions. Matthew continued to rebuff his requests, at one point bluntly saying he was lucky to have a roof over his head.

Resting upstairs later in his bedroom, with Bella curled up by the door, Matthew heard the Range Rover pull onto the gravel driveway. He looked out the window to see Hughes and Peter carrying in bags of groceries. Albert was at the door, arms out to help, and the three were already carrying on like old fraternity brothers.

"Tequila for everybody!" Hughes said with excitement from the kitchen below. "I've been waiting to get here to make a proper margarita."

"I surrender full control of the bar," Albert said with a smile.

"Where is the boy?" Peter asked.

"Napping," Albert said. "You know, this surfing life is tough business!"

The three guffawed as they walked inside. Matthew came down stairs and stood listening outside the kitchen while they unloaded the food.

"So, Matt tells me you're a painter," Hughes said to Albert.

"Starving artist would be more accurate," Albert said.

Hughes said, "Van Gough couldn't get twenty-five bucks for his paintings. I bet you're better than you're leading on. I'd love to see your work."

Matthew entered the kitchen with a smirk.

"He might get twenty-five bucks, but he's never tried," he said, surveying the room. "What a distinguished gathering!"

He went to Hughes and gave him a hug, greeting Peter over his neighbor's shoulder.

"Peter, I owe you a thank you," he said. "And an apology. Welcome to Las Palmas"

Peter waved him off. "Thank you. It worked out quite well, actually."

"I saw your pile of luggage," Matthew said. "Are you two planning on moving in?"

Hughes frowned. "Come on, Matthew! Where are your manners? I promised Peter we'd be warmly welcomed."

"Of course," Matthew said. "Stay as long as you want! Everyone else does!"

Matthew's sarcasm silenced everyone.

"I just can't believe you two are still talking," Matthew said to Peter, lightening the mood. "Hughes is a real treat to travel with, isn't he?"

Peter turned around from unloading groceries. "Let's just say it's been an adventure," he said with a grin. "At least we had Bella to break things up. Where is she, by the way?"

"Upstairs. She's afraid you're going to put her back in the car."

"We became pals, all those hours in close quarters," Peter said, "even with her bad gas. She was very patient. I think she knew we were coming to you."

They'd bought all the ingredients for a Mexican fiesta, with chicken and peppers and onions for fajitas, black beans, and cilantro, a half-dozen avocados for guacamole, a dozen limes and a half-gallon of high-octane tequila. Matthew was happy to turn the kitchen over to the new guests and sat at the table while Hughes filled the blender with lime juice, liquor, and agave syrup. The machine grinded away and when the ice was crushed, he poured four full tumblers of margaritas. Hughes loved any gathering that involved alcohol and was beaming amidst the hearty cheer. He raised his drink.

"To Pasadena! And all that she brings!"

They stood by the table exchanging smiles and clinked glasses.

"I sense a new beginning, Matthew, for you, your father, for Bella, and anyone else who might pop in," Hughes continued. "I'm reluctant to say this, but your California roots are coming through. You are the embodiment of the west coast ethos. Why, just look at you – you're a splendid specimen, a sun-tanned, surfing God!"

Matthew blushed, uneasy with the praise, and took an extended sip from his glass, the ice-cold tang hitting his palette with an explosion of lime. All three were beaming at him now as if he were some sort of museum exhibit. He looked to his father, gloating as if he were responsible. Peter and Hughes were nodding in acknowledgment, and Matthew, so intimidated by the sudden attention, turned and walked into the foyer where he called upstairs for Bella. When she didn't appear he climbed the two flights and found her asleep in his closet, curled up on top of a pile of laundry. He bent over to pet her and she rolled onto her back. He rubbed her belly until her hind leg began its phantom scratching, then he stood and told her to come down and join the party. She stood stiffly and followed him out. As they came down the stairs Matthew could hear the three conversing in low tones.

"Isn't our boy looking good?" he heard Hughes reiterate.

"That nasty laceration above his eye healed nicely," Peter said.

"I've been too afraid to ask," Albert said. "What happened to his face?"

Matthew was stopped now on the landing and could hear them clearly.

"The guy really clobbered him," Peter said. "Busted his nose, split it open. I see now I should have given him a stitch or two right then and there."

Matthew rushed down the stairs.

"Stop! That's none of your business!" He burst into the kitchen and Hughes jumped up from the table.

"We were only saying how good you look!" he said, "With all the sun and healthy exercise!"

Matthew snarled. "Yeah, right. I'm not deaf," he said from the doorway. "You were talking about Kane."

Albert said, "I plead ignorance. I know nothing about any of this. I'm going to stay out of it." He rose and looked as though he might leave.

Matthew didn't respond. He clipped a leash to Bella's collar and hastily led her out, slamming the door behind them.

"The boy's so sensitive," Hughes said when he was gone.

Albert sat back down and looked puzzled.

"So Julia was –"

"Oh dear," Hughes said. "I thought you knew."

Over the steady flow of potent margaritas, Hughes shared with Albert the highlights of Matthew's past nine months, a graphic, blow-by-blow depiction, every bit of it difficult for his father to hear. When he was done, Albert sat quietly absorbing the sad chain of events.

"No girlfriends since?" he finally said, wincing slightly.

"Just a woman from work," Hughes said. "She's sophisticated. And intelligent. But I don't think she's of any consequence. That is, beyond the occasional visit to his bedroom."

Matthew returned from his twenty-minute walk and silently rejoined the party, which quickly proved to be mistake. Hughes and Albert, red-faced and loud, were in an obscure debate about the intersection of Cubism and Dadaism. Peter kept the music going, playing Ella Fitzgerald loudly on a 1960s vintage console in the living room. The three barely noticed Matthew's return as he stood in the kitchen, quietly smoldering. As a diversion, he started frying the fajita ingredients. He sliced the chicken and the knife slipped, cutting his forefinger. He wrapped it in a wet paper towel and finished cutting the breasts. Hughes mentioned there was one more blender of drinks, and Matthew quietly helped himself to a double before chopping the peppers and onions.

By the time everyone was seated in the dining room and dinner was put on, the four were in various stages of acute intoxication, all cynical and louder, except for Peter who'd gone quiet.

Ingredients for the fajitas were passed and tortillas rolled and a bottle of wine was passed around the table.

"So, tell us," Hughes said partway through the meal. "How is it, living in the land of fruits and nuts?"

"Excuse me?" Matthew said.

"Isn't that what they call California? It seems apt, although I haven't met too many fruits yet." Hughes winked at Peter.

"Plenty of nuts, that's for sure," Albert piped in, glancing at Matthew.

"Takes one to know one Dad," Matthew said.

The room fell silent. Matthew had just issued a mixed signal, calling Albert *Dad* for the first time in however long, and it wasn't lost on anyone. The dining room was suddenly the size of a banquet hall. Its heavy oak table was fourteen feet long, able to seat a crowd, and the four of them were spread out ridiculously, one on each side. Matthew had claimed the armchair at the north end, leaving the opposite seat to Albert, who missed the fact that he'd been beaten to the patriarchal power seat, farthest from the kitchen. Their guests sat across from one another in the middle, with a black wrought iron candelabra suspended above holding ten ivory candles, all of which had been perilously lit by a wobbly Hughes. The room was cast in a sepia tone of the Moorish era and on opposite walls were hung portraits of Spanish priests, including Father Junipero Serra, founder of the missions along the California coast. Their gilded frames flickered in the candlelight.

"Matthew," Peter said, finally speaking up, "tell us about your ceramics. I was admiring your figurines earlier. I particularly enjoyed the otter."

Hughes interrupted, his mouth half full. "They remind me of Rembrandt Bugatti."

Matthew downplayed the praise. "They're practice pieces."

"Some practice!" said Hughes. "They have nuance. A sophistication I don't remember in your Hartford pieces."

Albert blurted out, "Bugatti – wasn't he the Italian sculptor who rented animals from the zoo? Was it Antwerp? He kept them in his apartment. Zebras and armadillos and the like. His brother was the car designer."

Hughes said, "Very good, Al. He was a crackpot, but bloody good. He was so traumatized by the slaughter of the animals during the Nazi invasion he turned on his gas stove and asphyxiated himself."

The room went quiet. Hughes filled everyone's wine glass, emptying the bottle.

Back in his chair, he broke the silence.

"So, we have the Hartford period, in young Matthew's canon of work. Now tell us, what are we to expect of the Pasadena period?" His words were slurring to the point of embarrassment.

A noticeable silence again fell across the table.

Peter, the least inebriated, attempted to redirect the conversation. "What shall we do tomorrow?" he asked.

Hughes went into the kitchen and retrieved another bottle of wine.

"I read about a fair in Pasadena," he said as he sat back down. "Native American arts and crafts. I'd like to support the local reservations."

Matthew sat up, blinking drunkenly. "What do *you* know about Native American Indian reservations?"

"I know enough to want to give back to an exploited, displaced band of indigenous peoples," Hughes said angrily. "The Franciscan missionaries uprooted tribes all the way up this coast, in the name of Christianity. Filthy heathens! That's all they were!" He was red-faced and slobbering as he scowled at a portrait on the wall across from him. "The biggest land grab in north American history!" He raised his glass to the painting in a mock toast. "Here's to you, you fucking colonialists!"

Matthew leaned into the table.

"I didn't ask for a damn history lesson Hughes."

Albert interrupted.

"For the record, I am a sixth-generation Californian. Matthew's the seventh. As you might expect, we have a few thoughts on the matter."

Matthew trained his glare to the far end of the table.

"Speak for yourself, mister international man of mystery. You're more of a *frog* than a Californian." His voice had risen to an uncomfortable level. He drained the last of his margarita. "What you should ask him is what it's like to live in the land of the snobby French. He knows all about the snobby French!"

Albert scowled. "I think it's time you changed your tone, young man," he said. "There's no need to be disrespectful. And I think you've had enough tequila for one night."

"Hear hear," said Hughes. "Show some respect for Señor Banks. And by the way, what's the consensus on these fajitas?"

Matthew jumped from his chair and carried his plate into the kitchen. A crash rang out as it shattered in the sink and he came storming back through the dining room.

"Whoever walks Bella, turn out the damn lights," he said without stopping on his way out the front door.

"You're not coming back?" his father called after him. "You're alright to drive?" The front door slammed shut and they heard the big white Cadillac start-up peel down the driveway.

✷ ✷ ✷

Albert climbed the basement stairs the next morning to a kitchen reeking of alcohol, lime juice, and fried onions. Dirty dishes were stacked in the sink. A pan with scraps of chicken and peppers sat on the stove. The waste bin, normally under the sink, was overflowing in the corner with the empty half-gallon bottle of tequila balancing on top.

He checked the garage for the big white Cadillac and saw Matthew had not come home. There was no sign of Bella, and he hoped she was on the third floor loyally waiting for him to return. There were stirrings above and he heard the toilet flush. A bright spring sun beamed through the kitchen windows, intensifying his headache as he began cleaning up.

"I guess we had some fun," Hughes said, standing in the doorway in his bathrobe without his prosthesis, hair standing on end, his face a pallid grey.

"No kidding," Albert said from the sink.

"Where's our boy?" Hughes asked.

Albert moved to the coffee maker and poured him a cup. Handing it to him he said, "Anybody's guess. Maybe his girlfriend's place at the beach."

Hughes' forehead puckered as he took the coffee.

"Is this new girlfriend serious?"

Albert said, "No idea. We don't talk about his personal life. I think they surf together."

"He seems awfully crabby. I wonder if something else is bothering him. He could do with a new girlfriend."

"Couldn't we all," Albert said. And then, "Well, I guess I'll speak for myself."

Hughes stood with his coffee, gazing out the window. The empty sleeve of his robe was neatly tucked into the side pocket.

"I was alone for so long," he said, staring dreamily into the yard. "I had forgotten what it feels like to have someone in your life. Then along came Peter, thank God. Now, take our Matthew – he thought he had someone in Julia, only to lose her in the crash. And then... *and then*, he lost her again when he found out about Kane – the rotten bastard."

Albert turned from the sink.

"I wish you'd fill me in on that sometime," he said. "I see now Matthew's been through a very difficult time. I know nothing about it, as painful as it is to admit."

Hughes gave him a caring smile.

"It's all quite simple, Al, when you boil it down," he said. "Death and betrayal. Two of life's elemental setbacks. Your son suffered them both, one on the heels of the other. A disillusioned wife goes adrift in her marriage, adds a dash of excitement with an ill-conceived affair, and *bang!* Her car is crushed, and with it Matthew's dreams. He finds out she was cheating, just as he's beginning to confront his grief. Don't you see? He wants to miss her, damn it to hell, but she's guaranteed that's a complicated option. Now the poor devil can't make heads nor tails of anything. It's a hell of a thing. It's bloody Shakespearean!"

The two sat in the quiet of the kitchen drinking their coffee. Hughes' clinical overview had momentarily silenced them.

"Of course," Hughes added moments later, "Matthew might see things quite differently."

Albert retreated deep into his thoughts while Hughes put more sugar in his coffee. The sad information about his son came to him as a many-headed snake, and now he was thinking about retreating to the basement to reflect further. The sprinklers switched on with a hiss and *tic-tic-tic* as it spat out the water just beyond the open window. Bella shuffled into the kitchen and went to her bowl and Peter appeared at the doorway, hair glistening from his morning shower, in shorts and a crisp white linen shirt.

"Well, look at you," Hughes said. "Fresh as a daisy."

"Not feeling so fresh," Peter said. "Whose bright idea was the tequila?"

"When in Rome," Albert said. "But you make a fair point Peter. We didn't need to finish a half-gallon jug."

"Of course we did," Hughes said.

Peter said, "I'm worried about Matthew driving last night. Did he make it home?"

"We're assuming he's with his friend at the beach," Albert said.

Hughes single handedly made another pot of coffee and put one of Albert's baguettes in the toaster oven. Albert decided against going downstairs and the three sat around the kitchen table talking for the next hour. Peter held court with graphic emergency room tales, one involving a naked man and woman stuck together with Crazy Glue. When they heard a car pull into the gravel driveway, they turned in their chairs to look out the side window. Bella started barking.

"Here's our boy now," Albert said, rising and sounding relieved. He walked back toward the garage door, expecting to greet the big white convertible. Instead, the doorbell at the front of the house rang. Albert turned around and hurried through the kitchen toward the foyer.

"Who in God's name..."

He opened the door as a taxi pulled away. A distinguished looking middle-aged woman, slightly rumpled and pregnant, stared back at him. By her side was a young boy, and at their feet several suitcases and a backpack.

"I'm looking for Matthew Banks," the woman said. "You must be Albert."

Chapter 30

Matthew and April were driving with the top down in the big white Cadillac along the Pacific Coast Highway, headed for Pasadena. The morning marine layer was burning off and several hundred feet below them the ocean was a deep blue field of sparkling diamonds. At midnight the night before, he luckily made it to her house, despite his condition, and when she didn't answer the door he was forced to sleep in the car. She claimed she'd passed out from too many Mai Tai's, and he was in no position to argue when she came outside to find him that morning. Now they were headed back to *Las Palmas* where she would drop him off. She had asked to borrow his car to move some items from her bungalow to a friend's house and wanted to take advantage of the enormous trunk. He agreed to her request but didn't trust her with it overnight.

"I need it back by six o'clock," he said as they made their way up the coast.

"I'll have Bo follow me. I'm seeing him after work."

Matthew turned to her sharply.

"He'll give you a hard time for driving my car."

"I'll make something up," she said.

He realized Bo had been hanging out at the beach more lately. He always showed up when the surf was decent, putting his expert skills on display, and had a way of ending up beside April, sitting on their boards during breaks. Although Matthew had no claim on her, this other man's desire tweaked him. She claimed they'd fallen off as a couple, but Matthew suspected the opposite. Bo was a woman chaser. Matthew knew that look of longing, of raw desire some men wear unabashedly. But he'd decided if Bo did have a burning need for April, considering all that was going on, he hadn't the time nor inclination to bother with her.

As they neared *Las Palmas,* Matthew's eyes blurred and his head throbbed. He had no sleep in the back of the Cadillac, and the margaritas had barely worn off. He could only guess at the overall mood at the house this morning, assuming the other three had carried on into the night. He was seriously considering going back to bed.

Turning into the driveway, he spotted the luggage on the front step. For a moment he thought Hughes and Peter had decided to leave early, but then saw the bags belonged to someone else. One was light blue, the other a duffle bag emblazoned with Red Sox logos. He pulled up to the garage, jammed the car into *PARK,* and climbed out.

"Remember, have it back by six," he said over his shoulder to April as he headed inside.

"Hello!" he yelled into the empty foyer. "*Hello!*"

The house was eerily quiet. He walked back to the kitchen and saw three mugs on the table. He could smell the toast. He heard someone coming down the stairs.

"If you're going to be a father, you'd better start acting like one," Albert said as he stood at the bottom of the steps. Matthew gave him a sour look, beyond the usual.

"What the hell are you talking about?"

"Come with me," Albert said, turning around and heading back upstairs.

Albert led his son to the back bedroom suite where a breeze was blowing in through windows flung open to the gardens. Matthew walked in and saw Madeleine lying on the bed with her feet raised on some pillows. Her face was pale and drawn. Peter was leaning over her pumping the bulb of a blood pressure cuff. Bradley was in a chair, pulled up to the bedside, peering worryingly down at his mother. Matthew froze, glued to the floor in the middle of the room.

"Your mother will be alright," Peter was saying to Bradley. "She needs to lay still for a while." Turning to Madeleine, with a serious look: "It was by the grace of God that you make it across the country today." He laid his hand flat on her rounded abdomen. "How are they now?"

"Less frequent," Madeleine said, referring to her contractions.

Now she gave a long look at Matthew. She saw how tan he was, and noticeably more fit. His hair was nearly blond, and what she saw before her was a pure Californian, better looking than she remembered, like someone in the movies, even with him glaring back at her icily.

"I know, *I know*," she whispered. "You have every right to be upset."

Matthew stuttered and paused.

"*Upset*?"

"I ignored the doctor's advice," she said. "I had to get out of Hartford."

"What could be so important?" Matthew said.

She nodded toward Bradley. Bradley stood from his chair.

"This is all your fault!" he shouted to Matthew.

Madeleine reached out and clutched her son's arm. "No sweetheart, we're in this together."

Peter interrupted.

"We're keeping Madeleine quiet now," he said directly to Matthew. "If her blood pressure gets one point higher I'll need to take her in. Everyone must leave the room. Bradley, you can stay."

Matthew was speechless as he scanned the room. His father looked detached, sitting back in an easy chair in the corner, wearing a look of disappointment mixed with mild shock, shaking his head slowly. Madeleine closed her eyes and began what sounded like breathing exercises. Peter was putting his medical instruments back in his travel bag and Bradley asked for something to eat.

Matthew backed out of the room. He climbed the stairs to the Crow's Nest, where he stretched out on the bed and tried to steady himself. Madeleine's arrival was a blow that now seemed surreal. It threatened to push him into a state of total disorientation, eternal alienation. Her justification for the perilous cross-country flight had to have been due to extraordinary circumstances. One reason would be her frustration with him, yes, but also she must have a desperate need to protect her son. Now he wondered if there was something more to Adam's story. Judging by the fear in her eyes, she was not only facing a medical emergency. She could be expecting her screwball ex-husband to show up with a gun, in a maniacal rage. That she brought Bradley made the situation more tenuous. It would require all of them to think twice about how they addressed issues like Madeleine's health, how to best shield him from the harshest realities. Was this a test for him, planned by Madeleine? How was the boy going to react to Matthew being the father? Based on what he'd seen so far, it wasn't going to be easy, that is if they were to stick around. Whatever the case, she and Bradley had arrived and were suddenly installed as the latest infestation of freeloaders at *Las Palmas*. The irony wasn't lost on him that somewhere above, Grampa Blevins was smiling, pleased to see the grand hacienda, a place of refuge he'd built for family and friends, was finally being put to its intended use.

* * *

Madeleine spent the afternoon resting in the back bedroom. Albert took Bradley to get hamburgers, borrowing Peter's Range Rover, and when they returned all but Matthew gathered at the kitchen table for a late lunch. Matthew had remained in his bedroom, door closed, hangover persisting as he tried to get a grip on what was happening and what to do about it.

"When's mommy coming downstairs?" Bradley asked as the group ate their lunch. The men looked at one another and Peter, who had assumed a position of command by virtue of his medical knowledge, offered an answer.

"It won't be for a while, Bradley. She seems stable. It doesn't look like your mother is going to have the baby now. But she needs her rest."

Bradley's face brightened.

"So, Mr. Banks, does this make you a grandfather?" he asked Albert.

Albert raised his eyebrows and a sly grin came over his face.

"Why yes, it sure does," he said. "It comes as a bit of a surprise, but I'll take it!"

Hughes said, "Al, it's a noble calling. My grandfather, God rest his soul, filled in for my parents when they weren't up to the task. It's what grandparents do."

Albert considered the observation and said, "Same for Harry Blevins, the man responsible for this house. He was a kind, bighearted man – the grand patriarch of our family. I wish he were here now."

He stood to get more lemonade. Bradley had gulped down the last of his burger and pushed his plate away.

"I just wish I had grandparents," he said.

The men looked at one another.

"Oh dear," Hughes said. "I'm so sorry." There was a hush at the table. "But you must be excited to have a little brother – or sister on the way!"

"Sister!" Bradley said. "Mom showed me a picture!"

Albert tried to temper his excitement. Not only had he just learned about becoming a grandfather; now he knew he'd have a granddaughter. Having raised a son, this posed all sorts of new opportunities. He sat at the table beaming when Matthew walked in.

"Did anyone think to get me some food?" he asked.

Hughes mentioned the leftover chicken from the night before. Matthew scowled as he rummaged through the refrigerator. Bradley pushed his unfinished bag of potato chips across the table.

"Here Mr. Banks, you can have these," he said to Matthew.

Mr. Banks. It was the first time the boy called him that. Who did Bradley think he was? Beyond his one-night role in creating the pregnancy, it was clear to everyone present Matthew wanted little to do with this situation. By rights, he should be considered something akin to the boy's stepfather, which was another consequence Matthew hadn't considered. He gave the boy a wink and took some chips from the bag.

"Call me Matt," he said.

Madeleine slept into the early evening. Peter was looking in on her every half hour, checking her blood pressure and various vital signs, and listening to her abdomen. Hughes and Albert took Bradley to a nearby Putt-Putt course to keep him occupied. They invited a neighbor boy to come along.

Peter was wary about how deeply he got involved in Madeleine's case. But he took the time to call around in search of the best neonatal facility, and when he found what he felt was equipped with the latest technology, he introduced himself to the director of the unit as a family friend and provided all the details of her prognosis. They had a bed for her, he was told, and would be expecting them any time. He had made a private decision that at the first sign of labor or any complication he would call for an ambulance to take her to the community hospital five miles from the house.

Although not in any real pain, Madeleine spoke only when she needed information. She was repeatedly asking for her blood pressure to be taken.

"Any sign of Matthew?" she asked Peter when he appeared just before 6 p.m.

"He's here somewhere," Peter said coolly.

"Can you tell him I need to see him?"

Peter put some instruments in his bag and sat at the foot of the bed.

"This is none of my business." He was studying her with added concern now. "Where do you plan to go from here? Do you have a plan?"

She turned away and looked out the window. There was a clear view of the tall palm tree that stood by the fountain, cast in silhouette. The sun setting directly behind it saturated the entire back yard with a tangerine glow.

"This was a complete surprise," she said.

"So I gathered," Peter said.

"Honestly Peter, I'm ashamed to say Matthew and I hardly know each other. I was supposed to counsel him through his grief – and I wound up in his bed. I'm so ashamed – and terrified for my profession. Career aside, I'm nothing but a sinner in God's eyes." She closed her eyes. "And then, there are my colleagues..."

Peter thought about what she said.

"'He who is without sin, let him be the first to throw a stone'."

"Book of John," Madeleine said. "So you follow the scriptures?"

"Not really. I just remember that one. Don't be too hard on yourself."

"I was raised in a convent. There's nothing that comes close to Catholic guilt."

"Oh, well –" He stopped and looked at her, not sure what to say.

"You have no idea," she said.

He fell to thinking.

"But now here you are," Peter said, his voice even. "You've no choice but to have this baby and create a safe, loving world for her. We both know that's exactly what you will do, with or without Matthew."

Madeleine looked frightened.

"I would like to say you're right," she said. "But I've already seen one child robbed of a father, and the damage that comes from it, for everyone. It happens too easily. I feel my son's pain every day."

Peter said, "But you will do your best."

He took her wrist and felt for her pulse. "Which is better than most. It's all Madeleine Batiste knows. It's how you've approached every challenge you ever faced. I know people like you – uncompromising, fiercely loyal, determined. You remind me of my mother." He smiled down at her. "That's a compliment I don't throw around casually."

Now Madeleine's eyes were welling with tears.

"This baby might kill me Peter," she said. "I know how this can go."

"Not while I'm here."

She looked out the window. A murder of crows had gathered in the palm tree and was raising a racket. She began to openly weep.

"Can you please find Matthew?" she said.

"Do you really think he'll be of any help?"

She didn't answer. Peter rose from the bed and drew the curtains.

"Bradley's down the street playing with his new friend," he said. "Seems like a good kid. Brent, or Bryce or something. I suggested he invite himself for dinner. I'll send Matthew up if I find him. You should rest now."

Downstairs, Hughes and Albert sat by themselves at the kitchen table.

"You were right," Albert said. "That Madeleine is a tall drink of water. I don't know how intelligent she is, getting tied up with my angry son, but she's got a way about her."

Hughes rose to rinse his coffee mug in the sink.

"I met her when she came to Matthew's place in Hartford. She'd left some jewelry on his nightstand. He asked me to let her in. We talked about art. Believe me, she's smart as a whip, and plenty sophisticated. And I like her. I was so happy to see Matthew get back on the horse."

"Back on the horse?"

Hughes turned around and smiled at him.

"You know what I mean."

* * *

Matthew was up in the Crow's Nest with the door closed, secretly packing. His plan was to leave with Bella the minute April returned the big white Cadillac. He would say he was going out for food and head south, going until he was in Mexico or beyond, maybe Costa Rica. He'd been stockpiling cash, plenty for a year, and it was stowed in his backpack. The house in Hartford would eventually sell and that would bring more, probably enough for another year, maybe longer. His father could stay at *Las Palmas*, the leech. Let him have the goddamn place. And good luck keeping it! Eventually, when it sold, at least half would be allotted to him, assuming the crack attorney Stan worked things out with the courts. By then he'd have returned to California, maybe down south, near La Jolla. He'd find a way to build a studio on the beach, become a bona fide sculptor with exhibitions in chic local galleries patronized by wealthy benefactors and pretty middle-aged housewives. He'd surf every day and get in the best shape of his life, with nothing and no one to answer to but Bella. As for Madeleine and Bradley and the baby? Hell, they needed a fresh start anyway, why not right here in Pasadena? Albert would let them remain at *Las Palmas* for now, the giddy new grandfather, glad to have another shot at raising a kid, which could absolve him of past negligence, not that he deserved it. And April? Oh – April, so young and willing. However you sliced it, their relationship was toast. She was a child. She should go with Bo, another child. They could catch waves and frolic on the beach forever, for all he cared. In the end, the whole damn lot of them would get exactly what they deserved.

His musings were cut off when Peter called up for him from the kitchen. Matthew didn't answer as he pulled together the last of his things. It was nearly six o'clock. He looked out the front window to the driveway. There was no sign of April.

A knock came on his door.

"Can I come in?" a voice said.

Matthew opened it a crack. It was Albert.

"What do you want?"

"Let me in."

Matthew eased open the door and his father shoved through and looked around. It had been years since he was in the Crow's Nest. The last time must have been when he tucked Matthew into bed, maybe after a summer barbeque. It was exactly as he remembered, complete with clothes strewn across the floor, empty water glasses, and an unmade bed. He noticed a suitcase on the chair.

"Going somewhere?"

Matthew didn't answer.

"Thinking about skipping town?"

"I don't have to answer you," Matthew said.

"You just did. Talk to me. Tell me what's going on."

Matthew hadn't heard this gruff tone since he was a child. He stuffed his hands in his pockets and looked out the window.

"You're all driving me insane," he whispered. "I need to go."

"Son, you don't have that freedom anymore."

"Oh yes I do."

"You think leaving is the answer?"

"It seemed to work for you."

Albert's face tightened.

"It was one of several choices," he said. "And no, it was not the right decision."

"A little late to admit that, isn't it?"

"It's never too late. Look – I can't change the past. Only what happens going forward. You have the opportunity to do the right thing, right now. Avoid the biggest mistake of your life, one you'll regret forever. Don't follow my path, for God's sake! If you don't learn from my mess-ups, what good is it all?"

Matthew looked his father up and down.

"Madeleine is not the innocent, God-fearing product of a convent she pretends to be, you know."

Now Albert's face flushed with anger.

"That's a cheap shot Matthew. Maybe Madeleine isn't so pure, but she certainly doesn't deserve the treatment you're giving her. And what about your child?"

Matthew didn't need to be reminded of his child. Just the mention of her sent a chill right through him. The two stood staring into each other's identical blue-grey eyes. Matthew spoke first.

"So, mister *do what I say not what I do*, what is the right thing?"

"I don't have to tell you," Albert said.

Matthew turned away, folded a pair of pants, and laid them in the suitcase. His father stood in the doorway, arms akimbo.

Hughes called up the stairwell.

"You have visitors!"

Matthew looked out and saw the big white Cadillac parked in the driveway. Bo's Land Cruiser, surfboards jutting out the back, was parked behind it. Matthew turned to leave. His father didn't move.

"Don't go, Matthew," he warned.

Matthew forced himself between his father and the door and vaulted downstairs.

In the foyer, April was standing in the corner and appeared upset. A line of black eye make-up dribbled down one cheek. Bo stood in his bare feet behind her, wearing shorts and a T-shirt. Hughes had disappeared into the kitchen.

"Bo wants to talk to you," April said in a whisper.

"Let's take it outside," Bo said.

Matthew followed him as he walked toward his Toyota.

"What's up?" Matthew said as they stepped onto the gravel drive. Bo turned with clenched fists and looked poised to punch him. Just then, Madeleine called from the upstairs window.

"Somebody – get Peter!"

She sounded terrified, calling out in a plaintive wail. In her pale-colored nightgown, she appeared ghost-like in the shadow of the frame.

April had stepped between Bo and Matthew. Bo shoved her aside, telling her to get into the jeep. Matthew glowered at him.

"Keep your hands off her!"

Bo stood with his fists at his waist, returning Matthew's scowl. Matthew turned toward the front door and saw Madeleine was downstairs now, standing in the foyer. The lower half of her nightgown was different shades of pink, her face a chalky white. She was slumped against the bannister. Matthew rushed inside and gently lowered her to the floor.

"Somebody please find Peter," she said again, this time calmly. She was sitting against the staircase with her knees pulled up. "I think the –" She gasped.

A gush of reddish fluid began pooling between her legs, covering the terra cotta floor. Matthew ripped off his shirt and stuffed it between her legs. She had slid down flat, with her back on the floor. Matthew cradled her head with one hand.

"Breathe Madeleine," he said, remembering a scene from a movie.

Bo was at the door peering inside.

"Dude – holy shit!" he said.

"Get the hell out of here Bo," Matthew said. "*Now!*"

Peter appeared from the basement where he had been admiring Albert's paintings. He quickly sussed what was happening and sprinted up to his bedroom and back down the stairs with his medical bag, kneeling at Madeleine's side. He began pulling out implements while Matthew was bent between Madeleine's feet.

"You're not bleeding," Peter said to her calmly. "Your water broke."

"Pull them off!" she cried, looking down at her panties.

"Can you take over?" Matthew said frantically to Peter.

Peter had stood and stepped back, seeing she wasn't in imminent danger. His arms crossed, as if attending a dance recital.

"You're doing fine."

Matthew gave him a look of shock combined with disbelief and turned back to Madeleine, pulled off her soaked underwear and flung them into the corner.

"Now get ready to receive the head," Peter said as the crown emerged.

"*Jesus Christ!*" Matthew was hyperventilating now.

Madeleine's legs were spread as wide as a gymnast's. Fully exposed for all of creation to see was a sight so primary, so raw, Albert and Hughes had to turn away. Matthew stared at Madeleine's anatomy. He was mesmerized by the energy coming from the confluence of her loins, the nexus of life, about to yield to the world his tiny daughter, as the mother host instinctively opened up to allow for the little being's exit (or is it entrance?) to break free into the wide-open coolness of the evening, to take her first breath. He wondered: Could she smell the star jasmine he'd planted last week, its perfume now wafting through the front door? And what about her brand-new eyes? What image would first pop onto her virgin retinas? She'd see a frightened man, peering down frantically, half responsible for all of this yet planning to cut and run. Now his emotions began to spill over. Tears pooled and ran to his jaw, warm, warmer than he remembered. When was the last time he cried? It was in Madeleine's office, a pathetic fool. He pushed that from his mind and now he was trying to mimic Madeleine, slowing his mind, breathing in rhythm with her. He studied her intently. Her eyes were shut as she continued her rhythmic breaths, deeper in concentration, willfully giving herself over to nature to comply with another of life's routine callings, so easily taken for granted. Their tiny daughter seemed to double her effort to escape, her head and shoulders now visible, both arms flailing, and she was making guttural sounds of some other order. Her hair was ink black, like her mother's. Her nose was short and compact – a Banks nose! Matthew had the random fleeting thought: Albert will be so thrilled! Madeleine let go a long, exhausted moan, an appeal to her child: *Come!* Matthew cupped the baby's slippery head with one hand, keeping it from the cold tile, and with the other gripped her miniature bottom, easing her from her mother's final clench. The baby slid out clean, a pea squeezed from a pod, and her bowed legs began kicking furiously. The blue ropy cord from her abdomen looked like butchers' offal, running mysteriously inside its larger host. The baby glistened, slathered with blotches of fluids and streaky blood, and Matthew, still on his knees, was now freely sobbing.

Albert was leaning against the stairs observing. Hughes was in the corner wiping off his pants after slipping on the wet tile, his prosthesis askew. In the distance they could hear a siren.

"Congratulations," Albert said to his son. "Welcome to fatherhood."

The baby's strangled cry barely filled the front hallway. Madeleine was arching her neck to see. The ambulance turned into the driveway and was charging toward the house, tires spitting gravel. Matthew held his impossibly tiny daughter in the palm of his hand now. Everything about her was perfect but her size, and a coating of goo. Peter was kneeling and had put on surgical gloves. He lifted Madeleine's bottom off the floor and laid several sterile pads under her. Two EMTs came in blue uniforms, pushing a gurney, one wheeling a tank of oxygen. Peter handed his shears to Matthew.

"Cut the cord," he said, "right here." He gestured to the spot between his thumbs.

Matthew looked at him as if he'd lost his mind.

"Come on, quickly now," Peter said.

Matthew snipped the rubbery cable and Peter took the oxygen mask from the technician and placed the small cup over the baby's nose and mouth. Her color quickly went from grey to pink, her little face grimacing as it twisted toward the evening light at the door.

"Let's get her into the ambulance," Peter said.

"I'm coming," Matthew announced.

Chapter 31

They arrived at the hospital in central Pasadena just as the sun was setting and the shift was turning over. Madeleine was rushed to the ICU to receive a blood transfusion and critical scans. Her uterus, ballooned with blood from a ruptured placenta, had released its contents on the way in. Peter had been correct in keeping her still in the foyer; any sudden movement during labor could have caused a fatal hemorrhage. The baby, barely to the point of viability outside the womb, was hurried to the NICU.

When the nurse first took her baby away, Madeleine became hysterical, yelling obscenities at the staff. Matthew intervened and calmed her, saying he would stay with the baby wherever she went. Madeleine's rage subsided after the nurses disappeared down the hallway with the portable incubator. Matthew walked behind them as they wound their way through the labyrinth of corridors, past examination rooms with sci-fi-looking diagnostic machines and costumed technicians, until they came to the Neonatal Intensive Care Unit, a separate wing bathed in its own ecosystem. The lights were dimmed and the air noticeably warmed and humidified. Through the window of the observation area several other new fathers stood nervously. He could see his alien-like daughter lying in her precisely controlled and monitored incubator. All others had names affixed. Since Matthew and Madeleine had never discussed what name she'd take, first or last, the label on her box only read "Baby B."

Matthew thought while sitting there he was looking into a giant half-lit aquarium. She was one of eight in two rows of acrylic boxes, tiny pink and brown bodies naked but for diapers no bigger than a cocktail napkin. They were all flat on their backs with spindly arms spread wide, laboring to breathe, each in their own distress, depending on the maturity of their lungs. As Baby B lay struggling, he could see her color had grown ashen, close to the bluish grey at birth, and her little mouth popped open and snapped shut like a guppy as she grabbed for air. Peter had warned Matthew the real concern was getting enough oxygen into her blood. Matthew motioned for one of the nurses to come out.

"I don't think she's getting enough," he said to the older, overweight nurse.

"She's getting just the right amount, Mr. Batiste."

"But her color –" he said, ignoring her oversight.

"It won't change for several hours, if at all. Her lungs are trying to catch up. If we see no progress, we'll give her something to speed it up." She turned and went back into the unit.

Matthew took a seat and picked up a magazine on parenting. He was too tired to read and tossed it to the table and put his head back against the wall. He stared blankly into the purplish glow of the NICU. Beyond the glass, a mass of machines blinked like arcade games. The nurses silently went about their jobs in practiced syncopation, attending to each tiny being in their private effort to survive through the night and hopefully, eventually thrive.

As the evening wore on the assemblage of parents thinned to just one other father with his nose pressed to the viewing window. Matthew took advantage of the quiet surroundings to slow his mind and reflect on the miracle of life that unfolded before him on the floor of his grandparent's house. It shook him to his core, how in the span of minutes he'd not just seen the essence of life materialize in real-time; he'd moved from a scheming deserter to a gawking father, bowing to the command of a power over which he had zero control. Again, a random confluence of people and events had created a massive shift in his world. His resentment toward Peter, for insisting he lead the delivery, had eased. He understood now why the savvy physician would so blithely stand by. This was Peter's plan, conceived in the moment, to force Matthew's engagement. His intentions were noble, but it was faint praise that he felt Matthew was up to the task. And Albert's passive support, albeit at arm's length, also suggested this was one hundred percent on Matthew. It was a stinging reminder of his self-obsession and the estrangement he'd created, now seen as inexcusable and shameful.

It was after midnight, and he had fallen asleep in a chair outside the NICU. A nurse holding a blanket woke him.

"There's a couch in the other lounge," she said.

"How is she?" Matthew said as he sat up, blinking.

"She's a fighter, that one."

Matthew accepted the blanket. "I'll stay here."

He would stand watch over the baby and Madeleine alternately for the next thirty-six hours, walking the hallways between wings all hours of the day and night. Staffers gave him fruit and bottles of water and chatted with him, all taken by his quiet concern and vigilance. With the baby, he was restricted to the viewing area while brief visits were permitted in Madeleine's room during which she was semi-conscious, barely acknowledging him.

The next morning, as he approached Madeleine's room, her nurse informed Matthew she was running a fever. They suspected an infection. He would be kept from seeing her for the time being. He immediately called Peter, who had already learned of it, and assured Matthew it didn't appear serious and that her treatment was appropriate.

* * *

Albert showed up at the hospital on the third morning. Matthew went to meet him at the main entrance.

"You look awful," Albert said as his son approached. "How's our little one?"

"They don't tell me much. But she looks more human, and if you ask me, more like a Banks."

"And her mother?"

"Not so well." He shared the latest information.

"Does she know you're here?" Albert asked.

Matthew nodded. "I think so."

"Want me to take over?" Albert said.

Matthew looked at his father, dressed in the same silly bohemian painter's clothes and his straw planter's hat, rested and eager to help, the opposite of Matthew, who was bone tired, hungry, and overcome by emotions he'd never felt. His lip quivered and he covered his eyes with one hand and began to weep. Albert stepped closer and put his arms around his son. Matthew accepted the hug without reciprocating and moments later a nurse approached.

"Mr. Banks," she said. "The doctor wants to see you."

Matthew, with Albert following, stepped into the NICU where the baby's doctor, an Indian woman named Kapoor with black hair and quick, similarly black eyes, told him to sit down. He took a chair in the corner.

"Go home," she said. "Sleep. Your baby is in good hands. Mom is still in the ICU. As the father, you need to be available, clear-headed. If necessary, we will call you." Her intense eyes pleaded with him to go.

He looked to his father.

"Listen to the doctor," Albert said. "I'm here for as long as you need me."

* * *

On the drive home, Matthew took a detour and headed to the beach. It was a sharply clear morning with modest waves. He wasn't thinking about surfing, or April or Bo. He was thinking about Cosimo.

He parked the big white Cadillac in the same spot as the day he met the man, where he handed him the lighter for his cigarette and listened to him talk of the green flash and the universe shifting. He sat in the car for some time replaying in his mind that momentous night. Some things Cosimo envisioned had come to pass; others remained on a list of unknowns. Matthew assumed the *'there is more'* comment referred to the baby. But what did he mean *'there are things to do'*? And the one that really threw him: he must accept *"all that she brings.'* The words echoed as if said minutes ago.

He climbed from the car and started walking along the water's edge in the direction of Cosimo's lean-to. As he approached, he could see among a stand of locust trees five faded Tibetan prayer flags strung on a line, rippling in the breeze. Blackened rocks and charred chunks of wood in a pit were all that remained of his camp. Matthew sat where they had drunk the powerful mescal. He felt beneath his shirt for the necklace. *My token of serenity for you.* He'd taken it off only once, at

April's bungalow. She tried it on without asking and wouldn't take it off. When he demanded it back, she was almost in tears. He hadn't removed it since.

✷ ✷ ✷

When Matthew pulled up to *Las Palmas*, Hughes and Peter were in the driveway loading suitcases into the Range Rover.

"You're leaving?" Matthew said, trying to appear disappointed.

"We've worn out our welcome," Hughes said. "You've got enough on your plate. Just look at you. Poor man. You're a wreck. You have important work to do."

Peter assured Matthew both mother and daughter were on track for a healthy outcome.

"Madeleine should be fine in a week or so," Peter said. "The baby will be in a few weeks longer. Your focus should be on them both."

"Oh, believe me –" Matthew said, mentioning he'd be returning to the hospital in a few hours. He reached into his back pocket and pulled out a tiny maternity ward photograph.

"Meet my daughter," he said, beaming. Hughes examined it, his eyes lighting up.

"My lord," he said. "She's just a *tiny* thing! No bigger than a dot!"

Peter stared smiling at it for a few moments. "You can reach me on the road if anything comes up. And the hospital has my number if they need me, which I'm sure they won't."

Albert appeared at the front door holding one of his paintings. It was a small canvas with a post-Impressionistic scene of a Provençal town square.

"Oh gosh, I just realized," Albert said, stopping in his tracks. "I should have brought two! Is there something in my studio that speaks to you, Peter?"

"I love the painting of Matthew at the beach," Peter said. "But I would never ask."

Matthew interrupted. "Please – take it," he said. "He made me look like –" He stopped and they waited for him to finish and then everyone chuckled awkwardly. Hughes began complaining that Albert had never offered to paint *him,* and they laughed some more even though Hughes was serious.

"I'll see you in Hartford in the not-too-distant future?" Hughes said.

"Not soon, but eventually, probably when I sell the house," Matthew said.

"I'll ship your painting," Hughes said.

"Painting?"

Hughes shook his head and said nothing. He gave Matthew his typical mechanical hug, the acrylic forearm jabbing into his back, and whispered in his ear.

"Take care of that precious little creature. You have everything it takes to be a good father, but you'll need to work at it. Take all the best things you learned from Albert."

He pulled away and looked Matthew in the eye. "And give the old man a break, will you?"

Matthew could see Hughes' eyes were moist. He gave his neighbor a wink, grabbed his good arm, and squeezed. Bella had jumped into the backseat of the Range Rover. Matthew leaned in to coax her out.

"Come out of there girl, you don't want to make that trip again! Things here can't be *that* bad!"

✶ ✶ ✶

Inside, Bradley was watching Scooby-doo.

"How's my mommy?" he said to Matthew from the couch, his eyes stuck on the screen.

"You know Bradley, your mother is very strong."

"I know," Bradley said. "How's my sister?"

Matthew's face softened. The newly minted brother had already bonded with his tiny sibling.

"Your sister is strong too, but she's going to need time in the hospital before she comes home."

Bradley continued watching the cartoon.

"Did my mom almost die?" he said after a few moments.

Matthew sat down, took the remote control and turned off the cartoon.

"She had a condition. That's why your sister was born too soon. And it was hard for her, she wasn't ready to come out yet. But Peter, and the good people at the hospital, made sure everything turned out okay."

"Did *your* mother have a condition?" Bradley said.

Matthew looked to the floor, astonished by the boy's precocious empathy.

"There are many different kinds of conditions, Bradley. Some are worse than others."

Bradley stared ahead at the blank TV screen.

"I'm almost nine," he said.

"Your mother told me."

"That's a lot older than my sister. Will I be allowed to play with her?"

Matthew smiled.

"You will do more than just play. You'll teach her to ride a bike and throw a baseball. You'll protect her from all the crazy boys in the neighborhood."

Bradley jumped off the couch and struck a boxer's pose.

"Anybody messes with my little sister – *POW!* Right in the nose!"

Chapter 32

Matthew was dressing to go back to the hospital when his cell phone rang.

"Is the old man still with you?"

It was Mel Goldman, calling to check in. It had been at least a month since they last spoke.

"I'll give you one guess," Matthew said.

"I'm still getting the dirt on him. Nothing too bad. The worst is the tax business," Goldman said. "I'll ask you one more time – what do you want me to do with this?"

"Water under the bridge," Matthew said.

"What?"

"I can't put him out on the street now. He's the grandfather to my newborn."

"What the hell are you talking about?"

Matthew explained.

Mel's escalating laughter rose through the phone and when he settled down he said something about Matthew being a real piece of work. Then he asked about Hughes.

"He was supposed to stop by my office," Goldman said. "Claimed he had a check for me. Did you know he was covering my retainer?"

Matthew didn't answer. He'd never mentioned Goldman's usurious fees, or how he'd be paid. Evidently, Hughes was too magnanimous to say anything.

"Good luck with the old man," Goldman said before hanging up, "and the new bambino."

At the hospital, Matthew was looking for Albert to send him home. He found him in Madeleine's room, sitting in a corner chair, watching over the mother of his granddaughter. Madeline was asleep, an IV in her arm and wire leads running beneath her gown.

"She's been asking for you," Albert said. "She's pretty out of it."

Matthew sat on the edge of the bed and touched her forehead. Her fever seemed to have gone. A nurse walked in and scolded him.

"You're not supposed to be here," she said.

"What about *him*?" Matthew said, nodding to his father.

"Mrs. Batiste was given permission for one visitor."

Albert looked at Matthew, his raised eyebrows suggesting innocence.

Matthew left the room and headed for the NICU. He would spend two more nights watching over the little girl he'd just decided should be named after Hughes' prescient description: "Dot", after his mother. The name on her birth certificate would be Dorothy Blevins Banks, as long as he could get Madeleine to agree.

Chapter 33

"Frère Jacques, frère Jacques. Dormez-vous?"

Albert Banks sat beside the crib singing to his five-week-old granddaughter. It was a routine he'd adopted soon after mother and child returned from the hospital's NICU days before. He insisted it was the beginning of her language lessons. Fifteen years in the French countryside had honed his nearly flawless adoption of the language. With the proper tutelage, he claimed, she would not only learn French; she'd have the added distinction of a dialect rooted in Provence.

Hearing the singing, Matthew stuck his head in the nursery as he walked by.

"You're spoiling her," he said to his father. "She'll never get to sleep on her own."

Albert was making goofy faces at his granddaughter. "She has no problem getting to sleep. She's growing like a tropical flower," he said.

In the spacious bedroom next door, Madeleine was fast asleep. Her recovery, still day to day, kept her in bed most hours of the day. Albert provided most of her care, making nutritious protein shakes and baking Parisian delicacies in an effort to get her weight up. She had lost over ten pounds after her stressful delivery and its aftermath, and her iron level remained dangerously low. Matthew quietly monitored the varied procedures, focusing mostly on the baby, who needed bathing and changing and to be at her mother's breast every several hours.

It might have been because she was too tired to debate, but Madeleine went along with Matthew's suggested name. The baby's full name would be Dorothy Batiste Blevins Banks, with Matthew happy to make a small concession so long as they could call her Dot. A nickname never seemed so apropos.

Bradley and the neighbor boy Brandon had become fast pals and he was spending hours each day in their swimming pool. The first thing the eager big brother did when he came home was check on his growing sister. He had learned to hold and feed her with the tiny bottle of supplemental formula, talking to her with the same sing-song voice he'd adopted from his mother.

The morning Matthew arrived home with Madeleine and the baby, Albert had greeted them at the door with great fanfare. A four-foot-tall pink stork had been placed in the front yard with a sign IT'S A GIRL!", ordered by Hughes and Peter. Pink and white bunting was strung around the front door and bright balloons gathered at the ceiling in the foyer. On the second floor, Albert and Matthew had filled the nursery with assorted infant *accoutrement,* mostly in pink. Colorful curtains with circus animals covered the windows; a Calder mobile, which Hughes bought, dangled above her crib, playful with moons and planets dancing mid-air. And there was the expensive Italian rocking chair with a cushioned ottoman Albert had found in a high-end boutique, all designed to make a warm, quiet nook where the baby could thrive just feet from where her mother convalesced. If it had been up to Madeleine, the baby's crib would be in her room at the foot of the bed. But her doctor insisted on separate rooms. Madeleine had exhibited a nearly obsessive attachment to Dot from the minute she came into the world. That she was such a fiercely devoted mother came as no surprise to Matthew, having witnessed her maternal commitment to Bradley, and with the arrival of her new daughter she was doubling down.

✶ ✶ ✶

Someone once told Matthew babies grow faster in their sleep, and this drew him to her nursery each morning, excited to check her development. One such morning, as he was changing her diaper, he called for his father to bring more wipes. Albert rushed from the hallway storage cupboard and handed them to his son and observed him cleaning her.

"I have to confess," he said, as Matthew threw the diaper in the bin. "I never was much for changing diapers."

"It isn't too late to learn," Matthew said, stepping away. "Finish her up."

Albert gave him a surprised look.

Holding her miniature ankles with one hand, he gently lifted her from the table and placed a tiny diaper underneath. He then tentatively spread the fine white powder on her bottom and lowered her, fastening the sides precisely. He looked to Matthew with raised eyebrows, anticipating his approval.

"See?" said Matthew. "Not so hard. You just doubled your skills as a grandfather."

With his father's eager assistance, Matthew would install an assortment of safety equipment to protect his fragile daughter, such as the audio monitor in his bedroom to hear her breathing from upstairs. He would not put a speaker in Madeleine's room, knowing she would never sleep. He'd read about crib death and didn't want to be overly paranoid, but still made sure everyone knew to place her on her back. He bought a special micron filter to put in the open window screen beyond her crib that ensured she was breathing only the purest air possible. A carbon monoxide and smoke detector was attached to the ceiling in the event the larger house alarm malfunctioned. To measure her growth, he bought the best digital infant scale, placed beside her bassinet, which charted her weight every day, which was steadily increasing ounce by ounce.

They spent their mornings together in the nursery overlooking the lush gardens, listening to the metronomic spitting of the sprinklers. He held her in his lap at intervals between feedings with her mother and naps, staring into the infant's milky blue eyes, convinced she looked more like a Banks every day. Her only response was a baffled gaze, returning his own look of wonder. Could she already be judging his qualifications, his willingness? Did she wonder where this person came from, or why he was even here? Or did she instinctively know and trust him, recognizing his scent, the pheromones, the tone of his voice heard through the walls of her mother's womb?

When the baby was sleeping and Madeleine had been attended to, Matthew spent much of his time reengaging with his craft. Now he went about it with renewed vigor, fueled by an unfamiliar kind of inspiration. He felt wildly creative, like never before, producing avant-garde shapes in his vases and bowls, some abstract, others more realist. Just like in the early days in Hartford, when working he lost any sense of time or place, entering a trance-like state where his hands moved as if remotely directed over the slippery clay. He wondered: did all new fathers feel this surge in their sense of what's possible?

* * *

One morning Albert walked into the room, struggling with his easel, rolled-up canvasses, brushes, and tubes of oils. Matthew heard him approach, turned around, and saw him set down the materials. As Albert stood his easel beneath the south-facing windows, Matthew said nothing. Albert finally broke the awkward silence.

"When are you going to let me add some color to your work?" he said. "We could do a set of bowls, maybe sell them at that ceramics gallery in town. I bet they'd bring some decent money."

Matthew didn't answer. He was trying to decide what to do; kick him out? Start another pointless argument? Instead he pretended to be deeply engaged with the piece he was working on, etching with a pencil-sized stylus the coarse feathers of a twelve-inch emperor penguin. Albert waited for a response that didn't come and turned back to setting up.

For the remainder of the morning they both leaned into their work quietly as the sun's rays, pouring through the arched window, advanced across the floor. When Matthew rose to make lunch he retrieved a finished piece from the drying table, a crudité plate in the shape of a lily pad, and silently placed it on the floor beside his father.

Chapter 34

On the first day of summer, Matthew was coming downstairs for breakfast when Madeleine called out from her bedroom.

"Can you come in here, please?"

He found her rummaging through her suitcase.

"I thought I brought a bathing suit. I guess not," she said.

"Planning on taking a swim somewhere?" he asked.

She straightened quickly and turned to face him. Her eyes were bright and smiling. She looked rested, more like the woman who had so captured his attention back in Hartford.

"I think it's time we took Dot to the beach. I've been here nearly three months and we've never been."

Matthew folded his arms across his chest.

"For good reason. I'm pretty sure they don't make swimsuits her size."

"Silly – Dot's not going in the water. But I might."

She went to her bedside table and picked up a catalogue that had appeared in the mail. "Let's see what the latest fashion trend offers. Do you think I could wear a bikini?"

"You're asking the wrong person."

Matthew turned and went on down to the kitchen to make coffee and she followed.

"I'm serious Matthew," she said, sitting at the table. "I think it's time we got out of the house. The doctor says it's safe for Dot, and we could use a change of scenery, don't you think?"

Matthew filled the grinder with beans and flipped the switch and the obnoxious high-pitched grating sound rang off the cupboards. When it stopped he scooped heaping spoons into the filter and turned to face her. The room instantly filled with the nutty smell of roasted beans.

"Do you realize I haven't been surfing since you got here?"

She put on an exaggerated frown. "You poor thing," she said. "I'm sorry if the premature birth of your daughter got in the way."

"Don't blame it on her. You know, I had a routine, before you showed up. There were people I hung out with. It was a nice break from this nightmare," he gestured to their surroundings.

"Which you helped create, I might add," Madeleine said. "So tell me, what happened to those people?"

"It was only at the beach. I really don't care if I see them again."

"Why do you suppose that is Matthew?"

He didn't answer.

"Then I don't know what you're complaining about. You can go anytime you like. You don't need permission."

She wasn't angry. In fact, she looked relaxed at the table, at home in her terrycloth robe, her hair pulled back, no make-up. She actually sounded more like a mother, although she was still able to summon that analyst tone, a concerned but judgmental attitude he looked forward to every Friday morning back in Hartford. How was it possible she'd come so far, across an entire continent, to sit here in his kitchen wearing nothing more than a bathrobe?

He switched on the coffee machine and it gurgled and began dripping the dark steaming liquid into the glass carafe.

"I'll think about it," he said.

"If you don't want to go, I'm sure Albert would be happy to take us," Madeleine said, standing to retrieve some mugs from the cupboard.

＊＊＊

Three days later, a box arrived at the front doorstep. Seeing the truck pull away from her window, Madeleine rushed downstairs to retrieve it. Matthew and Albert were in the solarium working on their most recent projects and Bradley was down the street with his new friend.

"Those must be the supplies I ordered," Albert said as Madeleine walked into the room holding the box. "You can leave them right there."

"Sorry Al," she said. "It's a swimsuit I ordered from Saks. Did Matthew mention he's taking us to the beach this week?"

Matthew put down a brick of clay he was cutting and walked to the sink to rinse his hands.

"What a great idea!" Albert said.

"We never really agreed," Matthew said.

"What's to agree? Albert said. "You used to practically live there." He stopped himself when he remembered there was another woman involved.

"Tomorrow is supposed to be the warmest day of the year so far," Madeleine said. "It will be perfect for Dot. And Bradley can try out the boogie board Albert bought him."

Matthew cleared his throat.

"They're calling for a western swell," he said, "a big storm up from Hawaii. Bradley's not ready. You wouldn't want him in that undertow."

"But would you check anyway?" Madeleine said.

"I'll bring an easel!" Albert said excitedly before Matthew could answer. "I've so missed my plein-air!"

Matthew left the studio without commenting and climbed to the Crow's Nest where he kicked off his shoes and laid down on the bed. Sleep would come easily now if he wanted it. Dot had an upset stomach, and he'd been up with her the last two nights while Madeleine slept through. He stretched out and stared at the ceiling and pulled out his phone to dial the surf report. Of course, there was no big storm from Hawaii, not even a western swell. Winds were expected to remain moderate through the next forty-eight hours and there would be modest two-foot waves at the coast. He put the phone down and dozed off until Miguel the gardener arrived with his noisy gang of mowers, crisscrossing the grounds of *Las Palmas*, their rotary blades whirring as they manicured the lush green grass.

★ ★ ★

They could fit everything but the dog in the big white Cadillac. Albert found a beach umbrella in a basement closet; Bradley had his boogie board and Madeleine packed a picnic basket with sandwiches and drinks. Matthew thought briefly about bringing his surfboard, but that would require him to put down the top, and Dot wasn't ready for all that sun and wind. He would only bring the used copy of *Anna Karenina*, bought in a local book shop. He was determined to finish it if he could find the time.

The morning had dawned grey with a quilted marine layer; cool and calm. The forecast called for clearing around midday with light to moderate winds. Temperatures at the beach would reach a high of 80, plenty warm for the baby. Albert was packing the car's trunk, as big as a sandbox, while Matthew strapped Dot's bassinet into the middle of the back seat. It would be just her second car trip, the other a brief run to the hospital early on, when they thought she had jaundice.

The seating was discussed. Albert and Madeleine would be on either side of the baby in the back while Bradley rode up front with Matthew, who was back inside taking care of the dog. Bella had watched all the proceedings with intense interest, following Matthew through the house as he prepared for the excursion, hopeful she'd be included. Feeling guilty, Matthew put some leftover hamburger from the night before in her bowl before saying goodbye.

After some final arranging of cargo, they all piled into the big white Cadillac. Matthew backed it out and eased down the long driveway. The car was riding low, its old shocks and springs giving under the unfamiliar weight. Bradley was bouncing in his seat, so excited for his first trip to the beach. Spirits throughout the car were running high.

"Can we stop at a department store?" Madeleine said as Matthew made his way through the neighborhood. "I need a sun hat." He explained there was a Target near the beach and they made their way west through moderate traffic steadily orienting south-southwest. The sky overhead was brighter by the minute.

At the shopping complex, they waited in the car while Madeleine went inside. Albert took the opportunity to explain to Bradley the difference between conventional studio painting and plein-air.

"Plein air is all about the here and now," he said, in his best instructor's voice, a tone that sounded all too familiar to Matthew. "You are standing in the element you're painting, taking in the air, sensing the weather, catching the *light*, all in real-time. And there are no do-overs

– you just paint what you see, and you paint it fast without too much thought."

Bradley was dreamily gazing out the window from the front, calling out every cool car he spotted.

"Maybe you'd like to try it sometime," Albert said.

"Okay," was all Bradley said.

Madeleine came to the car wearing an oversized straw hat with a black ribbon above a flouncy brim.

"You look like Audrey Hepburn," Matthew said as she got in. "I think she wore that hat in *Breakfast at Tiffany's*."

"I'll take that as a compliment."

He would take them to a quiet beach adjacent to where he used to go, in the early days of his move west. He didn't want to mingle with his old surfing group, especially April and Bo. They rarely came to this beach anymore, as he recalled, so it would likely be just the five of them plus a swimmer or two.

By the time they arrived just past noon, the sky was nearly clear, with a stretch of white clouds hovering at the western horizon. The open sun had lifted the temperature noticeably. Dot had fallen asleep, and Madeleine was unstrapping her car seat, gently coaxing her awake. Matthew and Albert began pulling everything from the capacious trunk while Bradley, boogie board clutched under his arm, charged toward the water.

"Wait for me!" Matthew yelled across the sand to him.

Albert said, "I suggest we set up on that little rise over there, with the tall grass." He was pointing to a dune pushed up against the edge of the beach.

"Madeleine will want to be closer to the water, but you go ahead," Matthew said. "Set up there if you want."

Albert, with folded easel, a palette of acrylics, and a canvas bag containing various *accoutrement*, trudged off to his chosen spot while Matthew grabbed the umbrella, cooler, and his book. Madeleine would carry Dot in her portable bassinet. The baby was serene, seemingly taken by the hush of the seaside, while her mother occasionally scanned the horizon, smiling broadly as though she'd just been released from a prison camp. Matthew was admiring the light robe she wore as a cover-up, and his curiosity about the type of bathing suit she had chosen was piqued.

"It's just so wonderful out here," she said, lifting her face to the sun.

"How close do you want to be?" Matthew said. "To the water?"

Madeleine pointed to a spot where twenty-five yards beyond modest waves were breaking. Matthew marched to the area and stuck the umbrella deep into the sand. When he slid the ring upward to open it, a small animal dropped to his feet.

"*Ewww*," Madeleine said. "What's that?"

Matthew bent down and saw it was a curled-up bat, desiccated and very dead. He kicked it away and quickly covered it over with sand.

"What was it?" Madeleine said.

"Just an innocent little creature that didn't ask to be born," he proclaimed.

She gave him a quizzical look and then spread a large blanket beneath the umbrella. Down at the water's edge, Bradley stood with his board, eyeing the waves.

"Wait for me!" Matthew yelled.

"Aren't you worried about the undertow?" Madeleine said.

"There isn't any now. We'll keep an eye on it."

He pulled off his shirt and tossed it onto a pile of towels then sprinted toward Bradley and didn't stop at the water, jumping over the waves like a steeplechase horse and then diving straight in. He came up seconds later and began a brisk stroke, swimming twenty yards out, stopped, and turned around to face the beach.

"Come in!" Matthew yelled to whoever was listening. "The water's perfect!"

Bradley dropped his boogie board into the shallow water and kneeled beside it.

"What do I do now?" he yelled above the sound of the crashing waves.

Matthew suddenly remembered it was the boy's first time and swam back to give him a quick lesson. Madeleine watched as he patiently instructed her son of another man, and with the brief attention span of any excited adolescent, how to catch the modest but steady waves. Mostly they washed out before Bradley could ride them, but after a dozen tries, he figured out the exact timing and was cruising atop of the bigger ones right to the end, giggling and kicking, jumping up immediately upon coming to a stop and heading back to do it again. Matthew would take the board every few turns and show him other techniques, and Madeleine could see by Matthew's easy maneuvering he was at home in the water, paddling, and diving amidst the churning surf like a sea otter.

Meanwhile, Albert had set up on the dune facing south beneath a high noontime sun that blazed down on a ribbon of beach that snaked all the way to San Diego. Barefoot, he was wearing a pair of loose linen shorts, his planter's hat, and a striped T-shirt. He even had a red bandana jauntily tied around his neck, completing the Picasso look. He could easily be standing on the beach in *Cote d' Azure*.

Madeleine was dozing in her black two-piece when Matthew and Bradley came up from the water and stood over her, dripping.

"Check out the beach babe," Matthew said.

Madeleine opened her eyes and pulled a towel across her chest. It was just a simple yet stylish two-piece, revealing enough to make her self-conscious.

"Be nice, please," she said.

"Mom, I think it's really awesome," Bradley said. "I can barely tell you had a baby."

Matthew and Madeleine traded adult smiles. He had to agree with the boy, although he couldn't help but note Madeleine's swollen breasts spilling over the top.

"Who's talking to Mr. Banks?" Bradley said, looking up toward the dune above them.

Matthew could make out a man and woman chatting with Albert. It was not unusual for passersby to stop and chat with plein air painters, so he didn't think much about it until he noticed the unique surfboard the man carried. Bo Diddley always had the latest designs and his familiar flaming orange shorts on.

"Stay here," Matthew said. He strode briskly across the sand and up the rising dune.

"Matthew! Say hello!" his father said as he approached. "These folks claim they were at Las Palmas when Dot was born, but I can't remember."

Matthew made a quick assessment. Bo had a surly smile. April was innocently looking out across the water.

"Yeah – they were at the house," Matthew said. "Briefly."

Bo began chuckling. "Dude, you were scared shitless!"

Albert shot a look at Bo, narrowing his eyes as he began to recall the afternoon.

"White as a sheet," Bo continued. "And your old lady – wow, she was sitting there against the stairs, her legs all spread out – dude, that was really wild!"

Albert put down his brush and wiped his hands on a rag.

"Watch your mouth young man," he said, turning toward Bo. Matthew stiffened but remained quiet. A gust of wind blew Albert's hat off. Matthew turned to check on Madeleine and saw the umbrella lift from the sand and begin bounding down the beach. He could hear Madeleine cry out. He turned to Bo.

"Why don't you two head over to the other beach? We're minding our own business here. You should do the same."

"I'll do that," Bo said, "if you promise not to come back here, *Connecticut guy.*"

Matthew ignored the juvenile request, and the stupid nickname.

Albert said, "We're not promising *anything*, punk."

Bo trained his cold stare at Albert.

"Oh, *okay.* You want to get into it, old man? Come on. Let's go."

He stepped toward Albert's easel and kicked a leg from under it, sending the canvas to the sand face down. Matthew jumped between them, grabbed Bo in a headlock, and wrestled him off his feet. He easily outweighed the skinny wave rider, pinning him on to the beach.

"Albert – go help Bradley with the umbrella," he said between grunts. "I'll take care of this." Bo continued squirming while April stood staring at them in disbelief. Matthew got Bo on his back and was straddling his waist, holding his wrists down on either side of his head, Bo bucking and heaving.

"Go!" Matthew yelled to Albert. *"Please!"*

Albert walked toward Madeleine, intermittently glancing back over his shoulder.

"What in God's name is going on up there?" she said as Albert approached.

"Nothing. Matthew's got it under control."

"But he's swinging at him!"

Albert looked up and saw Bo had freed one arm and was punching wildly at Matthew but not connecting. When he gave up, Matthew slid off. But Bo rose and jumped at him and Matthew took one step to the side and winding up, landed a roundhouse punch squarely on Bo's left ear, sending him to the sand in a bony heap. April shrieked. Bo lay still for several seconds. Matthew feared he'd knocked him out, but then he began to sit up.

"Stay there," Matthew said. "I don't want to hit you again."

Albert yelled to him from below.

"Let it go, Matthew!"

One hundred yards down the beach Bradley was running along the water's edge, chasing the wheeling umbrella. The wind had risen sharply now, and the waves more robust and coming in fast. The umbrella made its way into the water and was half-submerged, pulled under by the current. Bradley was about to wade in after it. Madeleine yelled up to Matthew.

"Bradley's going in!" she cried out as Albert approached. "The undertow!"

Bo was still down. When Matthew figured he was no longer a threat he turned to April.

"I'm sorry you had to see this," he said to her.

"Me too," she said. And then, "What's your baby's name?"

Matthew gave her a faint smile.

"Dorothy."

"Wasn't that your –"

"Yes," Matthew said.

By now Albert and Bradley had grabbed the pole and were dragging the umbrella through the surf up onto the beach. The waves were breaking at their waist and Bradley appeared excited to ride them.

"Can I get my boogie board?" he asked Albert.

"Ask your mother."

The boy ran to his mother while Albert furled the umbrella and tied it closed. Further down, Albert could see Bo and April walking away toward the other beach. April was carrying his surfboard while he trudged through the sand, head down, one hand cupping his ear. Up on the dune, Matthew had stood Albert's easel back up and was brushing off the canvas. Below him Madeleine was standing over Dot, keeping her in the shade. The baby was awake now and crying. Bradley was pleading to go into the water. Albert approached with the umbrella wedged under his arm.

"Listen to your mother, son. The wind has picked up. There could be rip currents. You might end up in Japan and it would be *sayonara* Bradley."

"Oh *man*," Bradley said.

Matthew joined them, rubbing his hand. He was thinking he didn't need to hit Bo so hard. It wasn't a fair fight. The kid was over his head. But now the situation was hopefully put to rest. He was glad Madeleine hadn't seen it; she would for sure have something to say, a psychiatrist's pointed questioning, forcing an uncomfortable answer, making him feel juvenile and small, and she'd probably be right.

"What was that all about?" Madeleine said.

Matthew looked to Albert, who stood behind her swiping at his throat, the universal gesture to remain silent.

"Just some guy harassing my father."

"Who do these people think they are?" Madeleine said, with a wave of her hand. "Aren't Californians supposed to be mellow?"

"We are," Albert said. "But you still have the occasional nut-job."

Matthew chuckled. Madeleine was studying his face, the mark on his cheek.

"Did he hit you?" she said.

He covered up a red spot where Bo harmlessly connected.

"It's nothing."

The wind was gusting forcefully now, making it impossible to keep the umbrella in the sand. They moved the picnic to the shade of some locust trees for the balance of the afternoon. Madeleine nursed Dot under cover of a giant striped beach towel while the others averted their glances while eating tuna sandwiches. Matthew and Albert drank cold Mexican beer and it seemed enough to just sit and enjoy the warm breezes, the sound of the waves.

After lunch, Albert returned to the dune, fixed a smudge on his canvas and finished his painting. It was a simple, lovely seascape that perfectly captured the day's light, the opaque haze that thickened further down the coast, the serenity of the open sea. Bradley asked if he would hang it in his bedroom. Albert said he'd be proud to do that. Matthew, after finding where he'd left off, was reengaged in the drama of *Anna Karenina*. Levin was in his vast fields threshing grass with his *muzhiks*, learning how best to work a scythe. "Watch out now master," one worker warns, "once you start, there's no stopping!"

As the sun moved past its apex, slowly moving their shadows across the warm sand, Bradley asked to return to the water one last time. Matthew offered to go with him. Three-foot waves were more challenging for the boy but also more fun. He proved to be a quick study, displaying his father's athleticism with his timing and agility, the way he zoomed flat atop the foaming water with the board beneath his slim torso, legs kicking wildly. Madeleine joined them briefly, leaving Albert to watch the baby. She tiptoed to the edge of the water, hugging her sides, her long legs lithe and toned, and tentatively waded in. Five yards out, she dove gracefully, surfacing and swimming freestyle for a ways before returning. She marched out of the water and onto the beach, a glistening sea goddess, as if she'd been doing this every day of her life.

"I love California!" she shouted above the sound of the waves.

They returned to the shadows of the grove and were lying about lazily, the wind gentle now and the afternoon sun softer behind a light haze. As Matthew began pulling things together to head home, he looked over to Madeleine. She was stretched out on her beach towel catching a nap while the baby cooed in her bassinet. He thought back to young Bradley's comment. Madeleine was indeed looking fine, more vibrant than ever. She filled out her suit as if she were modelling it. Her skin was already a shade darker, her Caribbean heritage showing after just a few hours outside. She appeared content and at peace. He'd never believe this proud, enigmatic woman just survived the emergency birth of a baby – his baby.

* * *

With everyone deep in slumber that night, exhausted from the sea and sun, Matthew lay in bed wide-eyed, staring into the blackness. The afternoon's events played out in his mind like a video loop. Aside from the incident with Bo, he'd had fun with this rag-tag group, the same people he vowed to evict just weeks ago. Although they didn't precisely qualify as a family, there were enough shared genes to call it more than a random group of strangers. He chuckled to himself, remembering a silly joke Bradley shared with the group: What do you call a cow with no legs? *Ground beef.*

At 3:11 he went down to the kitchen for something to drink. Walking by the darkened solarium, he could make out the silhouette of Albert's easel against the window holding his latest unfinished work. The room smelled of oils and baked clay. He'd fired the emperor penguin that evening, and the kiln still ticked as it cooled. The mingling scents were clean, promising. It carried him back to his childhood, when he first learned from his father how the church-like feel of a studio can help transform an idea into artistic expression; and when that art succeeds, it can change how people see things, even if in some small way.

He sat down in the dark kitchen with a glass of milk. The backyard was eerily illuminated by a waxing moon that hung on the opposite side of the house. Shadows of palm trees stretched across the yard like black felt cut-outs. In the wee hours of night, with the house and neighborhood so still, Matthew felt like the only soul awake in the entire universe. He pictured his mother lurching through this cavernous hacienda all alone, unable to sleep, a slave to her drink, sick and tired of being sick and tired. If he had come for her, would that have changed things? That was impossible to know, and something he'd rather not think about. But he did know this: he'd paid his dues, in his own empty house, sitting by the fireplace in the dark, watching the embers slowly die. He realized now was the time to sell the house in Hartford. He would say goodbye to Connecticut altogether, regardless of what happened with Madeleine and the baby.

His thoughts returned to the afternoon, possibly because his hand still buzzed from hitting Bo. His defense, not that he needed one, was that he reacted instinctually, taking control the second Albert's painting was kicked to the sand. Wasn't that the appropriate response to the rogue surfer's aggression? It never occurred to him he might have appeared protective of his father. And speaking of his father – what was he thinking, when he tried to hide the incident from Madeleine? Was he ashamed of his son? Or proud? Did it even register?

He finished his milk and climbed to the second floor, where he stuck his head in the nursery. Tiptoeing to Dot's crib, he lightly kissed her forehead and proceeded upstairs, where Bella was waiting in the darkened hallway. She licked his hand as he walked by, seemingly aware it was sore, and when he crawled under the covers, hoping for sleep, she returned to the closet, circled atop a heap of clothes and laid down.

Chapter 35

Albert was in Bradley's bedroom one morning helping him hang the painting he'd made at the beach. It was now mounted on cardboard with a modest wooden frame.

"Can I put it next to my Pedro Martinez poster?" Bradley asked.

Albert looked at the life-sized color photo of the Red Sox pitcher winding up.

"Actually," he said, "I think it would be lost next to Pedro. How about over your dresser?"

Just then Matthew walked by and stopped at the door.

"How about over your bed?" Matthew said. "That way you'll see it every time you come into your room."

"Bradley," Albert said with a warm smile, "put it where you want. I'm just happy you're hanging it up. So much of my work ends up in a closet."

Matthew sat on Bradley's bed.

"I've been meaning to ask you Al," he said. "Where's that plate I gave you to paint, and the pitcher?"

He'd been calling his father by the informal name, a sudden tongue-in-cheek acknowledgement of him as a legitimate human being. Another hint of growing harmony between the two: Matthew had shared several recent pieces with Albert after agreeing to jointly produce more finished and expressive pottery. The very first piece Matthew offered, the missing crudité plate, he'd painted a vibrant green with contrasting black hair-like veins, a modernistic rendition of a lily pad. It was Albert's first collaboration with his son since their early days in Pasadena. More followed, including a copy of the Picasso pitcher he'd seen in the Hartford exhibit, which he had sketched while standing beside it that snowy Sunday. Albert had matched the patterns of tan and black perfectly.

Albert sat on the bed beside Matthew.

"I was waiting to tell you when the time was right," he said. "I've put them on consignment at the Higgins Gallery downtown. I met with the chief curator a few weeks ago. She loved our work. In fact, someone came in and bought the lily pad while I was there."

Matthew grimaced.

"Don't you think you should have asked me first?"

"She got $175 for it."

"What?"

"The pitcher could go for $350, she thinks, and people are asking for more. She wants us to enter their annual show they hold every August. There's a competition. Only local artists."

"The pitcher's gone too?"

"Not yet, I told her to hold it. I knew you probably wanted to keep that, but we can make another."

Matthew studied his father. He'd regained some of the weight lost when he had the Marseilles bug, and several days at the beach painting had lent him a bronzed glow. He once again looked like a native southern Californian, the lifestyle obviously agreeing with him.

Matthew stood and walked to the door.

"I guess you could use the money," he said.

He turned to leave and Albert stopped him.

"Then we should talk now."

Matthew stopped in the hallway and turned and looked at him inquisitively.

"I've entered into an agreement with Higgins," Albert said.

"Oh really?"

"We verbally agreed to a dozen pieces a month. Miss Dawson – the cute and very well-schooled graduate student from USC who runs the place, wants to meet you."

"We? I can't believe you! You're making assumptions again. You shouldn't be out there making commitments you can't live up to.

"I'm not *out there* doing any such thing," he said.

"You sure as hell are."

"You should be happy I'm trying to earn a living."

Matthew had no answer for this. He hurried down the hallway and they heard him leave through the front door. Bradley began pounding a nail into the wall beside Pedro Martinez.

"Thanks Uncle Al!" he said, adopting a name his mother had suggested. He excitedly stepped back to look at his new wall decoration. "Doesn't it look neat there?"

Outside Matthew got into the big white Cadillac, put the top down, and headed to the coast. July in southern California was actually boring in its unrelenting sunshine and narrow range of temperatures. Albert had joked it was weather suited for a nudist colony; no need for clothes, day or night. Most mornings were clear, with only a marine layer hugging the coast until noon. Today the fog had burned off early, and as Matthew drove south on Highway 1, with the never disappointing Pacific below, he tried to imagine himself headed for Costa Rica with the bare essentials in the trunk, Bella beside him and a tank full of gas.

He wondered what it would be like if he'd run away that afternoon Madeleine went into labor. He would have vanished into thin air, after throwing his cell phone into the ocean to avoid being traced. But now the notion of missing the birth of his daughter, not being present for her in her early, perilous days, made him ashamed he'd come so close to leaving. If Albert hadn't come knocking on his door, he'd now be a free man in another country; a free and desperately alone man.

There was no denying the anxious feelings he still harbored toward his father. Things kept popping up that caused friction. For instance, a box recently arrived from Hartford. The return label showed it had come from Hughes. Albert signed for it and brought it to Matthew, claiming to know what it was.

"Obviously it's some sort of artwork," he'd said that morning in the foyer of *Las Palmas*. Matthew cut away the wrapping and when he peeled off the liner paper inside he saw it was the painting Hughes insisted on giving him that cold night in February. Albert was peering over Matthew's shoulder and came to his side to look more closely.

"Oh my God," he said, "it's a Turiot."

"You know this hack?" Matthew had said.

"Hack? He's the talk of the art world these days. There was an article in the Quarterly on him just last month. They say he's one of the most underrated European artists of the late 19th century. Why would Hughes give this up? It must be worth a small fortune."

Matthew continued staring at the painting.

"It was Julia's favorite. He meant to give it to her."

In his mind's eye, he pictured Julia looking at it, marveling, telling Hughes how much she loved it, while at the same time Hughes was conjuring to give it to her. The same anguished reaction washed over him he'd felt so strongly that night. The idea was so ill-conceived; it was so typical of Hughes to refuse to take no for an answer.

"Then maybe I'll sell it," Matthew said. "I'll split the money with you. Then we won't have to go to Higgins and hock our bowls and pitchers like a couple of amateurs."

Albert gave him a look of deep disappointment.

"I wouldn't let this painting out of the house," he said. "If you don't want it, I'll hang it somewhere out of the way where you don't have to see it."

Matthew handed it to him.

"It's all yours."

Later in the day, when he was working on a small obelisk, Matthew noticed the painting on the side wall beside Albert's easel, not in a prominent spot, but plainly in view.

Epilogue

Matthew would continue to get up for a glass of milk every night in the weeks that followed, adding a stop in the nursery to his routine. He would sit in the chair by Dot's crib, legs draped over the ottoman, listening to her tiny, steady exhalations. All around him were the distinct smells of a newborn: the sweetness of baby powder; the not entirely masked smell of the diaper bin, the tang of alcohol wipes. New gestures she made that day would play in his mind's eye; he'd remember an utterance, a word in the making. He sensed a sharp, opinionated personality emerging. How would father and daughter get along in years to come? Would she challenge him, question his authority, overlook his checkered past? Would she love him? There remained a troublesome list of questions beyond his grasp, but this much was for sure: his infatuation for this new addition to his life was growing faster than the baby herself, and he thanked the stars and the universe that she was healthy, well cared for, and quite likely, extraordinary.

✶ ✶ ✶

One night, Matthew stuck his head into Madeleine's room. The sound of her sleeping was altogether different; her breathing slower,

300

deeper. It would be so pleasant, he thought to himself, to just once lay beside her. Without thinking, he sat on the bed and lowered his head to the pillow. She flinched, mumbling something. He froze, staring into the dark, and she returned to sleep. It was interesting to compare the sounds and very different smells of her world with those of Dot's. In here were soothing applications and creams she pampered herself with, an unlit jasmine candle, the faint doughy scent of mother's milk. The intoxicating aromas put him to sleep.

When the greyness of pre-dawn gathered around the perimeter of the blinds, he awoke with a start. Madeleine lay in the exact position as before, the now familiar hint of a smile on her face. He silently left the room and went back upstairs.

* * *

When Madeleine was stronger, Matthew gave her the bad news. He had learned in a confidential call from Dooley that Adam Rich was found in a crack house in an abandoned part of New Haven. He'd been suspected in a string of burglaries and was at deaths' door from an overdose. They took him to the Emergency Room where recovery attempts continued for some time until they removed life support. He died alone in the hospital at Yale, where fifteen years earlier he'd completed his brilliant residency, a promising young surgeon.

She took it stoically, lying in bed with the early morning sun streaming in, as he stood at the door.

"Where's the body?" she asked coolly.

"In the New Haven city morgue. Dooley handled everything," Matthew said. Neither spoke for several moments.

"I can't travel for a while," she finally said. "I suppose his family will handle everything. Can you call Dooley?"

"I already have," he said. "There's no date for the burial."

Her face grew more sad.

"I need to decide, how do I tell Bradley?"

Matthew only shook his head.

"When do you think you'll go back?" he said.

"When do you want us to go?"

Matthew looked away.

Madeleine patted the bed. He walked over and sat down beside her. Up close he could see the very fine lines around her eyes, the strain. She had failed to gain the prescribed weight in the past weeks. The previous night Dot had been fussy. He'd brought her to Madeleine twice for feeding. They took turns rocking her to sleep. Now, with this latest news, she looked worse. As Matthew's concern deepened, a voice spoke to him: *The mother of your child should not travel.*

"We'll leave as soon as the doctor says it's safe to fly," she said softly. "It won't be long."

There was a hint of relief in her words.

"*No –*" Matthew said, as though agitated.

"Sorry?"

He took her hand. She was trembling.

"You mentioned once," he said, "when you first found out about the baby, we could build a life in Hartford."

He paused to construct the question. "Can't we do that here? Leave all our bad memories back east? Dot would have two full-time parents – something you and I never had. She deserves that, right? And Bradley – he's at home here already."

Madeleine's eyes were beginning to well with tears. He continued.

"There's no rule in your religion that says we have to be married, is there?"

A gentle breeze blew the curtains into the room.

"You've given this some thought," she said, searching his eyes. "Maybe now is a good time to share what you said to me the first night we met."

"I'd rather we forget that first night."

"But you said something so prophetic. I can still hear it. You said, 'you and I could make beautiful babies.' I was speechless. I can't believe you don't remember."

"Oh my God..." he said, remembering nothing. "And you still met with me."

Madeleine smiled.

"Boss's orders. I thought you needed help, and –" she stopped herself.

"And?"

"You were awfully handsome."

Matthew sat quietly, red-faced. A house fly the size of a kalamata olive bopped stubbornly against the window pane.

Madeleine said, "Reverend Mother Caroline would want Dot to be with her father." She was referring to her foster mother at St. Agatha's. "Which brings us to Albert."

Matthew gave her a look of surrender, a face she'd never seen.

"He can stay for as long as he wants," he said.

"I saw his easel upstairs."

Matthew's eyes brightened. "Isn't he amazing with Dot? I think she's babbling in French!"

The two shared a laugh for the first time since being rejoined in California.

Madeleine said, "She'll be speaking French before we know it, which has always been a dream of mine. I want to speak like a native.

I knew some, as a child, but it's gone. Do you think Albert could help me?"

Matthew smiled. "I haven't told him. That's part of the deal. He's going to teach us all."

The giant fly had left the room. Now the only sound was the travel clock ticking on her bedside table.

"Well?" he finally said.

Madeleine took a deep breath.

"First…"

"First *what*?"

"Tell me you love me."

FINIS

About the author

Toby Brookes was born and raised in the Midwest, and the family home in Maine is where he has always returned. A wide-ranging career in sales and marketing landed him in Cleveland, Minneapolis, London, Washington DC, and Northern California. In 2016 he left that world to write, completing a two-year novel writing program at Stanford University. He has four grown children and now splits his time with his wife and two dogs in Palo Alto and Carmel, California. This is his first novel.

Acknowledgments

The author wishes to thank the following people for their personal and professional guidance and encouragement, without which this book would not have been possible: Kelly Meldrum, wife and loving source of tireless support; Hadley, Jack, Spencer and Christian, for the boundless inspiration only children can provide; brothers Jeff and Jamie Brookes who suffered through early drafts, Scott Lax, Doug and Zoe Billman, David Crowther, Mary Holden Thompson, Joshua Mohr, Tom Jenks, Carolyn Crowell, Lloyd Greenberg, Mary Tsiara, David Plunkert, and the many friends who took such motivating interest along the way.